OUTLAWS

They were master of the holdup, the shoot-out, and the showdown. This collection captures the cunning and courage of the wicked evildoers who fought to keep the new frontier untamed.

THE BEST OF THE WEST

Anthologies of new and old stories written with gusto and realism by your favorite Western authors.

Another Fawcett Gold Medal Book
by Martin H. Greenberg and Bill Pronzini:

THE LAWMEN

OUTLAWS
THE

Edited by Bill Pronzini & Martin H. Greenberg

FAWCETT GOLD MEDAL • NEW YORK

Acknowledgments

"Charlie Bowdre," S. Omar Barker. Copyright © 1968 by S. Omar Barker. From *Rawhide Rhymes*. Reprinted by permission of the author.

"Assassin," Frank Gruber. Copyright © 1939 by Short Stories, Inc. Reprinted by permission of the agents for the author's estate, The Scott Meredith Literary Agency, Inc., 845 Third Avenue, New York, N.Y. 10022.

"Wine on the Desert," Max Brand. Copyright © 1936 by Frederick Faust. Copyright renewed 1964 by Jane F. Easton, Judith Faust, and John Frederick Faust. From *Max Brand's Best Western Stories*, edited by William F. Nolan. Reprinted by permission of Dodd, Mead & Company, Inc.

"Night on Don Jaime Street," Ernest Haycox. Copyright © 1940 by Ernest Haycox; renewed 1968 by Jill Marie Haycox. From *Rough Justice*. Reprinted by permission of the Scott Meredith Literary Agency, Inc., 845 Third Avenue, New York, N.Y. 10022.

"Posse," C. Hall Thompson. Copyright © 1951 by Esquire, Inc. First published in *Esquire*. Reprinted by permission of the Scott Meredith Literary Agency, Inc., 845 Third Avenue, New York, N.Y. 10022.

"Nobody's all Bad," W. R. Burnett. Copyright © 1930 by Crowell-Collier Publishing Co. First published in *Collier's*. Reprinted by permission of the Scott Meredith Literary Agency, Inc., 845 Third Avenue, New York, N.Y. 10022.

"Back Track," H. A. De Rosso. Copyright © 1956 by Better Publications, Inc. First published in *Ranch Ro-*

Contents

Introduction

The Outlaws is the second in a series of Fawcett-Ballantine Western Library anthologies dedicated to making available to contemporary readers the finest in short Western fiction. In the first book in the series, *The Lawmen,* we brought you stories of the famous, the near-famous, and the unsung among Old West peace officers; in these pages you will find some of the finest tales penned over the past century about Billy the Kid, Jesse James, Cole Younger, and a host of other wicked (and not so wicked) outlaws.

Future Fawcett-Ballantine Western Library volumes will contain stories about the working cowboy; the Indian, both good and bad; the men who built and rode and in some cases stole from the railroads and the great steamboats—stories by such important writers in the field as Owen Wister, B. M. Bower, O. Henry, Mark Twain, Clarence E. Mulford, Rex Beach, Alan LeMay, A. B. Guthrie, Jr., Elmer Kelton, Clay Fisher, Dorothy Johnson, Will Henry, Steve Frazee, Brian Garfield, and Conrad Richter.

May *The Outlaws,* and all the other anthologies in the series, give you many hours of reading enjoyment.

—Bill Pronzini and
Martin H. Greenberg

The sometimes humorous, sometimes sobersided, always entertaining rhymes of S. Omar Barker have been appearing in the better Western periodicals for nearly half a century. And his 1968 collection, Rawhide Rhymes, is chock full of such gems as this brief but pointed saga of an outlaw named Charlie Bowdre. Barker has also written much short fiction about the Old West; one of his stories, "Bad Company," from The Saturday Evening Post, won the Western Writers of America Spur Award as the Best Short Story of 1955.

Charlie Bowdre

S. Omar Barker

Over a hut near Stinking Springs,
Loud the clangor of battle rings.
Billy the Kid and his gang at bay,
Trapped in a hut of adobe clay,
Answer the posse shot for shot,
Curse as the lead hail waxes hot.

Slowly, surely, through the din,
Sheriff Garrett closes in.
Through chink holes in the 'dobe wall,
The Kid's keen eyes can see it all.
One man dies on his fallen face,
Another, shooting, takes his place.
Grimly the Kid foresees the end,
Turns with a curse to his closest friend:
"Slip out, Charlie, damn your hide!
Go for help, and by God, ride!"

Charlie Bowdre tries it, grim,
And Garrett's bullets riddle him.
Back he staggers within the walls,
Totters on his legs and falls.
Killed, yet living, there he lies.
Cold light gleams in Billy's eyes:
"Git up, Charlie! You can't last!
Git outside and git there fast!
You're done for, but not plumb dead!
Git out! Feed them coyotes lead!"

Shoved by his "friend" to face his foes,
Bleeding, dying, Bowdre goes;
With no ifs nor ands nor buts,
Dies an outlaw—but with guts!

Now the years have galloped on.
Long the Kid, too, has been gone.
Billy the Kid! What song and story
Men have conjured for his glory!
Bowdre's bones rot with the mold.
Rarely is *his* story told!

*The Cisco Kid as portrayed on television by Duncan Renaldo
was a dashing figure who regularly did battle with evildoers
and who was known as "the Robin Hood of the Old West."
The original Cisco Kid, however, as conceived by that master of the short story, O. Henry, was a much less benevolent
individual—a desperado who "had killed six men in more or
less fair scrimmages, had murdered twice as many (mostly
Mexicans), and had winged a larger number whom he modestly forbore to count." One of O. Henry's best stories, this
surprising and grimly ironic tale is like none that has ever
appeared on TV. . . .*

The Caballero's Way

O. Henry

*T*he Cisco Kid had killed six men in more or less fair
scrimmages, had murdered twice as many (mostly Mexicans), and had winged a larger number whom he modestly
forbore to count. Therefore a woman loved him.

The Kid was twenty-five, looked twenty; and a careful in-
surance company would have estimated the probable time of
his demise at, say, twenty-six. His habitat was anywhere between the Frio and the Rio Grande. He killed for the love of
it—because he was quick-tempered—to avoid arrest—for his
own amusement—any reason that came to his mind would
suffice. He had escaped capture because he could shoot
five-sixths of a second sooner than any sheriff or ranger in
the service, and because he rode a speckled roan horse that
knew every cow-path in the mesquite and pear thickets from
San Antonio to Matamoras.

Tonia Perez, the girl who loved the Cisco Kid, was half Carmen, half Madonna, and the rest—oh, yes, a woman who is half Carmen and half Madonna can always be something more—the rest, let us say, was hummingbird. She lived in a grass-roofed *jacal* near a little Mexican settlement at the Lone Wolf Crossing of the Frio. With her lived a father or grandfather, a lineal Aztec, somewhat less than a thousand years old, who herded a hundred goats and lived in a continuous drunken dream from drinking *mescal*. Back of the *jacal* a tremendous forest of bristling pear, twenty feet high at its worst, crowded almost to its door. It was along the bewildering maze of this spinous thicket that the speckled roan would bring the Kid to see his girl. And once, clinging like a lizard to the ridgepole, high up under the peaked grass roof, he had heard Tonia, with her Madonna face and Carmen beauty and hummingbird soul, parley with the sheriff's posse, denying knowledge of her man in her soft mélange of Spanish and English.

One day the adjutant-general of the state, who is, *ex officio* commander of the ranger forces, wrote some sarcastic lines to Captain Duval of Company X, stationed at Laredo, relative to the serene and undisturbed existence led by murderers and desperadoes in the said captain's territory.

The captain turned the color of brick dust under his tan, and forwarded the letter, after adding a few comments, per ranger Private Bill Adamson, to ranger Lieutenant Sandridge, camped at a water hole on the Nueces with a squad of five men in preservation of law and order.

Lieutenant Sandridge turned a beautiful *couleur de rose* through his ordinary strawberry complexion, tucked the letter in his hip pocket, and chewed off the ends of his gamboge moustache.

The next morning he saddled his horse and rode alone to the Mexican settlement at the Lone Wolf Crossing of the Frio, twenty miles away.

Six feet two, blond as a Viking, quiet as a deacon, dangerous as a machine gun, Sandridge moved among the *jacales,* patiently seeking news of the Cisco Kid.

Far more than the law, the Mexicans dreaded the cold and

certain vengeance of the lone rider that the ranger sought. It had been one of the Kid's pastimes to shoot Mexicans "to see them kick": if he demanded from them moribund Terpsichorean feats, simply that he might be entertained, what terrible and extreme penalties would be certain to follow should they anger him! One and all they lounged with upturned palms and shrugging shoulders, filling the air with *"quien sabe"*'s and denials of the Kid's acquaintance.

But there was a man named Fink who kept a store at the Crossing—a man of many nationalities, tongues, interests, and ways of thinking.

"No use to ask them Mexicans," he said to Sandridge. "They're afraid to tell. This *hombre* they call the Kid—Goodall is his name, ain't it?—he's been in my store once or twice. I have an idea you might run across him at—but I guess I don't keer to say, myself. I'm two seconds later in pulling a gun than I used to be, and the difference is worth thinking about. But this Kid's got a half-Mexican girl at the Crossing that he comes to see. She lives in that *jacal* a hundred yards down the arroyo at the edge of the pear. Maybe she—no, I don't suppose she would, but that *jacal* would be a good place to watch, anyway."

Sandridge rode down to the *jacal* of Perez. The sun was low, and the broad shade of the great pear thicket already covered the grass-thatched hut. The goats were enclosed for the night in a brush corral near by. A few kids walked the top of it, nibbling the chaparral leaves. The old Mexican lay upon a blanket on the grass, already in a stupor from his *mescal*, and dreaming, perhaps, of the nights when he and Pizarro touched glasses to their New World fortunes—so old his wrinkled face seemed to proclaim him to be. And in the door of the *jacal* stood Tonia. And Lieutenant Sandridge sat in his saddle staring at her like a gannet agape at a sailor-man.

The Cisco Kid was a vain person, as all eminent and successful assassins are, and his bosom would have been ruffled had he known that at a simple exchange of glances two persons, in whose minds he had been looming large, suddenly abandoned (at least for the time) all thought of him.

Never before had Tonia seen such a man as this. He seemed to be made of sunshine and blood-red tissue and clear weather. He seemed to illuminate the shadow of the pear when he smiled, as though the sun were rising again. The men she had known had been small and dark. Even the Kid, in spite of his achievements, was a stripling no larger than herself, with black, straight hair and a cold, marble face that chilled the noonday.

As for Tonia, though she sends description to the poor-house, let her make a millionaire of your fancy. Her blue-black hair, smoothly divided in the middle and bound close to her head, and her large eyes full of the Latin melancholy, gave her the Madonna touch. Her motions and air spoke of the concealed fire and the desire to charm that she had inherited from the *gitanas* of the Basque province. As for the hummingbird part of her, that dwelt in her heart; you could not perceive it unless her bright red skirt and dark blue blouse gave you a symbolic hint of the vagarious bird.

The newly lighted sun-god asked for a drink of water. Tonia brought it from the red jar hanging under the brush shelter. Sandridge considered it necessary to dismount so as to lessen the trouble of her ministrations.

I play no spy; nor do I assume to master the thoughts of any human heart; but I assert, by the chronicler's right, that before a quarter of an hour had sped, Sandridge was teaching her how to plait a six-strand rawhide stake-rope, and Tonia had explained to him that were it not for her little English book that the peripatetic *padre* had given her and the little crippled *chivo,* which she fed from a bottle, she would be very, very lonely indeed.

Which leads to a suspicion that the Kid's fences needed repairing, and that the adjutant-general's sarcasm had fallen upon unproductive soil.

In his camp by the water hole Lieutenant Sandridge announced and reiterated his intention of either causing the Cisco Kid to nibble the black loam of the Frio country prairies or of haling him before a judge and jury. That sounded businesslike. Twice a week he rode over to the Lone-Wolf Crossing of the Frio, and directed Tonia's slim, slightly lemon-tinted fingers among the intricacies of the slowly growing lariat. A six-strand plait is hard to learn and easy to teach.

The ranger knew that he might find the Kid there at any visit. He kept his armament ready, and had a frequent eye for the pear thicket at the rear of the *jacal*. Thus he might bring down the kite and the hummingbird with one stone.

While the sunny-haired ornithologist was pursuing his studies, the Cisco Kid was also attending to his professional duties. He moodily shot up a saloon in a small cow village on Quintana Creek, killed the town marshal (plugging him neatly in the center of his tin badge), and then rode away, morose and unsatisfied. No true artist is uplifted by shooting an aged man carrying an old style .38 bulldog.

On his way the Kid suddenly experienced the yearning that all men feel when wrongdoing loses its keen edge of delight. He yearned for the woman he loved to reassure him that she was his in spite of it. He wanted her to call his bloodthirstiness bravery and his cruelty devotion. He wanted Tonia to bring him water from the red jar under the brush shelter, and tell him how the *chivo* was thriving on the bottle.

The Kid turned the speckled roan's head up the ten-mile pear flat that stretches along the Arroyo Hondo until it ends at the Lone Wolf Crossing of the Frio. The roan whickered; for he had a sense of locality and direction equal to that of a belt-line street-car horse; and he knew he would soon be nibbling the rich mesquite grass at the end of a forty-foot stake-rope while Ulysses rested his head in Circe's straw-roofed hut.

More weird and lonesome than the journey of an Amazonian explorer is the ride of one through a Texas pear flat. With dismal monotony and startling variety the uncanny and multiform shapes of the cacti lift their twisted trunks and fat, bristly hands to encumber the way. The demon plant, appearing to live without soil or rain, seems to taunt the parched traveler with its lush gray greenness. It warps itself a thousand times about what look to be open and inviting paths, only to lure the rider into blind and impassable spine-defended "bottoms of the bag," leaving him to retreat, if he can, with the points of the compass whirling in his head.

To be lost in the pear is to die almost the death of the thief on the cross, pierced by nails and with grotesque shapes of all the fiends hovering about.

But it was not so with the Kid and his mount. Winding, twisting, circling, tracing the most fantastic and bewildering trail ever picked out, the good roan lessened the distance to the Lone Wolf Crossing with every coil and turn that he made.

While they fared the Kid sang. He knew but one tune and sang it, as he knew but one code and lived it, and but one girl and loved her. He was a single-minded man of conventional ideas. He had a voice like a coyote with bronchitis, but whenever he chose to sing his song he sang it. It was a conventional song of the camps and trails, running at its beginning as near as may be to these words:

> *Don't you monkey with my Lulu girl*
> *or I'll tell you what I'll do—*

and so on. The roan was inured to it, and did not mind.

But even the poorest singer will, after a certain time, gain his own consent to refrain from contributing to the world's noises. So the Kid, by the time he was within a mile or two of Tonia's *jacal,* had reluctantly allowed his song to die away—not because his vocal performance had become less charming to his own ears, but because his laryngeal muscles were aweary.

As though he were in a circus ring, the speckled roan wheeled and danced through the labyrinth of pear until at length his rider knew by certain landmarks that the Lone Wolf Crossing was close at hand. Then, where the pear was thinner, he caught sight of the grass roof of the *jacal* and the hackberry tree on the edge of the arroyo. A few yards farther the Kid stopped the roan and gazed intently through the prickly openings. Then he dismounted, dropped the roan's reins, and proceeded on foot, stooping and silent, like an In-

dian. The roan, knowing his part, stood still, making no
sound.

The Kid crept noiselessly to the very edge of the pear
thicket and reconnoitered between the leaves of a clump of
cactus.

Ten yards from his hiding place, in the shade of the *jacal,*
sat his Tonia calmly plaiting a rawhide lariat. So far she
might surely escape condemnation; women have been
known, from time to time, to engage in more mischievous
occupations. But if all must be told, there is to be added that
her head reposed against the broad and comfortable chest of
a tall red-and-yellow man, and that his arm was about her,
guiding her nimble small fingers that required so many lessons at the intricate six-strand plait.

Sandridge glanced quickly at the dark mass of pear when
he heard a slight squeaking sound that was not altogether unfamiliar. A gun-scabbard will make that sound when one
grasps the handle of a six-shooter suddenly. But the sound
was not repeated; and Tonia's fingers needed close attention.

And then, in the shadow of death, they began to talk of
their love; and in the still July afternoon every word they uttered reached the ears of the Kid.

"Remember, then," said Tonia, "you must not come
again until I send for you. Soon he will be here. A *vaquero*
at the *tienda* said today he saw him on the Guadalupe three
days ago. When he is that near he always comes. If he
comes and finds you here he will kill you. So, for my sake,
you must come no more until I send you the word."

"All right," said the ranger. "And then what?"

"And then," said the girl, "you must bring your men
here and kill him. If not, he will kill you."

"He ain't a man to surrender, that's sure," said Sandridge. "It's kill or be killed for the officer that goes up
against Mr. Cisco Kid."

"He must die," said the girl. "Otherwise there will not
be any peace in the world for thee and me. He has killed
many. Let him so die. Bring your men, and give him no
chance to escape."

"You used to think right much of him," said Sandridge.

Tonia dropped the lariat, twisted herself around, and curved a lemon-tinted arm over the ranger's shoulder.

"But then," she murmured in liquid Spanish, "I had not beheld thee, thou great, red mountain of a man! And thou art kind and good, as well as strong. Could one choose him, knowing thee? Let him die; for then I will not be filled with fear by day and night lest he hurt thee or me."

"How can I know when he comes?" asked Sandridge.

"When he comes," said Tonia, "he remains two days, sometimes three, Gregorio, the small son of old Luisa, the *lavandera,* has a swift pony. I will write a letter to thee and send it by him, saying how it will be best to come upon him. By Gregorio will the letter come. And bring many men with thee, and have much care, oh, dear red one, for the rattlesnake is not quicker to strike than is *'El chivato,'* as they call him, to send a ball from his *pistola.*"

"The Kid's handy with his gun, sure enough," admitted Sandridge, "but when I come for him I shall come alone. I'll get him by myself or not at all. The Cap wrote one or two things to me that make me want to do the trick without any help. You let me know when Mr. Kid arrives, and I'll do the rest."

"I will send you the message by the boy Gregorio," said the girl. "I knew you were braver than that small slayer of men who never smiles. How could I ever have thought I cared for him?"

It was time for the ranger to ride back to his camp on the water hole. Before he mounted his horse he raised the slight form of Tonia with one arm high from the earth for a parting salute. The drowsy stillness of the torpid summer air still lay thick upon the dreaming afternoon. The smoke from the fire in the *jacal,* where the *frijoles* bubbled in the iron pot, rose straight as a plumb line above the clay-daubed chimney. No sound or movement disturbed the serenity of the dense pear thicket ten yards away.

When the form of Sandridge had disappeared, loping his big dun down the steep banks of the Frio crossing, the Kid crept back to his own horse, mounted him, and rode back along the tortuous trail he had come.

But not far. He stopped and waited in the silent depths of the pear until half an hour had passed. And then Tonia heard the high, untrue notes of his unmusical singing coming nearer and nearer; and she ran to the edge of the pear to meet him.

The Kid seldom smiled; but he smiled and waved his hat when he saw her. He dismounted, and his girl sprang into his arms. The Kid looked at her fondly. His thick, black hair clung to his head like a wrinkled mat. The meeting brought a slight ripple of some undercurrent of feeling to his smooth, dark face that was usually as motionless as a clay mask.

"How's my girl?" he asked, holding her close.

"Sick of waiting so long for you, dear one," she answered. "My eyes are dim with always gazing into that devil's pincushion through which you come. And I can see into it such a little way, too. But you are here, beloved one, and I will not scold. *Qué mal muchacho!* not to come to see your *alma* more often. Go in and rest, and let me water your horse and stake him with the long rope. There is cool water in the jar for you."

The Kid kissed her affectionately.

"Not if the court knows itself do I let a lady stake my horse for me," said he. "But if you'll run in, *chica,* and throw a pot of coffee together while I attend to the *caballo,* I'll be a good deal obliged."

Besides his marksmanship the Kid had another attribute for which he admired himself greatly. He was *muy caballero,* as the Mexicans express it, where the ladies were concerned. For them he had always gentle words and consideration. He could not have spoken a harsh word to a woman. He might ruthlessly slay their husbands and brothers, but he could not have laid the weight of a finger in anger upon a woman. Wherefore many of that interesting division of humanity who had come under the spell of his politeness declared their disbelief in the stories circulated about Mr. Kid. One shouldn't believe everything one heard, they said. When confronted by their indignant menfolk with proof of the *caballero*'s deeds of infamy, they said maybe he had been driven to it, and that he knew how to treat a lady, anyhow.

Considering this extremely courteous idiosyncrasy of the Kid and the pride that he took in it, one can perceive that the solution of the problem that was presented to him by what he saw and heard from his hiding place in the pear that afternoon (at least as to one of the actors) must have been obscured by difficulties. And yet one could not think of the Kid's overlooking little matters of that kind.

At the end of the short twilight they gathered around a supper of *frijoles,* goat steaks, canned peaches, and coffee, by the light of a lantern in the *jacal.* Afterward, the ancestor, his flock corralled, smoked a cigarette and became a mummy in a gray blanket. Tonia washed the few dishes while the Kid dried them with the flour-sacking towel. Her eyes shone; she chatted volubly of the inconsequent happenings of her small world since the Kid's last visit; it was as all his other homecomings had been.

Then outside Tonia swung in a grass hammock with her guitar and sang sad *canciones de amor.*

"Do you love me just the same, old girl?" asked the Kid, hunting for his cigarette papers.

"Always the same, little one," said Tonia, her dark eyes lingering upon him.

"I must go over to Fink's," said the Kid, rising, "for some tobacco. I thought I had another sack in my coat. I'll be back in a quarter of an hour."

"Hasten," said Tonia, "and tell me—how long shall I call you my own this time? Will you be gone again tomorrow, leaving me to grieve, or will you be longer with your Tonia?"

"Oh, I might stay two or three days this trip," said the Kid, yawning. "I've been on the lodge for a month, and I'd like to rest up."

He was gone half an hour for his tobacco. When he returned Tonia was still lying in the hammock.

"It's funny," said the Kid, "how I feel. I feel like there was somebody lying behind every bush and tree waiting to shoot me. I never had mullygrubs like them before. Maybe it's one of them presumptions. I've got half a notion to light out in the morning before day. The Guadalupe country is burning up about that old Dutchman I plugged down there.''

"You are not afraid—no one could make my brave little one fear."

"Well, I haven't been usually regarded as a jackrabbit when it comes to scrapping; but I don't want a posse smoking me out when I'm in your *jacal*. Somebody might get hurt that oughtn't to."

"Remain with your Tonia; no one will find you here."

The Kid looked keenly into the shadows up and down the arroyo and toward the dim lights of the Mexican village.

"I'll see how it looks later on" was his decision.

At midnight a horseman rode into the rangers' camp, blazing his way by noisy "hallo"'s to indicate a pacific mission. Sandridge and one or two others turned out to investigate the row. The rider announced himself to be Domingo Sales, from the Lone Wolf Crossing. He bore a letter for Señor Sandridge. Old Luisa, the *lavandera*, had persuaded him to bring it, he said, her son Gregoro being too ill of a fever to ride.

Sandridge lighted the camp lantern and read the letter. These were its words:

Dear One: He has come. Hardly had you ridden away when he came out of the pear. When he first talked he said he would stay three days or more. Then as it grew later he was like a wolf or a fox, and walked about without rest, looking and listening. Soon he said he must leave before daylight when it is dark and stillest. And then he seemed to suspect that I be not true to him. He looked at me so strange that I am frightened. I swear to him that I love him, his own Tonia. Last of all he said I must prove to him I am true. He thinks that even now men are waiting to kill him as he rides from my house. To escape he says he will dress in my clothes, my red skirt and the blue waist I wear and the brown mantilla over the head, and thus ride away. But before that he says that I must put on his clothes, his *pantalones* and *camisa* and hat, and ride away on his horse from the *jacal* as far as the big road beyond the crossing and back again. This before he goes, so he can tell if I am true and if men are hidden to shoot him. It is a terrible thing. An hour before daybreak this is to be. Come, my dear one, and kill this man and take me for your Tonia. Do not try to take hold of him alive, but kill him quickly. Knowing all, you should do that. You must come long before the time and hide yourself in the little shed near the *jacal* where the wagon and saddles are kept. It is dark in there. He will wear my red skirt and blue waist and brown mantilla. I send you a hundred kisses. Come surely and shoot quickly and straight.

Thine Own Tonia

Sandridge quickly explained to his men the official part of the missive. The rangers protested against his going alone.

"I'll get him easy enough," said the lieutenant. "The girl's got him trapped. And don't even think he'll get the drop on me."

Sandridge saddled his horse and rode to the Lone Wolf Crossing. He tied his big dun in a clump of brush on the arroyo, took his Winchester from its scabbard, and carefully approached the Perez *jacal*. There was only the half of a high moon drifted over by ragged, milk-white gulf clouds.

The wagon-shed was an excellent place for ambush; and the ranger got inside it safely. In the black shadow of the brush shelter in front of the *jacal* he could see a horse tied and hear him impatiently pawing the hard-trodden earth.

He waited almost an hour before two figures came out of the *jacal*. One, in man's clothes, quickly mounted the horse and galloped past the wagon-shed toward the crossing and village. And then the other figure, in skirt, waist, and mantilla over its head, stepped out into the faint moonlight, gazing after the rider. Sandridge thought he would take his chance then before Tonia rode back. He fancied she might not care to see it.

"Throw up your hands," he ordered loudly, stepping out of the wagon-shed with his Winchester at his shoulder.

There was a quick turn of the figure, but no movement to obey, so the ranger pumped in the bullets—one—two—three—and then twice more; for you never could be too sure of bringing down the Cisco Kid. There was no danger of missing at ten paces, even in that half moonlight.

The old ancestor, asleep on his blanket, was awakened by the shots. Listening further, he heard a great cry from some man in mortal distress or anguish, and rose up grumbling at the disturbing ways of moderns.

The tall, red ghost of a man burst into the *jacal*, reaching one hand, shaking like a *tule* reed, for the lantern hanging on its nail. The other spread a letter on the table.

"Look at this letter, Perez," cried the man. "Who wrote it?"

"Ah, Dios! it is Señor Sandridge," mumbled the old man, approaching. *"Pues, señor,* that letter was written by *'El chivato,'* as he is called—by the man of Tonia. They say he is a bad man; I do not know. While Tonia slept he wrote the letter and sent it by this old hand of mine to Domingo Sales to be brought to you. Is there anything wrong in the letter? I am very old; and I did not know. *Valgame Dios!* it is a very foolish world; and there is nothing in the house to drink—nothing to drink."

Just then all that Sandridge could think of to do was to go outside and throw himself face downward in the dust by the side of his hummingbird, of whom not a feather fluttered. He was not a *caballero* by instinct, and he could not understand the niceties of revenge.

A mile away the rider who had ridden past the wagon-shed struck up a harsh, untuneful song, the words of which began:

Don't you monkey with my Lulu girl
Or I'll tell you what I'll do—

Beginning with his first novel, The Westerners *(1901),
Stewart Edward White wrote more than fifty expert and
evocative books about the Old West, each with a different
theme: Indian-fighting, logging, cattle-ranching, prospect-
ing, homesteading, trapping, etc. Among his notable works
are the novels* The Claim Jumpers, The Long Rifle, Gold,
and The Rules of the Game; *the collections* Arizona Nights
and Blazed Trail Stories; *and this memorable tale of cattle-
rustling in Arizona.*

The Two-Gun Man

Stewart Edward White

*B*uck Johnson was American born, but with *a black beard*
and a dignity of manner that had earned him the title of
Señor. He had drifted into southeastern Arizona in the days
of Cochise and Victorio and Geronimo. He had persisted,
and so in time had come to control the water—and hence the
grazing—of nearly all the Soda Springs Valley. His troubles
were many, and his difficulties great. There were the ordinary problems of lean and dry years. There were also the ex-
traordinary problems of devastating Apaches; rivals for
early and ill-defined range rights—and cattle-rustlers.

Señor Buck Johnson was a man of capacity, courage, di-
rectness of method, and perseverance. Especially the latter.
Therefore he had survived to see the Apaches subdued, the
range rights adjusted, his cattle increased to thousands,
grazing the area of a principality. Now, all the energy and
fire of his frontiersman's nature he had turned to wiping out

the third uncertainty of an uncertain business. He found it a task of some magnitude.

For Señor Buck Johnson lived just north of that terra incognita filled with the mystery of a double chance of death from man or the flaming desert known as the Mexican border. There, by natural gravitation, gathered all the desperate characters of three states and two republics. He who rode into it took good care that no one should ride behind him, lived warily, slept light, and breathed deep when once he had again sighted the familiar peaks of Cochise's Stronghold. No one professed knowledge of those who dwelt therein. They moved, mysterious as the desert illusions that compassed them about. As you rode, the ranges of mountains visibly changed form, the monstrous, snaky, sealike growths of the cactus clutched at your stirrup, mock lakes sparkled and dissolved in the middle distance, the sun beat hot and merciless, the powdered dry alkali beat hotly and mercilessly back—and strange, grim men, swarthy, bearded, heavily armed, with red-rimmed unshifting eyes, rode silently out of the mists of illusion to look on you steadily, and then to ride silently back into the desert haze. They might be only the herders of the gaunt cattle, or again they might belong to the Lost Legion that peopled the country. All you could know was that of the men who entered in, but few returned.

Directly north of this unknown land you encountered parallel fences running across the country. They enclosed nothing, but offered a check to the cattle drifting toward the clutch of the renegades, and an obstacle to swift, dashing forays.

Of cattle-rustling there are various forms. The boldest consists quite simply of running off a bunch of stock, hustling it over the Mexican line, and there selling it to some of the big Sonora ranch owners. Generally this sort means war. Also are there subtler means, grading in skill from the rebranding through a wet blanket, through the crafty refashioning of a brand to the various methods of separating the cow from her unbranded calf. In the course of his task Señor Buck Johnson would have to do with them all, but at present he existed in a state of warfare, fighting an enemy who stole as the Indians used to steal.

Already he had fought two pitched battles, and had won them both. His cattle increased, and he became rich. Nevertheless he knew that constantly his resources were being drained. Time and again he and his new Texas foreman, Jed Parker, had followed the trail of a stampeded bunch of twenty or thirty, followed them on down through the Soda Springs Valley to the cut drift fences, there to abandon them. For, as yet, an armed force would be needed to penetrate the borderland. Once he and his men had experienced the glory of a night pursuit. Then, at the drift fences, he had fought one of his battles. But it was impossible adequately to patrol all parts of a range bigger than some eastern states.

Buck Johnson did his best, but it was like stopping with sands the innumerable little leaks of a dam. Did his riders watch toward the Chiricahuas, then a score of beef steers disappeared from Grant's Pass forty miles away. Pursuit here meant leaving cattle unguarded there. It was useless, and the Señor soon perceived that sooner or later he must strike in offense.

For this purpose he began slowly to strengthen the forces of his riders. Men were coming in from Texas. They were good men, addicted to the grass-rope, the double cinch, and the ox-bow stirrup. Señor Johnson wanted men who could shoot, and he got them.

"Jed," said Señor Johnson to his foreman, "the next son of a gun that rustles any of our cows is sure loading himself full of trouble. We'll hit his trail and will stay with it, and we'll reach his cattle-rustling conscience with a rope."

So it came about that a little army crossed the drift fences and entered the border country. Two days later it came out, and mighty pleased to be able to do so. The rope had not been used.

The reason for the defeat was quite simple. The thief had run his cattle through the lava beds where the trail at once became difficult to follow. This delayed the pursuing party; they ran out of water, and, as there was among them not one

man well enough acquainted with the country to know
where to find more, they had to return.

"No use, Buck," said Jed. "We'd any of us come in on a
gunplay, but we can't buck the desert. We'll have to get
someone who knows the country."

"That's all right—but where?" queried Johnson.

"There's Pereza," suggested Parker. "It's the only town
down near that country."

"Might get someone there," agreed the Señor.

Next day he rode away in search of a guide. The third
evening he was back again, much discouraged.

"The country's no good," he explained. "The regular in-
habitants 're a set of Mexican bums and old soaks. The cow-
men's all from north and don't know nothing more than we
do. I found lots who claimed to know that country, but when
I told 'em what I wanted they shied like a colt. I couldn't
hire 'em, for no money, to go down in that country. They
ain't got the nerve. I took two days to her, too, and rode out
to a ranch where they said a man lived who knew all about it
down there. Nary riffle. Man looked all right, but his tail
went down like the rest when I told him what we wanted.
Seemed plumb scairt to death. Says he lives too close to the
gang. Says they'd wipe him out sure if he done it. Seemed
plumb *scairt*." Buck Johnson grinned. "I told him so and he
got hosstyle right off. Didn't seem no ways scairt of me. I
don't know what's the matter with that outfit down there.
They're plumb terrorized."

That night a bunch of steers was stolen from the very corrals of the home ranch. The home ranch was far north, near
Fort Sherman itself, and so had always been considered im-
mune from attack. Consequently these steers were very fine
ones.

For the first time Buck Johnson lost his head and his dignity. He ordered the horses.

"I'm going to follow that _____ _____ into Sonora,"
he shouted to Jed Parker. "This thing's got to stop!"

"You can't make her, Buck," objected the foreman.
"You'll get held up by the desert, and, if that don't finish
you, they'll tangle you up in all those little mountains down

there, and ambush you, and massacre you. You know it damn well.''

''I don't give a _____,'' exploded Señor Johnson, ''if they do. No man can slap my face and not get a run for it.''

Jed Parker communed with himself.

''Señor,'' said he, at last, ''it's no good; you can't do it. You got to have a guide. You wait three days and I'll get you one.''

''You can't do it,'' insisted the Señor. ''I tried every man in the district.''

''Will you wait three days?'' repeated the foreman.

Johnson pulled loose his latigo. His first anger had cooled.

''All right,'' he agreed, ''and you can say for me that I'll pay five thousand dollars in gold and give all the men and horses he needs to the man who has the nerve to get back that bunch of cattle, and bring in the man who rustled them. I'll sure make this a test case.''

So Jed Parker set out to discover his man with nerve.

At about ten o'clock of the Fourth of July a rider topped the summit of the last swell of land, and loped his animal down into the single street of Pereza. The buildings on either side were flat-roofed and coated with plaster. Over the sidewalks extended wooden awnings, beneath which opened very wide doors into the coolness of saloons. Each of these places ran a bar, and also games of roulette, faro, craps, and stud poker. Even this early in the morning every game was patronized.

The day was already hot with the dry, breathless, but exhilarating, heat of the desert. A throng of men idling at the edge of the sidewalks, jostling up and down their center, or eddying into the places of amusement, acknowledged the power of summer by loosening their collars, carrying their coats on their arms. They were as yet busily engaged in recognizing acquaintances. Later they would drink freely and gamble, and perhaps fight. Toward all but those whom they recognized they preserved an attitude of potential suspicion, for here were gathered the ''bad men'' of the border countries. A certain jealousy or touchy egotism lest the other man

be considered quicker on the trigger, bolder, more aggres-
sive than himself, kept each strung to tension. An occasional
shot attracted little notice. Men in the cow-countries shoot
as casually as we strike matches, and some subtle instinct
told them that the reports were harmless.

As the rider entered the one street, however, a more defi-
nite cause of excitement drew the loose population toward
the center of the road. Immediately their mass blotted out
what had interested them. Curiosity attracted the saunterers;
then in turn, the frequenters of the bars and gambling
games. In a very few moments the barkeepers, gamblers,
and look-out men, held aloof only by the necessities of their
calling, alone of all the population of Pereza were not included in the newly formed ring.

The stranger pushed his horse resolutely to the outer edge
of the crowd where, from his point of vantage, he could easily overlook their heads. He was a quiet-appearing young
fellow, rather neatly dressed in the border costume, rode a
"center fire," or single-cinch, saddle, and wore no chaps.
He was what is known as a "two-gun man": that is to say,
he wore a heavy Colt revolver on either hip. The fact that the
lower ends of his holsters were tied down, in order to facili-
tate the easy withdrawal of the revolvers, seemed to indicate
that he expected to use them. He had furthermore a quiet
gray eye, with the glint of steel that bore out the influence of
the tied holsters.

The newcomer dropped his reins on his pony's neck,
eased himself to an attitude of attention, and looked down
gravely on what was taking place.

He saw over the heads of the bystanders a tall, muscular,
wild-eyed man, hatless, his hair rumpled into staring confusion, his right sleeve rolled to his shoulder, a wicked-
looking nine-inch knife in his hand, and a red bandana
handkerchief hanging by one corner from his teeth.

"What's biting the locoed stranger?" the young man inquired of his neighbor.

The other frowned at him darkly.

"Dares anyone to take the other end of that handkerchief
in his teeth, and fight it out without letting go."

"Nice joyful proposition," commented the young man.

He settled himself to closer attention. The wild-eyed man was talking rapidly. What he said cannot be printed here. Mainly was it derogatory of the southern countries. Shortly it became boastful of the northern, and then of the man who uttered it. He swaggered up and down, becoming always the more insolent as his challenge remained untaken.

"Why don't you take him up?" inquired the young man, after a moment.

"Not me!" negatived the other vigorously. "I'll go yore little old gunfight to a finish, but I don't want any cold steel in mine. Ugh! It gives me the shivers. It's a reg'lar Mexican trick! With a gun it's down and out, but this knife work is too slow and searchin'."

The newcomer said nothing, but fixed his eye again on the raging man with the knife.

"Don't you reckon he's bluffing?" he inquired.

"Not any!" denied the other with emphasis. "He's jest drunk enough to be crazy mad."

The newcomer shrugged his shoulders and cast his glance searchingly over the fringe of the crowd. It rested on a Mexican.

"Hi, Tony! Come here," he called.

The Mexican approached, flashing his white teeth.

"Here," said the stranger, "lend me your knife a minute."

The Mexican, anticipating sport of his own peculiar kind, obeyed with alacrity.

"You fellows make me tired," observed the stranger, dismounting. "He's got the whole townful of you bluffed to a standstill. Damn if I don't try his little game."

He hung his coat on his saddle, shouldered his way through the press, which parted for him readily, and picked up the other corner of the handkerchief.

"Now, you mangy son of a gun," said he.

Jed Parker straightened his back, rolled up the bandana handkerchief, and thrust it into his pocket, hit flat with his hand the tousled mass of his hair, and thrust the long hunting knife into its sheath.

"You're the man I want," said he.

Instantly the two-gun man had jerked loose his weapons and was covering the foreman.

"*Am* I!" he snarled.

"Not jest that way," exclaimed Parker. "My gun is on my hoss, and you can have this old toad-sticker if you want it. I been looking for you and took this way of finding you. Now, let's go talk."

The stranger looked him in the eye for nearly a half minute without lowering his revolvers.

"I go you," said he briefly, at last.

But the crowd, missing the purport, and in fact the very occurrence of this colloquy, did not understand. It thought the bluff had been called, and naturally, finding harmless what had intimidated it, gave way to an exasperated impulse to get even.

"You _____ _____ _____ bluffer!" shouted a voice, "don't you think you can run any such ranikaboo here!"

Jed Parker turned humorously to his companion.

"Do we get that talk?" he inquired gently.

For answer the two-gun man turned and walked steadily in the direction of the man who had shouted. The latter's hand strayed uncertainly toward his own weapon, but the movement paused when the stranger's clear, steel eye rested on it.

"This gentleman," pointed out the two-gun man softly, "is an old friend of mine. Don't you get to calling of him names."

His eye swept the bystanders calmly.

"Come on, Jack," said he, addressing Parker.

On the outskirts he encountered the Mexican from whom he had borrowed the knife.

"Here, Tony," said he with a slight laugh, "here's a *peso*. You'll find your knife back there where I had to drop her."

He entered a saloon, nodded to the proprietor, and led the way through it to a boxlike room containing a board table and two chairs.

"Make good," he commanded briefly.

"I'm looking for a man with nerve," explained Parker, with equal succinctness. "You're the man."

"Well?"

"Do you know the country south of here?"

The stranger's eyes narrowed.

"Proceed," said he.

"I'm foreman of the Lazy Y of Soda Springs Valley range," explained Parker. "I'm looking for a man with sand enough and *sabe* of the country enough to lead a posse after cattle-rustlers into the border country."

"I live in this country," admitted the stranger.

"So do plenty of others, but their eyes stick out like two raw oysters when you mention the border country. Will you tackle it?"

"What's the proposition?"

"Come and see the old man. He'll put it to you."

They mounted their horses and rode the rest of the day. The desert compassed them about, marvelously changing shape and color, and every character, with all the noiselessness of phantasmagoria. At evening the desert stars shone steady and unwinking, like the flames of candles. By moonrise they came to the home ranch.

The buildings and corrals lay dark and silent against the moonlight that made of the plain a sea of mist. The two men unsaddled their horses and turned them loose in the wire-fenced "pasture," the necessary noises of their movements sounding sharp and clear against the velvet hush of the night. After a moment they walked stiffly past the sheds and cook shanty, past the men's bunk houses, and the tall windmill silhouetted against the sky, to the main building of the home ranch under its great cottonwoods. There a light still burned, for this was the third day, and Buck Johnson awaited his foreman.

Jed Parker pushed in without ceremony.

"Here's your man, Buck," said he.

The stranger had stepped inside and carefully closed the door behind him. The lamplight threw into relief the bold, free lines of his face, the details of his costume powdered thick with alkali, the shiny butts of the two guns in their

open holsters tied at the bottom. Equally it defined the reso-
lute countenance of Buck Johnson turned up in inquiry. The
two men examined each other—and liked each other at once.

"How are you?" greeted the cattleman.

"Good evening," responded the stranger.

"Sit down," invited Buck Johnson.

The stranger perched gingerly on the edge of a chair, with
an appearance less of embarrassment than of habitual alert-
ness.

"You'll take the job?" inquired the Señor.

"I haven't heard what it is," replied the stranger.

"Parker here—?"

"Said you'd explain."

"Very well," said Buck Johnson. He paused a moment,
collecting his thoughts. "There's too much cattle-rustling
here. I'm going to stop it. I've got good men here ready to
take the job, but no one who knows the country south. Three
days ago I had a bunch of cattle stolen right here from the
home-ranch corrals, and by one man, at that. It wasn't much
of a bunch—about twenty head—but I'm going to make a
starter right here, and now. I'm going to get that bunch
back, and the man who stole them, if I have to go to hell to
do it. And I'm going to do the same with every case of
rustling that comes up from now on. I don't care if it's only
one cow, I'm going to get it back—every trip. Now, I want
to know if you'll lead a posse down into the south country
and bring out that last bunch, and the man who rustled
them?"

"I don't know—" hesitated the stranger.

"I offer you five thousand dollars in gold if you'll bring
back those cows and the man who stole 'em," repeated
Buck Johnson. "And I'll give you all the horses and men
you think you need."

"I'll do it," replied the two-gun man promptly.

"Good!" cried Buck Johnson, "and you better start tomorrow."

"I shall start tonight—right now."

"Better yet. How many men do you want, and grub for
how long?"

"I'll play her a lone hand."

"Alone!" exclaimed Johnson, his confidence visibly cooling. "Alone! Do you think you can make her?"

"I'll be back with those cattle in not more than ten days."

"And the man," supplemented the Señor.

"And the man. What's more, I want that money here when I come in. I don't aim to stay in this country overnight."

A grin overspread Buck Johnson's countenance. He understood.

"Climate not healthy for you?" he hazarded. "I guess you'd be safe enough all right with us. But suit yourself. The money will be here."

"That's agreed?" insisted the two-gun man.

"Sure."

"I want a fresh horse—I'll leave mine—he's a good one. I want a little grub."

"All right. Parker'll fit you out."

The stranger rose.

"I'll see you in about ten days."

"Good luck," Señor Buck Johnson wished him.

The next morning Buck Johnson took a trip down into the "pasture" of five hundred wire-fenced acres.

"He means business," he confided to Jed Parker, on his return. "That caballo of his is a heap sight better than the Shorty horse we let him take. Jed, you found your man with nerve, all right. How did you do it?"

The two settled down to wait, if not with confidence, at least with interest. Sometimes, remembering the desperate character of the outlaws, their fierce distrust of any intruder, the wildness of the country, Buck Johnson and his foreman inclined to the belief that the stranger had undertaken a task beyond the powers of any one man. Again, remembering the stranger's cool gray eye, the poise of his demeanor, the quickness of his movements, and the two guns with tied holsters to permit of easy withdrawal, they were almost persuaded that he might win.

"He's one of those long-chance fellows," surmised Jed. "He likes excitement. I see that by the way he takes up with my knife play. He'd rather leave his hide on the fence than stay in the corral."

"Well, he's all right," replied Señor Buck Johnson, "and if he ever gets back, which same I'm some doubtful of, his dinero'll be here for him."

In pursuance of this he rode in to Willets, where shortly the overland train brought him from Tucson the five thousand dollars in double eagles.

In the meantime the regular life of the ranch went on. Each morning Sang, the Chinese cook, rang the great bell, summoning the men. They ate, and then caught up the saddle horses for the day, turning those not wanted from the corral into the pasture. Shortly they jingled away in different directions, two by two, on the slow Spanish trot of the cowpuncher. All day long thus they would ride, without food or water for man or beast, looking the range, identifying the stock, branding the young calves, examining generally into the state of affairs, gazing always with grave eyes on the magnificent, flaming, changing, beautiful, dreadful desert of the Arizona plains. At evening when the colored atmosphere, catching the last glow, threw across the Chiricahuas its veil of mystery, they jingled in again, two by two, untired, unhasting, the glory of the desert in their deep-set, steady eyes.

And all the day long, while they were absent, the cattle, too, made their pilgrimage, straggling in singly, in pairs, in bunches, in long files, leisurely, ruminantly, without haste. There, at the long troughs filled by the windmill or the blindfolded pump mule, they drank, then filed away again into the mists of the desert. And Señor Buck Johnson, or his foreman, Parker, examined them for their condition, noting the increase, remarking the strays from another range. Later, perhaps, they, too, rode abroad. The same thing happened at nine other ranches from five to ten miles apart, where dwelt other fierce, silent men all under the authority of Buck Johnson.

And when night fell, and the topaz and violet and saffron and amethyst and mauve and lilac had faded suddenly from the Chiricahuas, like a veil that has been rent, and the ramparts had become slate-gray and then black—the soft-breathed night wandered here and there over the desert, and the land fell under an enchantment even stranger than the day's.

So the days went by, wonderful, fashioning the ways and the characters of men. Seven passed. Buck Johnson and his foreman began to look for the stranger. Eight, they began to speculate. Nine, they doubted. On the tenth, they gave him up—and he came.

They knew him first by the soft lowing of cattle. Jed Parker, dazzled by the lamp, peered out from the door, and made him out dimly turning the animals into the corral. A moment later his pony's hoofs impacted softly on the baked earth; he dropped from the saddle and entered the room.

"I'm late," said he briefly, glancing at the clock, which indicated ten, "but I'm here."

His manner was quick and sharp, almost breathless, as though he had been running.

"Your cattle are in the corral: all of them. Have you the money?"

"I have the money here," replied Buck Johnson, laying his hand against a drawer, "and it's ready for you when you've earned it. I don't care so much for the cattle. What I wanted is the man who stole them. Did you bring him?"

"Yes, I brought him," said the stranger. "Let's see that money."

Buck Johnson threw open the drawer, and drew from it the heavy canvas sack.

"It's here. Now bring in your prisoner."

The two-gun man seemed suddenly to loom large in the doorway. The muzzles of his revolvers covered the two before him. His speech came short and sharp.

"I told you I'd bring back the cows and the one who rustled them," he snapped. "I've never lied to a man yet. Your stock is in the corral. I'll trouble you for that five thousand. I'm the man who stole your cattle!"

Frank Gruber, the author of many pulp stories and such expert Western novels as Peace Marshal, Outlaw, Fighting Man, *and* Fort Starvation, *offers in "Assassin" his own version of the life and death of Jesse James (redubbed here Jesse Carney). He also tells the tale of young Billy Mason, and of the lesson Billy learns from having ridden with Jesse on the outlaw trail. . . .*

Assassin

Frank Gruber

*T*he train screeched to a stop and Billy Mason swung up to the engine platform. He thrust his Frontier Model Colt into the face of the engineer and said, "Throw up your hands!"

Dick Small, a moment late as usual, came up from the other side and covered the fireman. "And damn quick about it!" he snarled.

The fireman's teeth chattered, but the engineer was made of sterner stuff. He raised his hands slowly. A scowl twisted his face.

He looked from Dick Small to Billy Mason and asked, "Which one of you is Jess Carney?"

Dick Small swore and struck at the engineer with the long barrel of his Colt.

Billy Mason struck out with his left hand and knocked the gun down. "Cut it!" he snapped. "You know the orders."

From the direction of the express car, a voice roared, "Open up, or we'll blow it open."

A gun roared; another. A man screamed in pain. Dick Small's face showed fright.

"Easy," Billy Mason cautioned.

The sharp, spiteful crack of a rifle was followed by a half-dozen duller reports, then Jess Carney's triumphant voice rang out: "All right, Sam!"

Billy Mason knew Jess was talking to Charley Ford, who was using the name of Sam, according to prearrangement. Billy knew, too, that the ring in Jess's tone indicated that the express messenger had surrendered.

Boots clattered alongside the engine and Billy risked a glance to the side. He saw the bearded face of Jess Carney and nodded.

"Another minute!" Jess said.

Charley Ford appeared carrying a half-filled wheat sack. "All right, Tom," he said to Jess.

Jess Carney cried out, "You engineer, start up. And if you stop inside of a mile I'll blow your head off."

The engineer said sullenly, "Which one of you is Jess Carney?"

Jess Carney snarled, "You think Jess Carney's the only man who can stick up a train?"

Billy Mason clambered down from the cab. Behind him came Dick Small. They lined up beside Jess and Charley Ford.

"Get going!" Jess ordered.

Steam hissed and the wheels of the engine began moving. The four bandits waited until the engine had gone perhaps fifty feet, then, as if by a signal, they turned and plunged into the thick brush that lined the roadway.

"Tom!" a voice called softly from ahead of them.

"All right," Jess replied.

They found Ed Mitchell already mounted on his horse, holding the reins of the other four. The men mounted swiftly and headed their horses in a northerly direction.

"Whew!" Ed Mitchell exclaimed in relief. "When I heard that shootin' I thought sure—"

"You think too much!" snapped Jess Carney. "I told you nothing would happen."

Ed Mitchell subsided, but after a moment Billy Mason asked quietly, "What happened, Jess?"

Jess Carney turned his head in the gloom. Billy could not see his features, but he sensed that the outlaw chief was trying to see his expression.

Finally Jess said, "The conductor opened on us with a rifle."

He did not add, "So I killed him," but Billy Mason knew that. When Jess Carney fired he shot to kill. He had always done so. He was a killer by instinct.

Billy Mason had never killed a man, but now the stigma was on him. He was tarred with the same brush that had blackened Jess Carney these many years. If he was captured he would receive the same treatment as Jess Carney.

Well, he had thought of all that before he had thrown in with Jess Carney. He had weighed everything and made his choice. Yet he had not thought it would feel—like this!

They came to a small stream and halted. "In a couple of hours everybody in fifty miles is going to be on the lookout for four or five men. I think we'd better break up here and meet again later on."

"Sure," said Dick Small, "but let's divvy up first."

"Why?" Jess Carney asked softly.

"Because—" Dick Small stopped short. He cleared his throat. "No reason at all."

"Anybody else wanta divvy now?" Carney went on.

"Whenever you say the word, Jess," Charley Ford said quickly.

Jess Carney snorted. "All right then, we'll split here. Billy, you come with me. The rest of you go east. We'll meet tomorrow night at your place, Charley. And now, remember—don't take any chances. I mean that particularly for you, Ed—don't get drunk!"

Jess Carney waited until the three men had gone off before he fell in beside Billy Mason. He said then, "Why I ever picked up a bunch of fellows like that, I don't know."

"Don't you think it went all right?" Billy Mason asked.

Jess Carney snorted. "The conductor killed and the express messenger wounded. Hell, there'll be plenty of noise over that. But you're all right, Billy, I was watching you. You were a lot cooler than Dick Small or Charley Ford.''

Billy Mason said nothing.

Jess Carney peered at him and asked, ''Well, how do you like it?''

''I don't know,'' Billy Mason said truthfully. ''I hadn't counted on anyone being killed.''

''It couldn't be helped. With Charley, Ed, and Dick so jittery, they got me nervous.'' He sighed wearily. ''If I only had a bunch like we had in 'seventy-six—Frank, Cole, Clell. Well, let's go on.''

'Seventy six, Billy thought. Yet that was the year the powerful Carney Federation had suffered its severest defeat. Eight of them, probably the outstanding outlaws of the day, they had descended upon Northport in Minnesota. Three had died and three had remained there, behind bleak, dank walls. Only two of the eight, Frank and Jess Carney, had escaped.

And now Frank Carney, in poor health, had gone into retirement and Jess Carney had gathered about him a new band, an inferior one, he said. It was the second job for Dick Small, Ed Mitchell, and Charley Ford, the first for Billy Mason. A hefty wheat sack on Jess's saddle was the result. And one man dead, another wounded.

They would howl about that; the newspapers and the law-enforcement bodies. Jess Carney, the terror of the countryside, outlaw and killer. He must be exterminated.

Billy Mason was riding with Jess Carney now. He had crossed his Rubicon, headed up the road from which there is no turning back. He was an outlaw, a member of the notorious Carney gang.

They rode through the woods and came out upon a narrow country road. Ahead and to the right, a tiny square of light showed in a larger rectangle of blackness. A dog barked.

''Easy, Billy,'' Jess Carney said quietly. But Billy Mason was not skittish. He had been cooler than Charley Ford and Dick Small back there on the train. Jess Carney himself had said that.

He rode beside Jess and said, "Do you suppose it's really safe to go back there to Ford's place?"

"It's as safe as anywhere," was Carney's reply. "The Fords have a bad reputation in their own neighborhood and people let them pretty much alone. They've got the local law bluffed."

"But what about the Wilkinsons?"

Jess Carney snorted. "Since 1875 Mr. William hasn't stepped out of his house in Chicago without a couple of bodyguards. He's afraid I'll get him. He does a lot of hollering but he does it at a distance. Shucks, Billy, I've been at this a long time. A long time."

He shook his head and went on: "I never really came in. I went out in 'sixty-three and this is 'eighty-two. Nineteen years and I'm only thirty-four now." He laughed harshly.

There were questions in Billy Mason's mind. He wanted to ask, *Do the faces of the men you've killed ever haunt you in your dreams? Do you ever wish you could look at a policeman and not be afraid? Don't you ever—ever yearn for peace?*

Billy wanted to ask those questions, but he didn't. Because he was riding beside Jess Carney, now. And soon he would learn the answers himself.

Morning. A golden sun creeping up over the freshly plowed farmlands. Smoke coming lazily from a chimney; a rooster crowing.

Jess Carney said, "Milltown's just ahead, but we'd better get some breakfast here."

"Here?"

"Why not? They don't know us. We are stock buyers. This sack"—he slapped it—"might contain grain for our horses."

They had thrown their linen dusters away during the night. They were now wearing broadcloth suits, with rather long coats, sufficiently long to conceal the pistols strapped about their waists. Many men dressed like this. Jess Carney was tall and slender. His beard, neatly trimmed, gave him a dignified appearance. Some might even mistake him for a minister. Certainly he didn't look like Jess Carney.

Jess Carney was a hulking, beetle-browed man with a fe-
rocious black beard and blazing black eyes. Women and
children quailed when he looked at them, strong men trembled. That's what people said.

They rode into the farmyard.

"Hello!" Jess called.

A man carrying a milk pail came out of the log barn.
"Morning, strangers," he said cheerfully.

"Good morning, sir!" Jess Carney replied heartily. "We
were just riding by and we wondered if we could beg a bite
of breakfast."

"Why, certainly," the farmer replied. "I imagine Florence is just about settin' the table. Light, won't you?"

Jess Carney swung easily to the ground. Billy Mason dismounted rather stiffly. He turned toward the door of the
house—and stopped.

A girl had come out, a tall slender girl with chestnut-
colored hair. She wore a gingham dress, and there was flour
on her bare forearms and a spot of it on the tip of her nose,
but her features were finely chiseled, her complexion
smooth and fresh. Her eyes smiled a welcome.

"I've just taken the biscuits out of the oven," she said.
"Won't you come in?"

"We certainly will," said Jess Carney. "Allow me to in-
troduce my assistant, Billy Mason. My own name's Tom
Howard."

"Howdy, Mr. Howard," said the farmer, "and Mr. Mason. I'm Jim King and this is my daughter, Florence. Traveling men, aren't you?"

"Something of the sort," Jess Carney shot a quick glance
toward the small log barn, then added, "I'm a stock buyer.
You haven't got fifteen or twenty good head you want to
sell, have you?"

"Gosh, no!" exclaimed Jim King. "I've got two cows,
that's all."

They went into the house and sat down at the table in the
kitchen. Florence King set out plates, poured coffee, and
brought crisp bacon, eggs, and fresh biscuits.

"Pitch in, gentlemen," said Jim King.

Jess Carney reached for the plate of biscuits, took one, and passed them to Billy Mason. Billy took a biscuit and broke it to apply butter.

Jim King said, "Heard about the holdup?"

Billy Mason's teeth closed on the biscuit. A ripple ran up his spine, paralyzed him. Then Jess Carney's matter-of-fact voice broke the spell. "What holdup?"

"Train holdup, over near Black Cut, last night. Jess Carney's gang."

"Doggone!" exclaimed Jess Carney. "So he's done it again. I don't see how he gets away with it."

"Neither do I," replied Jim King. "Except that everyone's so scared of him, they don't even chase him much. Paul Potter was by here a half hour ago. He told me about it. Carney got $50,000 out of the express car and the whole train crew was afraid to go after him."

"Fifty thousand!" exclaimed Jess Carney. "That is somethin'. Almost makes a fellow want to turn train robber, doesn't it?"

From near the stove, the voice of Florence King said crisply, "Why should it?"

Jess Carney turned. "Fifty thousand dollars is a lot more'n most people make in a lifetime of hard work."

"That's true," conceded Florence King. "But I don't imagine Jess Carney gets much enjoyment out of his money. He can't lie down in a bed at night and know that he'll still be in that bed in the morning."

"Why not? Your dad himself said folks are so scared of him they don't even dare go near him."

Florence King came a step closer to the table. "But what about his own men? Can Jess Carney trust them? With the huge reward the governor's placed on Carney's head, can Jess Carney go close his eyes at night and be sure that one of his own men won't creep up on him and send a bullet through his head?"

The light went out of Jess Carney's eyes. Billy Mason, sitting across from him saw that. He saw, too, the slight twitching of the muscles about the mouth, and he guessed suddenly that sheer nerve was carrying Jess through these days. The chase had been too hard, too long for Jess Carney. He was scared stiff—and as dangerous as death.

Billy said quickly, "I imagine Jess has made pretty sure of his men."

"Has he? No man can trust his best friend—if there's a huge premium for treachery."

Jess Carney laughed. Was there a slight touch of nervousness in his laughter? "Well, we don't have to worry about Jess Carney, do we? These biscuits are mighty fine, Miss King. Wish I could eat more of them."

He wiped his mouth on the damask napkin, pushed back his chair. "Thanks, folks. I guess me and Billy have got to be riding on." He tossed a silver dollar on the table. "Thanks, folks!"

Florence King came over, picked up the dollar, and handed it back to Jess. "Sorry, Mr. Howard. We're not running a hotel."

Jess Carney bowed. He started for the door. Billy Mason followed. At the door he turned.

"Thanks, Miss King—for the breakfast."

She smiled at him. "You're entirely welcome."

He hesitated. "Perhaps we'll be riding back this way in a couple of days." He knew he shouldn't have said it the moment the words were out of his mouth. He was Billy Mason, a member of Jess Carney's gang. A girl like Florence King must always be a stranger to Billy Mason.

But she said, "Stop in and say hello when you come back."

They rode until shortly before noon, when they entered a grove of poplars by a small stream. Jess dismounted and tied his horse to a sapling.

"We'll lay low here until dark."

Billy climbed from his horse and tethered it securely. Then he sat down on the bank of the stream and looked into the water.

"Better get some sleep, Billy," Jess said kindly.

"How about yourself?"

Jess shrugged. "Not sleepy. I'll sit up—and keep watch."

Was he thinking of what Florence King had said? That he couldn't close his eyes even in the presence of his closest friends—

Billy Mason dropped back. He moved his hat so it shaded his eyes. He tried to sleep but sleep wouldn't come. He was relaxed, but deep down in him a bell seemed to be tolling slowly.

Some time later, Jess Carney's voice asked softly, "Sleeping, Billy?"

"No," Billy replied.

"Thinkin'?"

"Yes."

"That you shouldn't have done it?"

Billy sat up. "No, of course not. I knew what I was getting into and I'm not sorry. I'd do it again."

Jess Carney was silent for a moment. Then he said, "How old are you, Billy?"

"Twenty-three. Why?"

"Just thinkin'. When I was twenty-three every sheriff in six states was lookin' for me. Lord, that was a long time ago. Eleven years. Sometimes it seems like fifty. I think I'll quit and go to California."

Billy Mason looked at him sharply. Jess Carney grinned.

"Don't worry, I went to California once before. I didn't stay very long. But I wish Frank'd come back. He was much better at this thinkin' business. He'd figure out a job and we'd pull it without any fuss. Then we'd go somewhere and have a good time."

"But you're married, Jess. What does Mrs. Carney think about it?"

Jess Carney's eyes blinked. "She doesn't say anything—anymore."

Billy Mason dropped back to the grass.

Shortly before sundown they started again. They rode for three or four hours, then Jess halted.

"One shade is up, one down. That means it's all right."

Billy Mason stared at the chink of light ahead of them. "They're here—?"

Carney nodded. "Yep! Now for the squabblin'."

They rode up to the house and Jess whistled. Instantly a door was jerked open and a woman looked out.

"Maggie?" Jess asked.

The woman disappeared and a tall youth appeared in her place. "Jess!" he exclaimed and came out.

"Hi, Bob," Jess said. He turned to Billy Mason. "Shake hands with Bob Ford, Billy. Charley's younger brother. Bob, this is Billy Mason."

Billy swung down from his gelding and Bob Ford's lean hand gripped his own. There was strength in the boy's grip. Billy looked into Bob's eager face. "Howdy, Bob," he said.

"Sure glad to know you, Billy," Bob Ford replied. "The boys were telling me about you."

"Put the horses away, will you, Bob?" Jess Carney asked.

He went into the house and Billy Mason followed. There were five persons in the room into which they entered, four men and the woman Jess had called Maggie. Charley Ford introduced a vicious-looking man of about fifty. "The old man, Billy. Call him Cap."

"And my wife," Dick Small said, nodding to Maggie.

Billy Mason turned to Maggie Small. He did not even make a mental comparison between Maggie and Florence King.

Jess Carney tossed the wheat sack on a bare table. "There she is, boys!"

Ed Mitchell reached avidly for the sack. Jess Carney lashed out with his fist and knocked Mitchell back. "I'll do the divvying!" he snapped.

Ed Mitchell's eyes glistened. "Some day—" he muttered.

Jess Carney caught hold of Ed's shirt. "What's that?"

"Nothin', Jess, nothin' at all!" Ed Mitchell exclaimed.

Jess released Ed and sniffed contemptuously. Then he up-ended the wheat sack upon the table. Exclamations of awe and delight went up. Billy Mason saw that young Bob Ford had come in. His eyes were shining as they took in the money on the table.

"Fifty thousand!" exclaimed Charley Ford.

Jess Carney snorted, "We'll be lucky if there's half of that."

"What do you mean?" cried Dick Small.

"You know damn well they always exaggerate the amount we get. If the papers say fifty thousand my guess is twenty thousand."

Ed Mitchell's eyes blazed. "That's what you say, Jess. There'd better be fifty thousand here, or—"

"Or what?"

Jess's words were toneless. His hands remained on the table. But Ed Mitchell looked into Jess's eyes and wet his lips.

"Nothin', Jess. I was just saying those newspapers lie like hell."

Jess Carney stacked the money on the table. His strong, lean fingers counted it swiftly. When he finished, he said, "They didn't lie so much this time. There's thirty-eight thousand. That's seven thousand apiece."

"Seven times five is thirty-five," said Bob Ford.

Jess Carney straightened. He looked at Bob Ford, then at Charley Ford. "Your kid brother's good at arithmetic,"

"I'll crack his teeth in if he don't keep his mouth shut," snarled Charley Ford. He took a step toward his younger brother. But Bob did not retreat.

"Try it some time, Charley," he said. "I'm taller'n you and—"

"Shet yore mouth, Bob!" said old Cap Ford.

"The extra three thousand goes to someone," Jess Carney said. "I told you boys about that. How do you think we know when there's money on a train?"

Bob Ford's eyes glowed. "Say, that's clever. I didn't know that—"

"Shut up, Bob," said Charley Ford.

"What for? I may as well talk now. Jess, I want to join up with you."

Jess Carney cocked his head to one side. "How old are you?"

"Twenty. That's more'n you were when you started."

"Maybe so, but it's too young—these days. Better wait awhile, Bob."

"What for?" demanded Bob Ford. He jabbed a finger at Billy Mason. "He ain't much older'n me. And I bet I can shoot better'n him."

"Can you now, Bob?" asked Jess Carney, showing his teeth. "Billy's the best man in the outfit—after me."

Instantly, Billy felt the hostile eyes of Ed Mitchell, Dick Small, and Charley Ford. Jess did not seem to notice. He divided stacks of bills.

"There you are, fellows. If you're smart you won't spend it all right away. One of these times—"

"When we spend it there's more where this came from," chuckled Dick Small.

Old Cap Ford went to a cupboard and brought out a bottle and a pack of greasy playing-cards. "How about some fun now, boys?"

Ed Mitchell grabbed the bottle and took a healthy swig. "That hits the spot," he said, smacking his lips.

Dick Small was already shuffling the cards. He did it dexterously, "All right, boys, ante up!"

Jess Carney put a hand to his mouth and yawned. "Count me out. I'm goin' to get some sleep."

"I think I will, too," Billy Mason said.

Jess Carney frowned. "Cap'll fix you up with a bed."

"Yep, you c'n use mine," Old Cap volunteered. He gestured toward a cot on one side of the room. Billy Mason looked at the dirty horse blanket that covered the cot.

"You'll need it yourself, Cap," Billy said.

"Naw, I'll prob'ly stay up and play poker with the boys."

Billy regarded the bed with disfavor. "I'd just as soon sleep out in your hayloft—" he began.

Jess Carney cut in, "No, you stay in here." But he moved to the door himself and went out abruptly.

Dick Small dealt cards, then said, "What's the matter with Jess? He afraid to sleep in the same house with us?"

Ed Mitchell sneered. "Maybe we're not good enough to sleep with. On'y good enough to do the dirty work."

"You know that's not so," Bill Mason said quickly.

Ed Mitchell banged his fist on the table. "You callin' me a liar, squirt?"

Billy Mason's hands dropped loosely to his sides. "If you want to take it up—yes," he replied softly.

Ed Mitchell pushed back his chair. Beside him, Charley Ford caught his arm.

"Cut it, Ed. He—he might be outside, listening."

Ed Mitchell's nostrils flared. "All right, Mason—but I'll remember that."

"I don't care if you do," retorted Billy. He walked to Cap Ford's smelly cot and dropped down on it.

But he did not sleep. The others played cards. They bickered and argued. Dick Small's wife wanted him to stop drinking and he cursed her furiously. Ed Mitchell picked a quarrel with Dick Small and Charley Ford again had to intercede to prevent a fight. Then both Mitchell and Small turned on Charley and it took the combined efforts of the three Fords to quiet them.

Billy Mason did not sleep. He stretched out on the cot, his eyes closed. Jess Carney was outside, probably sleeping in the woods. It was true, what Florence King had said. Jess Carney could not close his eyes in the presence of his own men. He could not trust them because the State of Missouri had offered so much money for his body—dead or alive—that he was afraid one of his men would make a try for the reward. For the reward and amnesty.

The gambling and drinking continued through the night. When the lamps were no longer necessary in the room, Jess Carney came in. Billy Mason looked at his face and thought that it was drawn. The eyes, he knew, were bloodshot.

He looked around the room and said, "Dick, get your wife to make some breakfast. I want to get going."

"Where to?"

"Clay County, first, then home. My advice to the rest of you is not to hang around here. Scatter and lay low for a month or so. I'll get in touch with you if I figure out anything new." He turned to Billy Mason, "What are you goin' to do, Billy?"

Billy shrugged. "I haven't made any plans. I might run over to St. Louis for a while."

"Oh, then you won't be coming my way?"

"I will, Jess," said Charley Ford. "I want to see a lady over near Independence."

"All right, Charley."

Maggie Small cooked breakfast and served it grudgingly. All the men ate, then Jess Carney got up from the table and nodded. "I'll be seeing you, fellows."

He and Charley Ford went out. Bob Ford followed. Ed Mitchell glared at the closed door. "He'll be seeing us!"

Dick Small shook his head. "He's gettin' mighty skittish."

"Don't blame him," rumbled old Cap Ford. "Ten thousand dollars is a mighty powerful bunch of money."

Bob Ford came in. His lean face was dark with anger.

"What's the matter, bud?" sneered Ed Mitchell. "Did he tell you you was still wet behind the ears?"

Bob Ford looked coldly at the outlaw. Billy Mason stepped to the door and went outside. There was a heavy dew on the grass and a nip in the air. He shivered.

He looked at the tumbledown log barn and littered, unkempt yard, then turned and regarded the exterior of the house, which he hadn't seen during the day. He sighed and shook his head. The Fords were a disreputable lot, he thought.

He walked through the wet grass to the barn and found his horse inside, his saddle tossed on the floor. He found a bin of oats and gave the gelding a half-measure, while he curried it. Then he saddled up and led the horse out to the yard.

Angry voices reached his ears. He frowned and wondered if it wouldn't be best just to leave without saying a word. But after a moment he shrugged and entered the house.

Dick Small and Ed Mitchell were facing each other in the middle of the room, their faces distorted with anger. Cap Ford and Maggie Small had gone to another room, but young Bob Ford stood to one side, watching the proceedings with a brooding look on his face.

Billy Mason inhaled sharply. "Cut it, fellows," he said

sharply. "First thing you know you're going to get into a fight."

"This is a fight!" snarled Ed Mitchell.

"Reach for your gun—if you've got the nerve!" invited Dick Small.

Billy Mason took a step forward. Then he leaped back.

Small and Mitchell had gone for their guns. Mitchell's was out first; it thundered and Dick Small staggered, but then he was firing. The room shook to the deafening explosions.

Billy whipped out his gun, yelled. "Stop or—!"

And then Ed Mitchell pitched to the floor. Dick Small, his left hand clutching his thigh, hobbled forward. "I got him!" he exulted.

Maggie Small bounced into the room, saw Ed Mitchell on the floor and screamed.

Dick Small turned toward Billy Mason, saw the Frontier Model in Billy's hand and hissed, "You sidin' with him?"

"No," replied Billy thickly. He felt suddenly sick with revulsion.

"He had it comin' to him," Dick Small said. "Didn't he, Bob?"

Bob Ford said evenly, "I guess he did, Dick. He wanted a fight and he got it. You hurt much, Dick?"

Dick Small looked down at the trickle of blood on his trouser leg. "Nah, just a scratch. I can hardly feel it." He lifted his head suddenly. "He drew first on me. Remember that!"

"What difference does it make?" asked Billy.

"It makes a helluva lot of diff'rence, if you was figurin' on tellin' Jess about it."

Billy moved to the door. "You tell him about it." He stepped outside, mounted his horse and rode away.

Calling at General Delivery in St. Louis for a letter, Billy Mason found one addressed to James Latimer. He tore it open and read:

*Dear Jim: I was talking to Tom Howard the other day
and he told me you were looking for a job. Jack Ladd
is looking for a man. The pay is good, I understand,
and the work not too hard. Why don't you go and see
Jack Ladd? Best wishes—*JOHN

Decoded, the message was to the effect that Jess Carney
had planned another holdup and that he wanted Billy Mason
to come to a certain place in Clay County, Missouri.

Billy took the train to Kansas City the same evening. Arriving at Kansas City in the morning, he bought a horse and
saddle and started eastward. This was familiar country to
him; his own home was not far from here. It was also Jess
Carney's country.

Jess had been born and raised twenty miles from here.
During the war he had skirmished through the entire section,
as a guerilla under Quantrell. Even today, hunted though he
was, Jess Carney could always find shelter in Jackson and
Clay Counties.

Before he was an hour out of Kansas City, Billy Mason
knew that the grapevine telegraph was reporting the presence of a horseman, riding eastward. His description was
going ahead of him and somewhere along the line someone
would identify him as Billy Mason, whose family lived in
Clay County. That he was a member of Jess Carney's gang
was not generally known.

He reached Liberty around noon, had a substantial lunch
in a restaurant, and took the northeast road out of town. A
mile, and Billy saw a horseman awaiting him beside the
road. It was Charley Ford.

"Hi, Billy," Charley greeted as he fell in beside Billy.

"Hello, Charley, what's new?"

"Nebraska, I think, although he hasn't made up his mind
definitely. He mentioned Butte, Montana, too, but that's too
far from here. None of us would know our way around."

"He's here?"

Charley nodded. "He was at his brother-in-law's with
me, last night. Don't know where he'll be tonight. You
know, he never sleeps twice in the same place." He shook

his head and shot a covert look at Billy. "He doesn't know about Ed Mitchell."

"How do you know?"

"Bob told me. He told me something else. That Dick Small's scared stiff Jess will find out he killed Ed and kill him. You think it'd be best to tell him?"

"I'm not a squealer, if that's what you mean," Billy replied shortly.

"I didn't mean anything of the kind," retorted Charley. "Only the kid's here and he was there when it happened."

"Bob's here?"

"Yes, Jess may let him come with us on the next job. Especially if one of the others doesn't show up—and Ed won't, of course."

They reached the little country village of Centerville after a while, but rode directly through it. People saw them, but gave no sign of recognition or salutation. That wasn't the custom around Centerville. You nodded at a stranger and he might turn out to be a Wilkinson man—or one of the "boys." Either way, it didn't do you any good.

Three miles out of Centerville, Charley turned in at a lane leading to a house almost out of sight of the road. "This is Hill's place; his sister's married to Jess's step-brother."

A man sat on the doorstep, whittling. He got up when Charley Ford and Billy dismounted.

"Shake hands with Billy Mason, Bud," Charley introduced.

Bud Hill held out a limp hand. "Harya!" He turned and yelled, "Donny! C'mon out here and put these horses away."

A barefooted boy of about twelve popped out of the house.

"I'll take care of my horse," Bill Mason said. He turned —and stopped.

Bob Ford and Jess Carney came out of the woods at the side of the house. "I see you got my letter," Jess said. He jerked his head to the trees and Charley Ford and Billy Mason followed him. After a moment Bob Ford came along. Jess did not order him back.

"I've got something good figured out," Jess announced. "Soon's Dick and Ed get here we'll start out. Unless I've got a bum steer, it'll make Black Cut look like small potatoes."

"Say, that'll be swell!" exclaimed Bob Ford.

Jess Carney frowned. "I haven't said yet I'd let you come along, Bob."

"But if one of the others don't show up?"

"They'll show up," Jess said confidently.

But Billy Mason knew that Ed Mitchell would not show up. Bob and Charley Ford knew that, too. The two brothers looked at one another uneasily.

Jess Carney said, "Charley, you come with me. The two young fellows can stay with Bud tonight."

Billy would have preferred to go with Jess, but the outlaw chief had not asked him. He turned back to the house, with Bob Ford.

The moment Jess Carney was out of sight, Bob Ford caught hold of Billy Mason's arm. "There's a dance up here at the schoolhouse tonight, Billy. Let's me and you go."

"I've been ridin' all day," Billy said. "I don't feel much like dancing."

"Aw, the exercise will do you good."

"Perhaps—but I don't think we ought to appear in a public place. Someone might—"

Bob Ford snickered. "Around here? Hell, half the people are related to Jess. And the rest'd be scared to open their mouths. Jess goes to these places himself, when he feels like it. Besides—" Bob Ford winked at Billy, "if I'm goin' to be one of the gang, we ought to get acquainted."

Billy Mason had no heart for music and laughter, but perhaps the gaiety of a country dance was just what he needed. It might relieve for a few hours the black oppressiveness that had been with him for days, since—yes, since he'd turned up the road.

He shrugged. "All right, we'll go to that dance."

The Hills were going, too, it seemed. Supper was early and immediately afterward there was a general washing, scrubbing, and dressing. Bud and Mrs. Hill and the three young Hills were all eager for the dance.

When they were ready, Bud Hill caught Billy's eye and walked to one side. "They usually leave their guns at home when they go to the dance. But if you don't want to do that, there's a woodpile behind the schoolhouse where you can stash your'n. Tell Bob."

The schoolhouse was only a mile from the Hill home and they all walked there. Before they reached it, they could hear the wail of a fiddle.

Bill drew Bob to one side and led him behind the schoolhouse. "Bud said to hide our guns in the woodpile."

Bob Ford looked toward the schoolhouse. "But suppose someone in there should try something?"

"If you think there's a chance of that, we'd better not go in."

Bob shrugged. Then he opened his coat and unbuckled a belt from about his waist. He rolled it around a long-barreled Frontier Model Colt and stuck the whole thing deep into the woodpile. Billy did the same with his own Colt.

Then they went to the front door of the schoolhouse where the dance was being held. The little room was crowded with thirty or forty men, women, and children. The desks and benches had been cleared to the sides and a number of couples were dancing to the music of a single fiddle.

They entered. And the first person Billy Mason saw was Florence King. She was standing on the side talking with another girl. When she saw Billy Mason her eyes opened wide and her nostrils flared a little.

Beside Billy, Bob Ford said, "There's a couple of good-looking girls. Let's ask them to dance with us."

Billy walked steadily toward Florence King. When he reached her he stopped and said, "Hello."

For a moment she just stared at him. Then she said in a voice that was strained. "You—"

"Will you dance with me?"

She hesitated, then nodded suddenly. He put his arm about her and moved to the center of the floor.

"I hadn't expected to see you here," he said.

She replied, "Who are you?"

"Billy Mason."

"But that boy you came in with—that's Bob Ford."

"You know him?"

"Yes, of course. You see, I'm visiting my uncle. I've been here before and I've met the Fords. But you—"

"My name is still Billy Mason."

"That man who was with you the other day. He's—"

"I'm sorry," Billy cut in, "but he told me his name was Tom Howard."

She stiffened. He felt it and turned cold inside. She tried to draw her hand away from his.

"Do you mind—?"

"I do," he said quickly. "Won't you step outside a moment?"

"No." But she let him lead her to the door and did not hold back there. He took her beyond hearing, into the shelter of a big oak tree. Her face was just a blur and he hoped she could not see his own distinctly.

He said, "You mustn't get the wrong ideas—"

"I haven't. But I remember now. Both of you were so interested in the Black Cut robbery and there was a wheat sack on his horse. The papers said—"

"No," he cut her off quickly.

In the gloom she laid her hand on his arm. "Look at me and tell me you're not a member of Jess Carney's gang. Tell me the man with you that day was not Jess Carney—or one of his men. Tell me that."

He couldn't tell her that. He couldn't say anything. And his silence told her the answer.

She inhaled slowly. "I must go inside."

"Florence—" he began and there he stopped. There wasn't anything he could say to her. Because he had ridden up the road with Jess Carney. He could never say anything to Florence King. The conductor who had died at Black Cut stood between him and this girl.

Yet he followed her to the schoolhouse. And at the door a hulking man who had inbibed too freely of corn whisky grabbed his arm and snarled:

''What's the idea takin' Flo outside?''

''Walter!'' Florence King exclaimed. ''Come inside.''

''I will, after I teach this squirt where he gets off foolin' around with my girl.''

Billy hit the big man then—hit him squarely in the mouth with all the strength in his powerful shoulders. The man reeled back, hit the door jamb, and recoiled. Billy Mason smashed him again. Behind Billy a man yelped and hit him back of the ear. Another of Walter's friends lashed at him from the side.

''Fight!'' someone roared.

Billy Mason took a stiff punch in his stomach, then lowered his head, and swung with both fists. They landed satisfyingly.

Bob Ford leaped through the door of the schoolhouse. ''I'm here, Billy!'' he cried.

One of Walter's friends smashed Bob in the face and the stripling fell forward. A terrific blow landed on Billy Mason's right ear and he bared his teeth. Walter and his two friends closed in on him. It was a tight spot for Billy Mason.

And then Jess Carney's voice rang out, cold and hard: ''Stop that!''

The attackers fell back. Billy Mason looked up and saw Jess Carney standing a few feet away, in the light cast by the open doorway. There was no gun visible on him. Perhaps these men didn't even know him by sight—but they could recognize the glaring eyes and the grim face and the timbre of the voice.

None said a word, but Billy Mason caught a glimpse of Walter's face and saw that it was slack and sickly-looking.

''What's going on here?'' Jess Carney demanded.

''Just a little fight,'' mumbled one of the men.

Bob Ford climbed to his feet, cursing. ''Who's the fool that hit me?''

''Shut up, Bob!'' snapped Jess Carney. ''The fight's over.''

The men who had attacked Billy Mason plunged into the schoolhouse. A woman's face appeared in the doorway for an instant, then was jerked back. Jess Carney was alone outside, with Bob Ford and Billy Mason.

"Come over here," Jess said, jerking his head toward the gloom.

The two followed. When they were under the tree where Billy had spoken with Florence only a few minutes ago, Jess said:

"Dick Small's given himself up!"

Billy Mason gasped. "Surrendered?"

"Bob, where is Ed Mitchell?"

Bob Ford stammered. "Ed? Why—why, I don't—"

"Don't lie!"

Billy Mason said, "He's dead, Jess."

Then Bob Ford burst into a torrent of words. "After you left the other day, Dick and Ed got into a fight. Ed drew on Dick and Dick killed him. He was afraid to tell you. I guess—I guess that's why he gave himself up."

"Yes?" snarled Jess Carney. "Or because he expects to get a reward for snitching?"

"I don't know, Jess, honest I don't!" Bob Ford exclaimed. "He left the same morning. I haven't seen him since. Neither has Charley, I know."

Jess turned to Billy. "Why didn't you tell me about Ed?"

"Because I don't play the game that way, Jess."

Jess was silent for a moment, then he said bitterly, "What a bunch of chicken thieves I've picked for men."

Billy said stiffly, "All right, if—"

Jess Carney made a savage gesture in the gloom. "Not you, Billy. You're the only man I've got any faith in. Ed and Dick and—" he hesitated—"that yellowbelly, Dick Small. He'll talk his guts to Wilkinson. We've got to clear out of here."

"We've got our guns in the woodpile," said Bob Ford.

"Get them. No—wait, I'll come with you."

He didn't trust them out of his sight. The finger of suspicion had stabbed at Jess Carney. The thing he had been fearing so long had happened. One of his men had turned traitor. Another might do so. He couldn't trust anyone now.

They walked to the woodpile and Bob Ford got out the

two pistols rolled up in their belts. He handed one to Billy Mason.

"All right, Jess."

"You come with me, Bob," Jess ordered. "Billy, you go back to Bud's place. Charley Ford will pick you up there. He'll bring you to St. Joe." He stopped. After a moment he sighed.

"I trust you, Billy."

He didn't. The very fact that he said so proved that. But he couldn't help himself.

Billy Mason walked back alone to the cabin of Bud Hill. It was dark and quiet, but Charley Ford materialized out of the gloom and said, "Billy?"

"Yes."

"Where's Bob?"

"Jess came to the dance and took him off with him. You know about Dick?"

"Yes, I was with Jess at his mother's place when the news came. Damn that dirty Dick. He was afraid Jess would find out about Ed and kill him. So he turned rat and went to the police."

"Who'd he surrender to?"

"Marshall Gray of Kansas City. And Sheriff Liggett."

"How long ago?"

"This morning. The newspapers haven't got it yet, but it came over the grapevine. It's true, all right."

"But if he surrendered this morning, how come— Well, it's strange Liggett and Gray haven't done anything. Dick knew we were gathering here."

"Yes, but the sheriff of Jackson County doesn't come out to Jess Carney's house. A sheriff did that ten years ago. Jess met him up the road. No, they'll get him somewhere else."

"What makes you so sure they'll get him at all? Jess has been around a good long while."

"Yes, but he's been overdue a long time. Up to now, the people've been friendly. He—we could go to any old Confederate soldier and he'd put us up and wild horses wouldn't make him squeal. But since the governor's issued that big reward and offered immunity—"

"Immunity," said Billy Mason softly. "Yes, that's it. Dick was between two fires. The law wanted him for a killing and Jess wanted him. The law offered immunity for turning traitor."

"The yellow dog!" But there was no vehemence in Charley Ford's epithet. It was too dark to see his face.

Charley Ford went into the house and got a lantern. By its light they went to a stable behind the house and saddled horses. It was then that Billy Mason touched the butt of his Frontier Model. He drew it from the holster.

"Bob got our guns mixed!" he exclaimed. He recalled now Bob had dug the two guns rolled up in their holsters from under the woodpile. Billy had taken the one offered him and strapped it about his waist.

Charley Ford looked at the gun. "What's the difference? It's the same model as yours; newer, though."

"Yes, it is." Billy held the butt of the gun under the lantern. "What're these initials on the butt—*H. H. G. ?* Where'd Bob get this gun?"

Charley Ford cleared his throat. "Well, I wouldn't exactly want Jess to know, but Bob and Jim Cummings over near Richmond pulled a couple of small jobs. Bob got this gun in one of them—"

Billy shook his head and holstered the gun. "I'll change with Bob when I see him. I'd prefer my own, even if this is newer."

"Yeah, sure."

They mounted their horses and rode into the night. They would always ride in the night, from now on. From now on, it would be dangerous for Billy Mason to show his face in daylight, among men. The finger had been pointed at him by Dick Small. He was known now, as a Carney man. And what did the governor's proclamation say about Carney men?

. . . and five thousand dollars reward for any member of Jess Carney's band, dead or alive.

They rode until morning, then hid in the woods. At nightfall they came out, along with the other beasts of prey.

Three days, and on the third night they reached St. Joseph. But they did not go into the city until dawn was breaking.

The house rented by "Tom Howard" was at the edge of the city, on a little hill. It was a white frame building with a large, sagging barn behind it. The closest house was a hundred yards away.

Charley Ford and Billy Mason led their horses to the barn and put them inside. As they came out of the barn, Bob Ford stepped out of the kitchen door, his right hand under his coat.

He exclaimed in relief when he recognized his brother and Billy. "Say, but I'm glad to see you."

"Je——Tom inside?" Charley asked.

Bob Ford shot an uneasy glance over his shoulder, then motioned toward the barn. Charley and Billy followed him.

"What's up, Bob?" Billy asked sharply. "Something wrong with Jess?"

"Yes, he's breaking, I think. Ever since we've been here he's been as nervous as a cat. Stays in the house all day, in his room, then spends half the night prowling around, outside. You can't even talk to him without his snapping your head off."

"Well," said Charley Ford, "he never was very even-tempered. What's Zee—his wife, say?"

"Hardly anything. But she's plenty worried. Wouldn't surprise me if she pulled out with the kids."

It was telling on Jess Carney. He didn't even trust anyone in his own house. He prowled outside at night, afraid of shadows, yet forcing himself to investigate and prove they were only shadows. He was afraid. The accumulated years of outlawry, living in constant danger, had worn his nerves to a frazzle.

Billy Mason could understand that—even though he had been on the dark road for only a few weeks. His nerves were steady, but deep within him, something gnawed at his vitals. In time it would tell on him, too. He had an object lesson in Jess Carney.

"Is he here now?" Billy asked.

Bob Ford shook his head. "No, we went to bed together

last night—in the same bed—but inside of an hour he was up and prowling around the house. I went down—to get something to drink—and discovered he'd left the house.''

''What's the news of Dick Small? We haven't seen any newspapers in three days.''

''Nothing,'' replied Bob Ford. ''Jess's been getting the papers every day and there hasn't been a single word printed about Dick Small. I'm not so sure that Dick gave himself up.''

''But Jess said Dick had been seen in Harry Gray's office!'' exclaimed Charley Ford.

''Gray?'' asked Billy. ''Who's Harry Gray?''

''Police Commissioner of Kansas City. Jess had some connection in his office. Don't know exactly what it is.''

Harry Gray—was there a middle initial? A chill fell upon Billy Mason. Deliberately, he drew his gun. ''Bob,'' he said, ''you mixed up our guns the other night at Centerville—''

''I know it. Discovered it the next morning. Here—'' Bob reached under his coat and brought out Billy Mason's own Frontier Model. ''They're the same make except that mine's newer.''

Billy Mason smiled. ''Yes—but it doesn't have your initials, I notice.''

Charley Ford said sharply, ''I told you about that. What're you trying to do—rub it in?''

''Of course not. I was just—'' He stopped.

A tall, slight woman had suddenly appeared in the doorway of the stable. Her face was drawn and her eyes suspicious. ''Who are these men, Bob?''

''My brother, Charley, Mrs. Car—— I mean, Mrs. Howard. And Billy Mason.''

''How do you do, Mrs. Howard,'' Billy said, bowing. He stared at the wife of Jess Carney. She looked—why, yes, give her a bit more color and take away about fifteen years and she could pass for Florence King's sister.

She was aware of his eyes upon her and, catching his, held them a moment. Then she relaxed. ''You're a—friend of Tom's? Won't you come in and have some breakfast?''

"We'd appreciate it, Mrs. Carney."

They left the barn, walked through the little backyard, and entered the house by the kitchen door. Mrs. Carney busied herself swiftly at the stove, while Charley Ford and Billy Mason washed some of the travel dirt from their faces and hands. By the time they were finished Mrs. Carney had set food on the table.

But Billy Mason never ate any of it. Hardly had he seated himself at the table than Jess Carney slammed into the house.

"Billy! Charley!" he cried. "We've got to clear out of here. Dick Small's confessed. Look—!" He threw a newspaper on the table and dashed into a room off the kitchen. "Zee!" he cried from there.

Billy Mason caught up the newspaper. *Member of Carney Gang Confesses!* screamed a headline.

"Read it out loud!" exclaimed Bob Ford, behind Billy Mason.

Billy Mason read: *"Police Commissioner Harry H. Gray admitted tonight that the mysterious man who surrendered to him last week is none other than Dick Small, lieutenant of the notorious Jess Carney band of bank and train robbers. Small, the commissioner stated, has made a complete confession, which it is believed will result in the eventual arrest of every member of the outlaw gang. The story is an astonishing one—"*

Harry H. Gray, Police Commissioner of Kansas City— H.H.G. Billy Mason put down the newspaper and pushed back his chair.

At that moment, Jess Carney, coatless, came out of the bedroom. "Boys," he announced, "we haven't got any time to lose. We've got to—"

"Jess," said Billy Mason. "I must talk to you."

"Later, Billy. We've got to—"

"This won't wait. You've got to hear it now!"

Something in Billy's tone caught Jess Carney's attention. His bloodshot eyes seemed to look right into Billy Mason's brain. He nodded, almost imperceptibly. Billy Mason stepped swiftly to the door and Jess Carney followed.

"Wait, Jess!" exclaimed Charley Ford. "Don't go out like that. Somebody might see your guns. Your coat—"

Jess Carney turned back. "All right, Billy, I'll be out in a moment."

As he walked to the barn, a warning knell struck somewhere deep within Billy Mason. He stopped, turned.

And then a gun thundered in the house.

"Oh, Lord!" cried Billy.

He plunged toward the kitchen door, tore at it, and burst into the house. In his first wild glance he thought the room was empty. But then his eyes went to the floor, beyond the table —and a cry of horror was torn from his throat.

Jess Carney lay there, blood streaming from a horrible wound in his head.

In the front of the house a door slammed. Feet pounded on stairs, and Zee Carney burst into the kitchen.

"Jess, oh, my God!" she screamed and threw herself upon the man on the floor.

Billy Mason leaped past her and tore through the house. He jerked open the front door and sprang out upon the porch. He saw them running, already more than a hundred feet away. He saw, too, in that one glance, a woman and a man in front of the neighboring house. And he knew it was too late—even for vengeance.

He went back into the house and found Zee Carney sitting on the floor beside the body of her dead husband. Jess Carney, dead at the hand of an assassin.

"You didn't do this?" Zee Carney moaned.

"No. The Fords—"

"It was Bob," Zee Carney said dully. "I didn't like him right from the start. His eyes—they couldn't ever face me. He was planning it all along."

"Yes," said Billy Mason. "I knew it. I—I was calling Jess outside to tell him. I knew for days but didn't tumble to the significance of it, until Jess brought in that paper. I was going to tell—" He broke off and his eyes saw the leather belt on the table, the belt with a holster on each side, one containing a Navy Colt, another a Smith & Wesson. "They got him to take off his guns."

"The first time he took them off in years." Zee Carney's face twisted and a bitter, hysterical laugh came from her lips. Suddenly she got to her feet.

"It's all over, the thing I've dreaded and feared for eight long years. He's dead, and—Jesse!" The face of a small boy showed in the door leading to the front part of the house. Zee sprang toward him, shoved him back into the other room. Then she hurried back to Billy Mason.

"You've got to go! The neighbors have heard the shot. The police will be here."

"It's all right," Billy said dully. "I'm willing to surrender. I—I didn't like it, anyway. I'll take what's coming to me."

"You won't have a chance, Billy Mason!" cried Zee Carney. "Dick Small's turned traitor. Bob and Charley Ford will turn against you. You'll take it all alone. You mustn't—"

"It doesn't make any difference. There's no one—"

"No one cares for you?" cried Zee Carney. "You haven't got a sweetheart? There's no one whose heart would break like mine did during these years—no one?"

There was someone.

Billy Mason wasn't an outlaw—not one at heart. He'd known that the moment he had first thrust his gun at the head of that railroad engineer, so long ago. He'd ridden down the road with Jess Carney, but he hadn't thought as Jess Carney had thought.

Billy Mason straightened. He said, "Good-bye, Mrs. Carney!" and leaped to the door. With his hand on it he whirled and said softly:

"Good-bye, Jess Carney!"

"Wine on the Desert" has been called a perfect short story—carefully crafted, beautifully characterized, full of irony, with an ending that is both haunting and unforgettable. It is the best known and, many feel, the best of Max Brand's (Frederick Faust) many stories. During the twenties and thirties, Faust was the premier writer of pulp and slick magazine Westerns, having published the equivalent of 215 full-length novels under the Max Brand name and other pseudonyms; many of his longer works have been reprinted for the enjoyment of modern readers, among them such classics as The Untamed, Destry Rides Again, Montana Rides!, *and* Silvertip.

Wine on the Desert

Max Brand

*T*here was no hurry, except for the thirst, like clotted salt, in the back of his throat, and Durante rode on slowly, rather enjoying the last moments of dryness before he reached the cold water in Tony's house. There was really no hurry at all. He had almost twenty-four hours' head start, for they would not find his dead man until this morning. After that, there would be perhaps several hours of delay before the sheriff gathered a sufficient posse and started on his trail. Or perhaps the sheriff would be fool enough to come alone.

Durante had been able to see the wheel and fan of Tony's windmill for more than an hour, but he could not make out the ten acres of the vineyard until he had topped the last rise, for the vines had been planted in a hollow. The lowness of the ground, Tony used to say, accounted for the water that

gathered in the well during the wet season. The rains sank
through the desert sand, through the gravels beneath, and
gathered in a bowl of clay hardpan far below.

In the middle of the rainless season the well ran dry, but
long before that, Tony had every drop of the water pumped
up into a score of tanks made of cheap corrugated iron. Slender pipelines carried the water from the tanks to the vines
and from time to time let them sip enough life to keep them
until the winter darkened overhead suddenly, one November
day, and the rain came down, and all the earth made a great
hushing sound as it drank. Durante had heard that whisper of
drinking when he was here before; but he never had seen the
place in the middle of the long drought.

The windmill looked like a sacred emblem to Durante,
and the twenty stodgy, tar-painted tanks blessed his eyes;
but a heavy sweat broke out at once from his body. For the
air of the hollow, unstirred by wind, was hot and still as a
bowl of soup. A reddish soup. The vines were powdered
with thin red dust, also. They were wretched, dying things
to look at, for the grapes had been gathered, the new wine
had been made, and now the leaves hung in ragged tatters.

Durante rode up to the squat adobe house and right
through the entrance into the patio. A flowering vine clothed
three sides of the little court. Durante did not know the name
of the plant, but it had large white blossoms with golden
hearts that poured sweetness on the air. Durante hated the
sweetness. It made him more thirsty.

He threw the reins of his mule and strode into the house.
The water cooler stood in the hall outside the kitchen. There
were two jars made of a porous stone, very ancient things,
and the liquid which distilled through the pores kept the contents cool. The jar on the left held water; that on the right
contained wine. There was a big tin dipper hanging on a peg
beside each jar. Durante tossed off the cover of the vase on
the left and plunged it in until the delicious coolness closed
well above his wrist.

"Hey, Tony," he called. Out of his dusty throat the cry
was a mere groaning. He drank and called again, clearly,
"Tony!"

A voice pealed from the distance.

Durante, pouring down the second dipper of water, smelled the alkali dust which had shaken off his own clothes. It seemed to him that heat was radiating like light from his clothes, from his body, and the cool dimness of the house was soaking it up. He heard the wooden leg of Tony bumping on the ground, and Durante grinned; then Tony came in with that hitch and sideswing with which he accommodated the stiffness of his artificial leg. His brown face shone with sweat as though a special ray of light were focused on it.

"Ah, Dick!" he said. "Good old Dick! . . . How long since you came last! . . . Wouldn't Julia be glad! Wouldn't she be glad!"

"Ain't she here?" asked Durante, jerking his head suddenly away from the dripping dipper.

"She's away at Nogalez," said Tony. "It gets so hot. I said, 'You go up to Nogalez, Julia, where the wind don't forget to blow.' She cried, but I made her go."

"Did she cry?" asked Durante.

"Julia . . . that's a good girl," said Tony.

"Yeah. You bet she's good," said Durante. He put the dipper quickly to his lips but did not swallow for a moment; he was grinning too widely. Afterward he said: "You wouldn't throw some water into that mule of mine, would you, Tony?"

Tony went out with his wooden leg clumping loud on the wooden floor, softly in the patio dust. Durante found the hammock in the corner of the patio. He lay down in it and watched the color of sunset flush the mists of desert dust that rose to the zenith. The water was soaking through his body; hunger began, and then the rattling of pans in the kitchen and the cheerful cry of Tony's voice:

"What you want, Dick? I got some pork. You don't want pork. I'll make you some good Mexican beans. Hot. Ah ha, I know that old Dick. I have plenty of good wine for you, Dick. Tortillas. Even Julia can't make tortillas like me. . . . And what about a nice young rabbit?"

"All blowed full of buckshot?" growled Durante.

"No, no. I kill them with the rifle."

"You kill rabbits with a rifle?" repeated Durante, with a quick interest.

"It's the only gun I have," said Tony. "If I catch them in the sights, they are dead. . . . A wooden leg cannot walk very far. . . . I must kill them quick. You see? They come close to the house about sunrise and flop their ears. I shoot through the head."

"Yeah? Yeah?" muttered Durante. "Through the head?" He relaxed, scowling. He passed his hand over his face, over his head.

Then Tony began to bring the food out into the patio and lay it on a small wooden table; a lantern hanging against the wall of the house included the table in a dim half circle of light. They sat there and ate. Tony had scrubbed himself for the meal. His hair was soaked in water and sleeked back over his round skull. A man in the desert might be willing to pay five dollars for as much water as went to the soaking of that hair.

Everything was good. Tony knew how to cook, and he knew how to keep the glasses filled with his wine.

"This is old wine. This is my father's wine. Eleven years old," said Tony. "You look at the light through it. You see that brown in the red? That's the soft that time puts in good wine, my father always said."

"What killed your father?" asked Durante.

Tony lifted his hand as though he were listening or as though he were pointing out a thought.

"The desert killed him. I found his mule. It was dead, too. There was a leak in the canteen. My father was only five miles away when the buzzards showed him to me."

"Five miles? Just an hour. . . . Good Lord!" said Durante. He stared with big eyes. "Just dropped down and died?" he asked.

"No," said Tony. "When you die of thirst, you always die just one way. . . . First you tear off your shirt, then your undershirt. That's to be cooler. . . . And the sun comes and cooks your bare skin. . . . And then you think . . . there is water everywhere, if you dig down far enough.

You begin to dig. The dust comes up your nose. You start screaming. You break your nails in the sand. You wear the flesh off the tips of your fingers, to the bone.'' He took a quick swallow of wine.

"Without you seen a man die of thirst, how d'you know they start to screaming?'' asked Durante.

"They got a screaming look when you find them,'' said Tony. "Take some more wine. The desert never can get to you here. My father showed me the way to keep the desert away from the hollow. We live pretty good here? No?''

"Yeah,'' said Durante, loosening his shirt collar. "Yeah, pretty good.''

Afterward he slept well in the hammock until the report of a rifle waked him and he saw the color of dawn in the sky. It was such a great, round bowl that for a moment he felt as though he were above, looking down into it.

He got up and saw Tony coming in holding a rabbit by the ears, the rifle in his other hand.

"You see?'' said Tony. "Breakfast came and called on us!'' He laughed.

Durante examined the rabbit with care. It was nice and fat and it had been shot through the head. Through the middle of the head. Such a shudder went down the back of Durante that he washed gingerly before breakfast; he felt that his blood was cooled for the entire day.

It was a good breakfast, too, with flapjacks and stewed rabbit with green peppers, and a quart of strong coffee. Before they had finished, the sun struck through the east window and started them sweating.

"Gimme a look at that rifle of yours, Tony, will you?'' Durante asked.

"You take a look at my rifle, but don't you steal the luck that's in it,'' laughed Tony. He brought the fifteen-shot Winchester.

"Loaded right to the brim?'' asked Durante.

"I always load it full the minute I get back home,'' said Tony.

"Tony, come outside with me,'' commanded Durante.

They went out from the house. The sun turned the sweat of Durante to hot water and then dried his skin so that his clothes felt transparent.

"Tony, I gotta be damn mean," said Durante. "Stand right there where I can see you. Don't try to get close . . . Now listen . . . The sheriff's gunna be along this trail some time today, looking for me. He'll load up himself and all his gang with water out of your tanks. Then he'll follow my sign across the desert. Get me? He'll follow if he finds water on the place. But he's not gunna find water."

"What you done, poor Dick?" said Tony. "Now look . . . I could hide you in the old wine cellar where nobody . . ."

"The sheriff's not gunna find any water," said Durante. "It's gunna be like this."

He put the rifle to his shoulder, aimed, fired. The shot struck the base of the nearest tank, ranging down through the bottom. A semicircle of darkness began to stain the soil near the edge of the iron wall.

Tony fell on his knees. "No, no, Dick! Good Dick!" he said. "Look! All the vineyard. It will die. It will turn into old, dead wood, Dick . . ."

"Shut your face," said Durante. "Now I've started, I kinda like the job."

Tony fell on his face and put his hands over his ears. Durante drilled a bullet hole through the tanks, one after another. Afterward, he leaned on the rifle.

"Take my canteen and go in and fill it with water out of the cooling jar," he said. "Snap into it, Tony!"

Tony got up. He raised the canteen, and looked around him, not at the tanks from which the water was pouring so that the noise of the earth drinking was audible, but at the rows of his vineyard. Then he went into the house.

Durante mounted his mule. He shifted the rifle to his left hand and drew out the heavy Colt from its holster. Tony came dragging back to him, his head down. Durante watched Tony with a careful revolver, but he gave up the canteen without lifting his eyes.

"The trouble with you, Tony," said Durante, "is you're

yellow. I'd of fought a tribe of wildcats with my bare hands, before I'd let 'em do what I'm doin' to you. But you sit back and take it.''

Tony did not seem to hear. He stretched out his hands to the vines.

''Ah, my God,'' said Tony. ''Will you let them all die?''

Durante shrugged his shoulders. He shook the canteen to make sure that it was full. It was so brimming that there was hardly room for the liquid to make a sloshing sound. Then he turned the mule and kicked it into a dog-trot.

Half a mile from the house of Tony, he threw the empty rifle to the ground. There was no sense packing that useless weight, and Tony with his peg leg would hardly come this far.

Durante looked back, a mile or so later, and saw the little image of Tony picking up the rifle from the dust, then staring earnestly after his guest. Durante remembered the neat little hole clipped through the head of the rabbit. Wherever he went, his trail never could return again to the vineyard in the desert. But then, commencing to picture to himself the arrival of the sweating sheriff and his posse at the house of Tony, Durante laughed heartily.

The sheriff's posse could get plenty of wine, of course, but without water a man could not hope to make the desert voyage, even with a mule or a horse to help him on the way. Durante patted the full, rounding side of his canteen. He might even now begin with the first sip but it was a luxury to postpone pleasure until desire became greater.

He raised his eyes along the trail. Close by, it was merely dotted with occasional bones, but distance joined the dots into an unbroken chalk line which wavered with a strange leisure across the Apache Desert, pointing toward the cool blue promise of the mountains. The next morning he would be among them.

A coyote whisked out of a gully and ran like a gray puff of dust on the wind. His tongue hung out like a little red rag from the side of his mouth; and suddenly Durante was dry to the marrow. He uncorked and lifted his canteen. It had a slightly sour smell; perhaps the sacking which covered it had grown a trifle old. And then he poured a great mouthful of lukewarm liquid. He had swallowed it before his senses could give him warning.

It was wine!

He looked first of all toward the mountains. They were as calmly blue, as distant as when he had started that morning. Twenty-four hours not on water, but on wine!

"I deserve it," said Durante. "I trusted him to fill the canteen. . . . I deserve it. Curse him!" With a mighty resolution, he quieted the panic in his soul. He would not touch the stuff until noon. Then he would take one discreet sip. He would win through.

Hours went by. He looked at his watch and found it was only ten o'clock. And he had thought that it was on the verge of noon! He uncorked the wine and drank freely and, corking the canteen, felt almost as though he needed a drink of water more than before. He sloshed the contents of the canteen. Already it was horribly light.

Once, he turned the mule and considered the return trip; but he could remember the head of the rabbit too clearly, drilled right through the center. The vineyard, the rows of old twisted, gnarled little trunks with the bark peeling off . . . every vine was to Tony like a human life. And Durante had condemned them all to death!

He faced the blue of the mountains again. His heart raced in his breast with terror. Perhaps it was fear and not the suction of that dry and deadly air that made his tongue cleave to the roof of his mouth.

The day grew old. Nausea began to work in his stomach, nausea alternating with sharp pains. When he looked down, he saw that there was blood on his boots. He had been spurring the mule until the red ran down from its flanks. It went with a curious stagger, like a rocking horse with a broken rocker; and Durante grew aware that he had been keeping the mule at a gallop for a long time. He pulled it to a halt. It stood with wide-braced legs. Its head was down. When he leaned from the saddle, he saw that its mouth was open.

"It's gunna die," said Durante. "It's gunna die . . . what a fool I been. . . ."

The mule did not die until after sunset. Durante left everything except his revolver. He packed the weight of that for an hour and discarded it, in turn. His knees were growing weak. When he looked up at the stars, they shone white and clear for a moment only, and then whirled into little racing circles and scrawls of red.

He lay down. He kept his eyes closed and waited for the shaking to go out of his body, but it would not stop. And every breath of darkness was like an inhalation of black dust.

He got up and went on, staggering. Sometimes he found himself running.

Before you die of thirst, you go mad. He kept remembering that. His tongue had swollen big. Before it choked him, if he lanced it with his knife the blood would help him; he would be able to swallow. Then he remembered that the taste of blood is salty.

Once, in his boyhood, he had ridden through a pass with his father and they had looked down on the sapphire of a mountain lake, a hundred thousand million tons of water as cold as snow. . . .

When he looked up now, there were no stars; and this frightened him terribly. He never had seen a desert night so dark. His eyes were failing, he was being blinded. When the morning came, he would not be able to see the mountains, and he would walk around and around in a circle until he dropped and died.

No stars, no wind; the air as still as the waters of a stale pool, and he in the dregs at the bottom. . . .

He seized his shirt at the throat and tore it away so that it hung in two rags from his hips.

He could see the earth only well enough to stumble on the rocks. But there were no stars in the heavens. He was blind: he had no more hope than a rat in a well. Ah, but Italian devils know how to put poison in wine that will steal all the senses or any one of them: and Tony had chosen to blind Durante.

He heard a sound like water. It was the swishing of the soft deep sand through which he was treading; sand so soft that a man could dig it away with his bare hands. . . .

Afterward, after many hours, out of the blind face of that sky, the rain began to fall. It made first a whispering and then a delicate murmur like voices conversing, but after that, just at the dawn, it roared like the hoofs of ten thousand charging horses. Even through that thundering confusion the big birds with naked heads and red, raw necks found their way down to one place in the Apache Desert.

The ability to capture the true essense of life in the Old West is what set Ernest Haycox apart from other Western writers of his time, and what continues to make his work popular with modern readers. His stories and novels invariably have an unsurpassed sense of realism and truth about them. "Night on Don Jaime Street," the story of an eleven-year-old boy named Ben and of Curly Jack, an outlaw "whose name was spoken carefully by grown people so that he would not be angry at them," is a perfect case in point.

Night on Don Jaime Street

Ernest Haycox

*H*is *mother's voice, never rising above a note of patient* self-control, boosted him out of the front door. "The first bell is ringing, Ben. That's a new shirt—try not to get in a scuffle today."

As he crossed the street he looked behind to watch the print his shoes made in the deep dust; he made an exact turn at Mrs. Ketchum's gate and another when he reached the corner of Stafford. From the round brick-colored hills behind town came the steady grind of ore moving along the mine conveyors, like the grumbling of a great chained beast. He made up a picture of how such a beast would look and meanwhile tried not to hear the school bell's brass-gong tolling.

He was eleven, tall for his years and blackened by the

Arizona sunlight. He wore long trousers, a pair of shoes with brass eyelets, and a blue, double-breasted flannel shirt which was the same kind of shirt sported by Ike Ball, driver of the Tucson stage, who was a god sitting on boyhood's highest throne of worship. Halfway along Stafford he closed his eyes and began to count, and when he counted forty he opened his eyes and turned into Lode, which was Dragoon's main street. At this early hour shadows lay beneath the board awnings and the whole town seemed deserted. Beyond the end of Lode the desert glittered under winter's bland sunlight.

He crossed Lode and entered Don Jaime Street, a narrow way connecting Lode with Border. All of Don Jaime was saloons and dance halls and buildings that his mother merely referred to as "those other houses." Now that the school bell had ceased to ring, a kind of sleepy feeling lay over everything, and when he stamped his shoes against the loose boards of the walk, echoes rattled all around. He kept his head down, fascinated by the shining of the brass eyelets on his shoes. Then a man said, "Feelin' ornery, bub?" and he raised his head and saw Curly Jack leaning against the front of the Louvre saloon.

"No, sir," he murmured, and was shaken by an insecure feeling. This man was danger itself; he was An Outlaw whose name was spoken carefully by grown people so that he would not be angry at them. His legs were very long; his hat lay on the extreme back edge of thick yellow hair, and cigar smoke drifted in gray ribbons around his face, and as he smiled his eyelids moved close together until the light came out of them in bright streaks.

"You're Gerrish's boy," said Curly Jack. "You're Ben. You know me, Ben?"

"Yes, sir."

Curly Jack seemed to laugh inwardly and he seemed to be pleased. The cigar angled upward between his lips. "What you going to be when you get older, Ben?"

"Maybe," said young Ben, "I'll drive stage."

Curly Jack's silent laughter showed more strongly. "Come to me when that happens, Ben, and you'll never have trouble on your trips." He took something from his pocket and pressed it into young Ben's hand. Young Ben said, "Thank you," and moved on. Opening his hand he saw that he held a $2.50 gold piece and halted dead in his tracks, knowing at once trouble would come of this. Curly Jack called after him, "That's all right, Ben, I gave it to you," in the voice of one who would not be disobeyed.

Young Ben crossed from the north to the south walk, passing saloon doorways from which drifted the rank-bitter smell of chewed cigars and spilled whiskey. The town bum lay sound asleep on the walk, his mouth a toothless opening in a gray, seamed face. A liver-colored pup sat near the painted window of the Pavilion dance hall and watched young Ben come on, his tail threshing the board walk. Young Ben paused to rub the pup's long ears and cut around the corner of the newspaper shop into Border Street. He stopped here, listening to the scrubbing run of the pup's feet. The pup rounded the corner and crossed his front legs and fell over and sat up, his tongue hanging out like a red shoe flap. Young Ben took him under an arm, went by the great dark arch of the stage barn, and moved slowly to the gaunt school building sitting alone in its yard. The second bell sent out a single clap as last warning, and he dropped the pup and said, "Stay there," and went up the school steps.

Curly Jack watched the boy turn the corner and his glance thereafter moved along Don Jaime Street, carefully touching the shade-drawn windows and the narrow alleys lying between buildings. The cigar teetered between his teeth; his lips drew back from the cigar. Behind him in the Louvre a swamper grumbled over a broom and the barman's murmuring talk rubbed against the emptiness of the place. Curly Jack pushed himself from the wall and paced down Don Jaime, moving in and out of the other saloons and dance halls to leave his brief greeting. Turning into Border he paused at the edge of Curran's barn and had a thorough look at the horses.

As soon as he departed from the precincts of the Louvre the swamper came to the doorway and watched him. The swamper said over his shoulder, "What's he doin' in town this time of mornin'?"

The barkeep murmured, "Doc Halliday's comin'."

"Ah," said the swamper and stroked his stained mustaches with the back of a hand.

Curly Jack stopped at Curran's barn for a moment, watching one man wheel a barrow along Border's dust. Out beyond the end of Border, morning sun streamed across the desert's tawny dust and silver cacti; in the distance a haze lay over Old Mexico. Curly Jack strolled on to the north side of town and paused momentarily by Boot Hill, idly considering the unmarked and inglorious mounds of those who had died by violence and in shame. Afterwards he crisscrossed Dragoon, prowling through alley and street like a restless cat, and at last came to the end of Lode Street and put his shoulder to the corner of Schermerhorn's butcher shop, once more indifferent.

Life moved thin and slow through Dragoon. One woman—the heavy and handsome Poker Belle—came out of Don Jaime and entered Lanahan's general store. Mrs. Gerrish and her daughter Hope appeared at the head of Stafford and moved forward with their parasols lifted against the sun. Curly Jack watched the girl, who was nineteen, with an appreciative eye and then he looked at Mrs. Gerrish and the indifference changed to wonder as though something new disturbed him. These two women turned the corner and went on toward Lanahan's, serene and untouchable in the dust and rawness of this town, leaving behind the clearest picture of immaculate grace.

Mrs. Gerrish said, "We'll stop at Lanahan's first to see if the ginghams came in from Tucson. You should walk with your shoulders straighter, Hope."

Beyond Lanahan's, a young man paused in the doorway of the Wells Fargo office, black arm protectors half covering his white shirt sleeves. He stood still with his eyes on Hope Gerrish and could not catch her attention; just before she passed into Lanahan's with her mother she looked over her shoulder and smiled at him.

In the half shadows of Lanahan's store dark shelves ran to

a high ceiling, and the odors of leather and coffee and fabric blended to make a pleasantly stale air. At the far end of the counter Poker Belle gave her order to Lanahan in a brusque voice. Poker Belle's glance went to Mrs. Gerrish covertly appraising her, and her voice dropped a full tone. Mrs. Gerrish stood at the counter with a sweet unawareness of the other woman's presence; in a moment, having finished her business, Poker Belle departed from Lanahan's, leaving behind the rustle of her broad-striped silk dress and the rank emanation of lilac cologne. Hope Gerrish cast an oblique glance at her mother, conveying a dramatic distaste.

The ginghams had not come. Mrs. Gerrish moved to the street and paused. "Hope," she said, "it is not good manners to express your feelings in public."

"The odor was rather strong."

"Where would she learn good taste?"

Hope said, "I think I'll walk to Father's," and moved down Lode with her parasol swaying daintily under the sun. Mrs. Gerrish tarried before Lanahan's to make certain minor adjustments to her dress. From the corner of her eyes she saw her daughter go slowly past the Wells Fargo doorway and stop and show a lady's charming surprise when young Neal Curzon came through the doorway to speak to her. Mrs. Gerrish silently said, "That was properly done," and went along Don Jaime Street, keeping to the outer edge of the walk. The town drunkard lay asleep by the Pavilion and the Louvre's swamper brushed the refuse of an evil night across the walk in rank clouds. Of this street Mrs. Gerrish had a most complete knowledge and yet walked through it and seemed to see nothing. She had been striking when young and now was gray and sedate and still pretty; but beneath her air of soft composure lay the inflexible commandments of a gentlewoman.

At the newspaper office she left the information she wished printed regarding an oyster supper at the church, and was squired gallantly to the door by Dragoon's eccentric whiskeydrinking editor, Sam Gault. Returning up Don Jaime she met her daughter in front of the freight office, which was her husband's business. The two of them strolled leisurely homeward under the streaming sunshine.

"Neal is coming over tonight."

"You arranged it very well," said Mrs. Gerrish. "It is important never to let a man know he is being sought. Your manners are excellent, though I think you should speak of him as Mr. Curzon and not use his first name until you are engaged. Men set a value on those niceties, though they do not know it. Now we shall bake cookies. I must teach you how to make the date-filled nougat. My mother gave me the recipe many years ago when we lived in Cleveland."

"You are very fond of old things," said Hope.

"They are," murmured Mrs. Gerrish, "like little lamps shining far over the desert."

Curly Jack followed Don Jaime to the last gray house sitting opposite the newspaper office and entered it without notice. He rolled up the front room's window shade to command a view of the street and pulled two chairs together, stretching himself on them; lighting a fresh cigar he lay back in comfort. Poker Belle came downstairs in her silk dress and went obediently to him, attractive and buxom, with great black eyes now carefully studying his humors.

She said, "I hear Doc Halliday's coming to Dragoon," and by the streaky laughter of his eyes she had her answer. "Curly," she added, "you better bring your boys in. If Doc comes he won't come alone."

"Belle," he said, "get yourself a new dress. Make it a little plainer, make it—"

"Like Mrs. Gerrish's." Poker Belle looked upon him with an unresenting wisdom. "It isn't the dress."

"Something else? Well, get it."

"I'd have to start fifteen years back to get it, and if I had it I wouldn't be here. This is Don Jaime Street. They live up at the head of Stafford."

He rolled back in the chair. He worked the answer around his head, the mask of strange speculation returning to his face. His lids crept nearer together. "I run this town but they don't know we're alive. Why's that? What makes it that way—"

She reached out a hand to ruffle his hair. "Ah, don't think about that. It won't do you any good."

He looked up, sharp now. "You ever think about it?"

"Quit talking about it, Curly—just quit."

The noon whistles were blowing from the mines as Ben Gerrish came along Don Jaime with the liver-colored pup behind him. He turned and said, "Stay there," and reached Lode in time to see the Tucson stage enter the street, its four horses slacking down from a dead run. Flat against the wall of Lanahan's store young Ben watched Ike Ball tool the stage exactly before the hotel porch and clap on the brake. A solitary passenger encased in a long yellow overcoat crawled from the stage, bearing marks of travel. Ike Ball threw down the reins to a waiting hostler and descended, a wire-drawn man with a set of agate, autocratic eyes set in a mahogany face whose features had an Indian inexpressiveness. A goatee pointed his chin. He saw young Ben and said, "Hello there, son," and young Ben said in a smothered voice, "Yes, sir," and walked homeward with his head down, in imagination flicking flies off the ears of the stage's lead horses with the sweep of a fifteen-foot whip.

The gold piece was a round, small weight in his pocket while he ate noon meal; the problem of it had been with him all morning. In time of hurt, when he needed sympathy, it was his mother he sought; but this was a practical matter before him now, and therefore he kept it to himself until he walked back toward Lode Street with his father. "Curly Jack gave me this," he said, taking the gold piece from his pocket.

He knew what his father would say, yet dreaded to hear it. His father looked down at the gold piece. "Did you earn it, Ben?"

"No, sir. He just gave it to me."

"Ah," said his father in that cool tone young Ben knew so well. They crossed Lode into Don Jaime, seeing Curly

Jack come from the Pavilion, and as they went forward the warm day grew cold to Ben and his heart began to swell against his chest. Curly Jack's face came about with that streak of brightness in the narrow apertures of his eyes.

"My son has something for you, Jack," said Gerrish.

Young Ben brought out the gold piece and held its round coldness in the warm sweat of his palm. Curly Jack faced Gerrish, his body stiff and his chest arched. He was like a wild horse, head lifted and everything in him keen and alert and unafraid. He no longer smiled. His face showed Gerrish a dark affront.

"I gave it to the boy."

"Tell him why you can't keep it, Ben," said Gerrish, unbreakably courteous.

"I didn't earn it," said Ben.

Curly Jack moved his shoulders. "It was a gift. It was free."

"Nothing's free," answered Gerrish.

The expression of puzzled wonder again broke vaguely across Curly Jack's face. He stood still, as though searching for an answer to this strangeness, and presently lifted the gold piece from young Ben's palm and wheeled away, and young Ben rubbed his wet hands against his shirt, feeling the quick tap of his heart. But the dread left him. His father had stared back at Curly Jack's streaky eyes and his father's voice had been, for a moment, harder than Curly Jack's. He looked up at his father and was very proud. The liver-colored pup came forward, all bones and skin and feet; he sat down at Ben's boots and his tail threshed the walk. Young Ben said tentatively, "He doesn't belong to anybody, Father."

"Don't be late," repeated Gerrish and turned back to Lode. Young Ben watched him move away and observed that his father was a tall man; his shoulders were as big as Curly Jack's shoulders. Young Ben tucked the pup under his arm and went on to the school. He left the pup at the foot of the steps and said, "Stay there."

Gerrish walked to his office. He paused at the door with his thoughts remaining on his son, and presently he turned about and went up Stafford. When he stepped inside the house, his wife came from the kitchen, startled because of this break in routine. "What's wrong?"

"It's a dog that Ben wants. He has spoken of it before."

"A dog would be good for him."

He said, "I happen to know it is Poker Belle's dog. I'd have to make a bargain with her."

Mrs. Gerrish straightened her shoulders. "No, I don't want him to touch anything that belongs to Don Jaime Street. I hate that dirty, beastlike place. It has destroyed every decent thing in Dragoon. I lie awake thinking how vile an atmosphere young Ben walks through on the way to school—the fear and lust and degraded morals that reach out from that place and touch us all. How can we raise our children decently? It is like living on the edge of a swamp, deadly things crawling toward us, nearer and nearer. No, I don't want—"

"He has taken a fancy to that dog," said Gerrish gently.

She showed him the strain and dark worry she had never permitted her children to see. She watched him a long while and at last dropped her shoulders. "If you think best," she murmured and went back to the kitchen. Gerrish returned down Stafford and walked directly to Poker Belle's house.

The sun moved west in the bluest, clearest of skies, and heat began to press down through town and slowly the town livened. The solitary passenger from the Tucson stage strolled into the newspaper shop and introduced himself to Sam Gault.

"Name's Aaron Shotwell, member of Congress from New York State, member of the committee on public lands, touring the West."

"Honored," said Sam Gault, suppressing his habitual irony. "Take the least dusty chair, Congressman."

"So this is the Babylon of the desert—the wildest town between St. Louis and the Pueblo of Our Lady of the Angels?"

"Babylon," observed Sam Gault, "was a camp before my time. Still, I imagine Dragoon might spot it a few points and come out with the most balls in the rack."

"Seems quiet."

"Sin keeps late hours. Have you had a drink lately, Congressman?"

"A man for breakfast," said the congressman. "Is that true?"

"Some mornings we're disappointed."

At four o'clock this afternoon the Louvre's professor had his breakfast of rye whiskey and chile beans at the free lunch counter and sat down to the piano to limber his fingers. Over at the Pavilion High-Pocket, Bill scattered his wax flakes on the dance floor, and shades began to lift from second-story windows to let in a breath of day before it went away and those women whom Sam Gault referred to in his columns as "ladies of the hetaera" moved in casual promenade along the street. Don Jaime stirred from its long lethargy in preparation for the night.

A dusty man with a great hank of hair hanging below his hat brim rode in from the desert and pulled up at McSwain's watering trough. While his horse drank, this rider rolled himself a cigarette, his eyes striking at the town from beneath the concealment of the hat brim. He put a match to the cigarette and his turning head stopped its motion when he found Curly Jack stationed idly by Lanahan's store. He looked upon Curly Jack with a complete blankness and turned the horse and loped out of Dragoon.

Curly Jack threw away his half-smoked cigar and chose a fresh one. Another man walked from McSwain's stable and stopped by. Curly Jack motioned at the disappearing rider. "He'll go back to tell Doc Halliday I'm here. They'll be in tonight, Link."

"I'll go get the boys," said Link.

"Yes," said Curly Jack, the smile dancing in his eyes. From his place by Lanahan's he watched young Ben Gerrish come up Don Jaime from the school and turn to his father's office, the liver-colored pup close following. A six-horse team climbed out of Pedro Wash and stopped at the end of Border, a small crowd slowly drifting toward it. Sam Gault sauntered up Don Jaime and joined Curly Jack; the two of them walked to the wagon.

"That the piano?" asked Sam Gault.

"Yeah," said the teamster. Curly Jack's cigar tilted upward between his teeth. He looked curiously at the thick mahogany legs, curved and bowed, showing beneath the protective tarps. "What piano?"

"Gerrish's," said Gault. "First piano in town. Civilization comes to Dragoon, Curly."

"Not the first," contradicted Curly Jack. "There's a piano in the Louvre."

"The Louvre's on Don Jaime Street, Curly. This is the first piano in a genteel home. You see the difference?"

"No," said Curly Jack. "What is the difference?"

"Sometime when I'm drunk," said Sam Gault, "I'll tell you. The universe is very clear to me then. Gentility is of the spirit, and I have to be drunk to speak of the spirit. Halliday comin' in tonight?"

"Maybe," said Curly Jack.

Gault said, "If you survive, look me up and we'll drink on your luck. If you die, I'll preach your sermon—because the minister won't."

He went away. Curly Jack watched the wagon and four horses go up Stafford Street with his eyes almost shut, reaching out to catch that one thing which had troubled him since morning.

Young Ben passed the freighting office, saw his father beckon, and went in. "The dog," said his father, "belongs to Poker Belle, but she has no use for it. You are to carry twenty armloads of wood from her shed to her back porch. Then you may take the dog home."

"Yes, sir," said young Ben and turned out. His father's voice called him back. "Ben," he said, "always do more than you promise. Make each armload a full one."

Young Ben went down Don Jaime Street with the liver-colored pup obediently behind, turned into a short alley, and came to Poker Belle's shed. It was fifty feet from shed to back porch, and the twenty armloads, faithfully performed, took him an hour. There was an old piece of clothesline rope on the ground, and this he tied around the liver-colored pup's neck. But the lessons of his father were all explicit, reminding him that nothing had been said about the rope; therefore, he removed it and left it in the yard, tucked the pup under his arm and returned home. The quitting whistles were blowing in the mines.

In his own shed behind the house, young Ben found another rope with which to tie the liver-colored pup. "Just for a few days, so you won't go back to Don Jaime." He discovered a burlap sack and made a bed for the pup. He crouched down, tugging the pup's soft long ears; when he stretched them under the pup's jaws the ends touched. The pup edged nearer and his long tongue licked across young Ben's mouth. Young Ben's mother called him out of his deep preoccupation; he went into the house.

The new piano was a great, black-shining square of elegance under the light. His mother sat on the piano stool, her fingers running along the keys. She had her eyes shut. She pressed one key softly, and then her fingers formed a chord and she turned about and young Ben was astonished to see that she was near to crying. His father moved over the room, smiling down. He said, "Like home, Rose?"

She said, "I'll teach Hope to play. I'll teach Ben." She was suddenly, terribly in earnest. "We must never let them forget anything."

At eight o'clock, night closed about Dragoon, soot black, velvet surfaced. Elsewhere the land lay empty, shadow and shadow pressing upon it, discreet in its mystery and beautiful, the formless edge of mountains shaped against lesser black. The stores on Lode were closed, presenting blank walls to the glitter of Don Jaime Street's saloons and dance halls. On that short way men moved in errant waves from walk to walk; they batted through the swinging doors, their feet made a steady shuffle on the boards, their aimless traveling brought up the street's alkali dust. From the Pavilion rolled the steady melody of guitar and violin, the tramping of dancers, the call of voices and the sharp laughter of women. Out of the night, up Border into Don Jaime, moved a steady procession of horsemen to populate this bright, glittering core of warmth. One man, early drunk, stood in the

middle of the dust, swinging his arms around in destructive
circles; somewhere a woman stridently cried and the music
went on and a gun exploded and all this revelry was like the
beat of blood in the jugular, echoing along Lode and drying
against the withdrawn, distant life at the head of Stafford.

The night marshal came into the jail office on Border
Street, fresh from sleep, and found the day marshall ready to
be relieved. The night marshal was a slight, blond man with
gray-green eyes on whose dry face latent danger lay as a
shadow. He said, "Anything new?"

"Curly Jack's in town. Doc Halliday just arrived. Both
got some boys with them."

"So," said the night marshal. He took pains with his cigar; he strapped on his gun. "That's been comin' a long
while."

"You want me to hang around?"

"No," said the night marshal.

The day marshal turned out of the office. The night marshal lifted and dropped the gun in its holster to test it, gave
himself a short glance in the wall mirror and stepped into the
street. Coming to Don Jaime, he had his practiced look at
the crowd, saw the things that needed to be seen, and set out
on his nightly rounds.

In his room at the hotel the congressman poured a pair of
drinks, one for himself and one for Sam Gault. He stood at
the window, viewing the sullen shining of light on Don
Jaime and the dust rising like clouds of brimstone and sulphur around the moving mass of men. The tremor of Don
Jaime, its shrill echoes and its growing undertone, came
through the window at him.

"Nothing," said the congressman, being half-drunk and
very clear of head, "could be like that. It is a scene out of
Dante, upon my soul. In a town like this not one decent
thing could thrive, no kind impulse take root."

"Congressman," said Sam Gault, "you travel with good
whiskey. Let me have that bottle."

Curly Jack crossed Don Jaime, moving men aside with a
push of his shoulder, and stopped in the alley shadows be-

side the Pavilion. He searched Don Jaime with his glance, closely watching the double shadow of two men standing at the Louvre corner. Somebody moved past the Pavilion and paused by the alley's mouth, murmuring, "Halliday's in Kilrain's place—he's standing at the bar," and moved on into the crowd.

Curly Jack went along the alley to a side door of the Pavilion and opened it; he stood against the wall until Poker Belle left her partner on the floor and came obediently to him, sequins glittering around the low-cut front of her dress, her skin white against piled-up black hair. He said irritably, "Come on," and led her into the alley.

"What's up, Jack?"

He didn't answer. They walked side by side through the alley, turned across Lode at its dark end and moved out toward the low hill behind town.

She said, "Halliday's in town. Curly, I wish—"

They were at the head of Stafford; they were in the shadows, looking across the width of a thirty-foot street whose width was a bay and on whose far shore the houses of the genteel showed strange and distant lights.

"A funny thing," he said. "You can't hear Don Jaime Street when you're standing here."

"Let's go back."

He faced the Gerrish house and was long silent, struggling with his wonder, annoyed by it but held by it. A young couple moved in from the edges of town—Neal Curzon and Hope Gerrish—walking arm in arm. They stood by the porch, softly laughing and gently whispering, and passed into the house.

"Listen," said Curly Jack. "That piano."

"There's a piano in the Louvre, Curly. Let's go back."

"I do what I please in this country, Belle. I can make a man smile and I can make him beg. Nobody in this town has got nerve enough to touch me. I could turn Don Jaime Street inside out if I wanted. But those people in that house—they don't know I'm alive. Why's that, Belle?"

"Come on," she said. "We don't belong here."

"Why not?" he said, in a resentful voice. "I walk where I please. Nobody stops me. Why not?"

But she pulled him around into Stafford. At the corner of Lode he stopped, looking across at the mouth of McSwain's stable. He said, "Go on, old girl. I'll see you later."

She took his arm, her strong perfume rising to him. Her shoulders lifted and her face in these shadows was pale. She was a big and emotional woman, but she held back her feelings, as she had learned to do, and turned across Lode to Don Jaime.

He had seen the blur of motion in McSwain's. He moved over Lode and threaded an alley and arrived at a side door of Kilrain's saloon. He opened the door and looked in. Halliday had been here but Halliday was gone, and so now he retreated and ducked along the rear alleys to Border and entered Don Jaime from the lower end. Light touched him briefly as he moved forward through the crowd; it flashed against his eyes and showed the faint sweat damp on his face. He passed the night marshal and said, "Hello, George," and came to the head of Don Jaime and crossed to Lanahan's. He placed his back to the store, watching Don Jaime. In a few minutes he was tired of waiting and moved to Stafford again, going along it toward the Gerrish house— impelled by the puzzle that wouldn't leave him.

He had his left flank close against the side of a building. He watched his right—the darkness over there and the break of building walls. The voice, when it arrived, shocked him immeasurably.

"Hello, Curly."

He wheeled full around, seeing nothing. He wheeled again and froze when he heard laughter above him and looked up to see shoulders poked half through the second-story window of the butcher shop. He heard the voice again, Halliday's cool and provoking voice: "So-long, Curly," and as he drew his gun in one futile motion Halliday's bullet tore through his chest and dropped him.

The noise of Don Jaime Street came forward in faint murmuring waves. The gun's echo ran on and on and died in the silence beyond town. Chest down on the walk, he heard

Halliday's boots rattle through the butcher shop and fade. er
that he was alone. He turned on his side and he pushed himself to his knees, facing the head of Stafford; from this position he saw the lights of the Gerrish house shining out and he
heard the tinkle of the piano. Someone ran toward him with
a gasping breath, and in a moment Poker Belle's big warm
arms enclosed him.

"Curly, why did you let him—!"

"Listen, Belle. Hear that piano?"

"It's from the Louvre, Curly."

"Louvre piano never sounded like that. Belle?"

"What you want, Curly?"

"Why don't they stop that damned piano. I'm out here.
I'm dying. Don't they know that?"

"Curly," she said and watched his head bob down. She
sat in the dust, this heavy woman, with her bare shoulders
bowed over a dead man, crying and saying things to him he
had never heard while alive. Nobody came along. She was
alone in the shadows of Stafford Street.

Mrs. Gerrish sat before the piano, thinking of tunes she
had played as a young girl in the East. A single shot broke
on Stafford somewhere, its echo creeping through the house
wall. She sat still, rigid inside, and presently turned—
holding dread out of her eyes. Neal Curzon and Hope sat on
the sofa, alternately taking turns at the stereopticon; she saw
them touch hands as though by accident, and look at each
other with an absorption that made nothing else important.
Young Ben sat on the floor with the pup spraddled on his
lap. He rubbed his hand down the pup's silk ears and his
face was held in its dream. They had not heard the shot.
Looking across to her husband she caught his nod, and
turned back to the piano, relieved. Inside the four walls of
this house Don Jaime Street was only an echo which meant
nothing.

This account of a vicious killer named Billy Reo, who had
witnessed a hanging as a youngster and who had a morbid
fear of dying at the end of a rope, is both grim and powerful,
and its ending is not one you'll soon forget. C. Hall Thomp-
son, who wrote weird fiction as well as first-rate Westerns,
also published a novel featuring a character with the same
name as the protagonist of this piece, A Gun for Billy Reo
(1955), which is considerably different in tone and conclu-
sion than "Posse."

Posse

C. Hall Thompson

*B*illy Reo *was dreaming again. The pain in the small of his*
back where buckshot had riddled the intestines seemed far
away now, and he was not lying in the loft of an abandoned
barn; he could not smell the hay nor hear the rats squealing
in the empty stalls below.

He was back in a town in the Panhandle and he was
nineteen and had never watched a man die. A mob jostled
along the main square. He could see the red, mustached
faces of furious men and hear them yelling, "Lynch the
murdering greaser! Bust into the cell and string him
up!"

Then he saw two townsmen come out through the jail
door, dragging the Mexican boy between them. He heard
the boy praying and moaning, and followed the mob across
the dusty wide square to the big oak. The boy was crying
softly and someone larruped the flank of the pony and it

jolted out from under and the boy screamed only once before the hemp snapped his spine.

And, here in the barn loft, Reo could see the boy's face, twisted at a crazy angle by the knot under the left ear. Only now it was his own face; it was Billy Reo who danced there above the stiff white masks of the mob.

''No!''

He lurched to a sitting position.

The stab of fire along his back brought him full awake. Sweat wilted the blond bristles of his jaw. It stung his eyes. He sank back, breathing too hard.

Get hold of yourself, he thought. *Let them form their damned posse. They'll never find you here.*

They had never caught him before. In the ten years since he had drifted north into the territories, Billy Reo had killed four men. Riding from one gun town to the next, he had learned the lightning downsweep and rise of hand that could put three slugs into a man's belly before he sprawled in the dust. And the killing had been a safe, secret thing. People had looked at him and wondered, maybe, but no one had ever been able to prove his suspicions.

Safe and easy, his mind said. And this time was no different.

Only this time *was* different. This time it had been in a grubby saloon in Alamosa with a mob of witnesses right on the spot.

He hadn't figured the greenhorn to call his bluff. The greenhorn, a spindly kid named Reckonridge, had looked as if he never left mama's side. Reo and Jack Larnin had idled into the bar to wash the red dust out of their tonsils and had seen this kid sporting a load of double eagles. It wasn't hard to talk up a game of deuces wild. It should have been easy to slip that deuce off the bottom when the pot was at its peak.

But Reckonridge had a quick eye and a temper to match. He had cursed and dropped one hand below the table. Reo never stopped to argue. A beer-blown blonde had screamed. The shots had sounded very loud and Reckonridge had gone over backward, still seated, with two small holes in his chest.

The saloon crowd had not moved. Elbow to elbow, guns level, Reo and Larnin had backed through swinging doors to the ponies at the hitch. They had swung up and wheeled west, and in that moment Reo had seen the long, loose-limbed man come running through the moonlight; glimpsed the lifting shotgun, the flash of a metal star against a black vest.

"Ride, Jack! Ride like hell!"

Slapping heels to the roan's flanks, he had bent low. But not low enough. He had felt the fire needles burn into his back almost before he heard the slam and echo of the double barrels. Somehow, he had kept the roan haunch to haunch with Larnin's pinto. Somehow, he had ridden.

Reo was sweating again. The blood-wet flannel shirt stuck to his back. His legs had a numbness that frightened him. *Witnesses,* he thought. This time there was proof. This time, the man in the black vest would talk. The citizens of Alamosa would swear in as deputies. Before daylight, the posse would lead out. Maybe even now . . .

"Damn," he said hoarsely.

His head rolled from side to side. He could see the Mexican boy very clearly; the hard, implacable faces of the mob, the sudden, singing wrench of the rope.

"Billy."

His body stiffened. A hand clawed for the pistol that lay by his hip. He caught the scrape of boots on the ladder; a light shaft cut up through the loft trap. Then the lean, flat-planed face and narrow shoulders came into view, one fist holding high the lantern, and Jack Larnin said, "Easy, Billy. Just me."

The gun hand relaxed.

Larnin set down the lamp. It was hooded so that only a thin yellow beam broke the darkness.

Reo's eyes narrowed. "Well?"

Larnin stood tall above him. A rat rustled in the hay. Light shimmered on the dainty needlework of a spider's web. Larnin said, "How's the wound?"

Reo looked at him. "The wound's all right. I'm not thinking about the wound."

The silent question hung between them. Reo felt sweat cold along his ribs.

Finally Larnin looked away, said, "I went up along the rise. You can see Alamosa from there. It don't look good, Billy. They started already. I seen torches moving out of town; high, like they were carried by men on horseback."

"Posse," Reo whispered.

Larnin's boots shifted. "You better let me take a look."

"The hell with the wound!"

Reo hauled himself to one elbow. The effort cost him plenty. There was a red-brown stain where his back had crushed the hay.

"What're the chances?" he said.

Larnin shook his head. "We got three, four hours on them, Billy. But we was riding too hard to cover trail. We left sign a blind man could follow."

Reo wet his lips. In the dark stillness now, a wind was rising and he could hear a voice praying high and shrill in Spanish and then cracking to dead silence.

Reo set his elbows, shoved himself erect. His teeth shut hard against the pain.

Larnin helped him. The numbness made his legs heavy and awkward. His insides burned. He held the pistol in a white-knuckled grip. He leaned against the wall, coughing for breath.

Larnin's face went uncertain. "Listen, Billy."

Pale eyes swung up. "I'm listening."

A minute passed. Their glances held. Then Larnin said, "Maybe it'd be better if you didn't run. You need a doctor, Billy. If you just waited here . . ."

"For the posse?" Reo said. "Sit here and wait for the mob to drag me out?" Fever made his stare too bright. "Wait for the rope?"

"I'm only saying . . ."

The gun hand lifted a fraction. "You said it. Now forget it."

"Sure, Billy, but . . ."

"But—you'd like to back down?"

"Billy, you got me wrong."

The gun was level with Larnin's belt buckle now. "Maybe," Reo said. "But you get me right. We're going to move. We're going to keep moving. They won't get me. Remember that, Jack. No mob'll ever get me."

Wind soughed in the stalls below. A rat skittered into the hay.

Larnin nodded. All he said was, "You still need a doctor."

"We'll head for Monte Vista. There's old Doc Carson."

Larnin frowned. "We ain't got much money. The doc mightn't want to . . ."

Billy Reo's hands moved light and smooth with the gun, broke it and checked the cylinder, snapped the breech shut again. He looked at the gun for a long time, then said, "He'll want to."

Shadows followed them. The moon was high and cloud-pierced and, behind them now, the pale meadows were restless with shadows that might have been wind bending the tall grass; or the groping movements of a posse.

Reo tried not to look back. Turned north and west toward the far reaches of the San Juan range, his face set rigid against thought and the memory of a sun bleached Panhandle town. The jogging of the saddle played hell with his back. He could feel the wounds seeping slowly; hot fingers clawed up from his belly and made breathing a torture.

Lifting gradually under them the land climbed toward distant foothills. The horses were wearing thin. The moon went down and winking stone-cold stars gave little light. Larnin took to shifting against the pommel, peering over his shoulder. Reo had drawn the Winchester from its saddle boot; he held it ready across his lap. Under the muffled dusty beat of hoofs, a Mexican tongue whimpered *Madre de Dios, socorro*, save me. *Madre de . . .*

"Shut up," Reo said aloud. "Shut up."

Larnin glanced at him sharply. A white edge fringed Reo's lips. He shook his head dully.

"Nothing. I was . . . Nothing."

Dawn was a pearl-gray cat paddling down from the west-

ward mountains. A ground mist swirled rump-high to the
ponies, made a cottony haze along the rim of Monte Vista.
They reined in at the east end of the main street.

Reo felt dizzy. The numbness of his legs was worse.

"Jack. The poncho. In case we meet somebody."

Larnin unstrapped the latigos and slipped the oilskin over
Reo's shoulders. It hid the dark clotted stain of the shirt.

"All right," Reo said. "Let's go."

They didn't meet anybody. Monte Vista was curled up in
sleep. A memory of stale beer and bought laughter drifted
through dim saloon doorways. Even the red lights of the
western skirt of town had gone dead. A dog high-tailed
across a side lane. Morning wind stirred the lazy dust.

The riders swung south along Don Paulo Street. Doc Carson's house was at the far end, gray, sand-eaten, set back in
weeds. They hitched the ponies in the shelter of a sad willow
and walked around to the kitchen door.

Reo moved slowly. Each step sent pain splintering
through his chest and stomach. In the shade of the back
stoop, he leaned against the wall, sucking deep lungsful of
air. Larnin waited.

Finally, Reo said, "Now."

They didn't knock. The latch was up. The kitchen
smelled of rancid coffee grounds. They went down the side
hall. A thick, wet snoring led the way to the bedroom. Reo
stopped on the doorsill. His palm rested lightly on the low-
slung pistol.

The doc lay among crumpled quilts, fully dressed and
booted. His string tie was undone and gray stubble matted
his sunken cheeks. His mouth hung open. When he breathed
out, a stink of whiskey tainted the air.

Reo made a sign. Larnin crossed to the window and drew
the blind. In the dark now, Reo leaned at the foot of the bed.
Larnin stood just beside the pillow. Reo nodded, Larnin
lifted the Colt and pressed the small muzzle under the hinge
of Doc Carson's jaw.

Long bony fingers knotted in the patchwork. The doc's
eyelids twitched and opened very slowly.

"Quiet," Reo said. "Nice and quiet, Doc."

Carson sat up carefully, drawing back from the touch of the gun. "Reo. What is this?"

Reo set a smile against the biting twinges of the wound. "A professional visit, Doc."

Carson let out a long sigh, but he kept watching the gun. Some of the liquor-haze cleared from his eyes. "Law on your tail?"

The smile faded. "A misunderstanding," Reo said flatly. "There was a kid. He didn't trust me. I don't like it when people don't trust me."

The doc's stare wavered. The voice went shrill. "Well, what do you want with me? I can't . . ."

Reo turned around and pulled aside the poncho. Carson whistled, swung his feet to the floor. "Sit down," he said. "I'll look."

For a second, Reo didn't move. Finally, he sat on the bed.

Carson said, "I'll need light."

Larnin looked at Reo and then brought a lamp from the washstand and set fire to the wick.

The doc peeled off Reo's shirt. Flesh tore where flannel stuck to the edges of the wound. Reo sat still, head down, sweating. Carson's fingers prodded; his loose mouth pursed. He straightened.

Reo said, "So?"

Doc Carson scratched his jaw. "It won't be no cinch, Reo."

"You can do it?"

"There'll be a lot of pain."

Reo said, "You can do it."

The doc went to the clothes chest. He uncorked a bottle, drank and swabbed his mouth with a shirt sleeve. At last, he said. "This is against the law. I never handle these things, unless . . ."

Reo said, "You'll be paid."

A smile cracked wet lips. "Five hundred?"

Larnin's gun started to lift. "You lousy cheating . . ."

Reo shook his head. Larnin stood still. Reo looked at the doc.

"All right. Five hundred."

The smile broadened. Carson took a step forward.

"Not now," Reo said flatly. "Later. When this blows over."

Carson said, "Maybe you better get somebody else. I got nothing to ease the pain and . . ."

Abruptly, Reo stood up. His insides twisted and burned; nothing showed in his face. His hand hung over the thigh-thonged Colt. Carson went back a step.

"Like I told you," Reo said, "I don't like it when people won't trust me."

The lamp wick flickered. Morning was a pale yellow crack fringing the dark blind. Somewhere, a rooster crowed the day.

Doc Carson again tilted the bottle. The drink was a long one. He punched the cork home with his palm and said, "I'll get the instruments ready."

Reo sat down heavily. His head throbbed. He shut out the buzzing of his ears and looked up at Larnin. "Circulate," he said. "Ride out a ways. See if you can get wind of the posse."

Larnin flicked a glance at Doc.

Reo said, "I'll handle him."

Carson kept working over his leather case. The instruments chinked as if his hands were trembling.

"How long?" Larnin asked.

Reo swung his gaze to Carson.

"An hour," Carson said. "Maybe two."

Reo's square face tightened. "That long?"

"I told you. Probing for that shot won't be no picnic."

Reo's breathing had picked up a beat. He managed to steady it and then he nodded at Larnin.

Larnin sheathed the gun and crossed to the hall. "I'll be back." The door closed.

The room was quite still. Reo could hear the rasp of his own lungs. He sat there, watching Carson spread bright tools on a towel on the bedside chair. Carson turned up the lamp wick and filled the washbasin with water from a cracked ewer. He rolled back his sleeves.

"On the bed," he said. "Belly down."

Reo sat still. Their eyes held. Reo drew the Colt and lay down, right arm stretched wide, the gun in his fist. His cheek pressed the greasy pillow, eyes turned toward the lamp. Carson's hands moved over the instruments, forced a thin wood splint against Reo's lips. "Bite when it gets bad." Carson lifted a needle-fine probe, bent over the bed. "This is it."

The probe went deep. The splint snapped between Reo's teeth.

They were coming. The posse was riding down on him and he could not move. He lay there, watching the hoofs rear and crash down at his face. They did not hang him at once. They drove white-hot pokers into his back and dragged him over live coals and then the rope burned his neck. He was praying in broken Spanish and the mob laughed when the knot jerked taut under his ear . . . .

It lasted an hour and twenty minutes. Then the blackness went away. He could see the lamp, made pale now by the blaze of sun against the blind. The splint was gone. He tasted salt where his teeth had dug into the lower lip.

Stitches and plaster held him in a vise. Far off Monte Vista stirred with morning life. On the main drag, a pianola wrangled.

Doc Carson sat in the rocker by the window. "Sixteen buckshot," he was saying. "Don't know how you ever got this far."

Reo's lips burned. He licked them with a dry tongue. "Jack?"

"Yeah." Spurs chinked. "Here, Billy." Larnin brought him a tumbler of whiskey.

"Watch it," Carson said. "Watch them stitches."

Reo gained one elbow. His back seemed to tear apart, but the liquor helped. He looked up at Larnin. "Any luck?"

Larnin took the glass and refilled it. "If you'd call it that."

He drank. Reo waited.

''I was up to the saloon. Ran into this Express rider. He'd passed a party on the east road.''

''And?''

''Posse,'' Larnin said. ''Pony-boy says they was riding down a gunny. Lost his trail back in the meadows, then picked it up again. They're heading this way, Billy.''

''How far behind are they?''

''Twenty miles when he saw them; moving slow, asking questions at every cabin they passed.''

''Then we got time.'' Abruptly, Reo swung his legs out of bed. His mouth twitched with pain.

Doc Carson jumped up. ''God A'mighty, man! Easy!''

Reo sat there, head low, hands clutching the mattress edge. ''We ride,'' he told Larnin. ''We make the mountains. They'll never track us through shale and rock.''

Larnin said, ''Billy, Maybe . . .''

''We won't go over that again,'' Reo said thickly. ''We ride.''

''Ride?'' Carson shrilled. ''Are you loco? Half an hour in the saddle and them stitches'll bust wide open. Your back'll be a sieve. And if you hemorrhage inwardly . . .''

Reo said, ''Shut up.''

''I tell you, it's one sure way to die.''

Reo's mouth paled. ''I can think of worse ways.''

''But, my money . . .''

''Shut up!'' Reo caught hold of the bedstead and rose very slowly. The room pitched wildly, but he did not fall. ''I'll need a clean shirt, Doc.''

It took a long while to get dressed. Finally teeth set against a rising inward ache, Reo faced Larnin. ''The horses?''

''All ready.''

Reo lifted his pistol from the tangle of red-flecked covers. He turned to Carson. His eyes showed no emotion at all.

The doc's loose mouth went to pieces. ''Listen, Reo.'' It was a dry whisper. ''No hard feelings, eh? You know me. I'm a businessman. It ain't that I didn't trust . . .'' Carson swallowed noisily and forced a smile. ''Ain't that right, Reo? No hard feelings?''

"Yeah."

The gun went up fast and down. Carson saw it coming. He sidestepped too late. The barrel got him along the ear. He went down head first against the bed.

"Sure," Reo said softly. "No hard feelings."

Larnin wet his lips. "Look, Billy . . ."

The eyes stopped him. They were too brilliant and hard. "It gives us time," Reo said. "It'll remind him to keep his lip buttoned."

They went out through the kitchen. Reo waited in the warm shade of the stoop. Far up the street, a Mexican woman was stringing out wet wash. She did not look their way.

Larnin led the horses around. They had been fed and watered, but they didn't look rested. Reo frowned. There was no helping it. Trading for new mounts would only attract attention.

He caught the roan's stirrup and stepped up. The skin of his back stretched tight. Plaster cramped his ribs and he felt a wet ribbon run down his spine. He told himself it was only sweat, but he knew it was fresh blood. His jaw muscles corded. He gave Larnin the nod.

They rode along an alley to the south edge of town, then swung west. Reo sat with one hand resting on the butt of his Colt. Morning sun struck fire from the watchful slits of his eyes. They did not pass anybody. Far away, at the center of Monte Vista, a school bell chimed, clean and cool sounding.

When they hit open ground, Reo turned once. He saw the main drag, pale and dusty under a yellow sky. Wagons rumbled up with kegs from the brewery. Grangers lounged and smoked outside the barbershop and a fat woman waddled home with a basket of greens. There was no sign that anyone had noticed the passing of two strange riders.

The pain was a network of burning wires that jerked taut with every roll of the saddle. The wetness was thick along Reo's back now, soaking slowly into the bandages. He cursed Doc Carson for a bungler; he cursed a quick-tempered greenhorn and a man with a star pinned to his black vest. A nerve twitched his mouth.

"The hills," he said. "We make the hills and we're safe."

Larnin frowned. "It's a rough climb."

Reo seemed not to hear.

"We make the hills and we're all right," he said.

Larnin's frown deepened, but he didn't speak again.

Just before noon, they hit the first spur of the San Juans. Larnin hadn't been wrong. The going was steep and treacherous with tangleweed and shale. The horses didn't help. Reo's roan was whiteflanked and frothing at the bit. It walked head down, laboring against sun and the steady rise. Its feet were no longer sure.

Larnin was in the lead when they came onto the ledge. The pitching trail hung like the rungs of a ladder to the mountain face. The ledge was less than five feet wide with sheer wall to the left and, on the right, a drop of jagged rock to the next bench, thirty feet below.

Larnin heard the sudden slither of hoofs. Behind him, the roan shrilled and Reo yelled, "Jack!" He swung in the saddle, saw the roan already plunging over the rim, pawing for a grip. Reo twisted violently, trying to jump clear, but his right boot heel snagged the stirrup.

Man and horse went down together. Their screams echoed high above the rattle of shale, pierced the billow of rising dust. A few pebbles danced in their wake and the screaming stopped.

Larnin back-tracked on foot. It took time. Dust had settled; the lower bench lay still under the blistering sun. He saw the roan first. It had struck the ledge head-on; its neck was snapped and twisted at a foolish angle.

"Jack."

It wasn't more than a whisper. Reo lay against a boulder, legs stuck out straight before him, arms folded hard across his belly. The tear wasn't only skin-deep anymore. There was a hot, wet feeling in his chest.

The grit-streaked face went crooked when Larnin tried to lift him. The legs wouldn't move at all. He tried to speak and the wetness welled into his throat. A bubble of red broke past his lips, trickled down into the blond beard. Larnin let go of him. Reo sat there, choking back the wetness, his eyes on Larnin. After a long time, he said, "So this is it."

Larnin did not answer. Uneasily now, his glance moved down the long ramp of the spur. He took a deep breath. "Listen, Billy . . ."

The pale eyes didn't blink. "Go on. Say it."

Larnin's mouth worked. "I didn't have nothing to do with this, Billy. I never done no killing. We were friends. All right. I helped you while I could. But now . . ." The narrow jaw tightened. "Now I want out, Billy." He started to turn away.

"All right," Reo said. "You want out."

Larnin stared at the gun in Reo's fist. "Billy, you're crazy."

"I told you once. Whatever happened, it'd never be the posse. The mob'll never take me."

Slowly, the meaning got to Larnin. He shook his head. "I don't like it, Billy. I don't want your murder on my hands. You got a gun. You can do it yourself."

"Maybe," Reo said. "Only I can't be sure. It ain't easy to put a bullet through your own head. At the last minute, I might lose nerve." His gaze switched down to the blanched eastward flats. His voice went sharp. "Then they'd come with their goddam rope. They'd . . ."

It ended in a coughing fit. Bright red drained down his chin. The gun hand didn't waver.

"I'm not sure, Jack. You're going to do me a favor. You're going to make me sure."

"Billy . . ."

"That's how it is." The muzzle came belly-high on Larnin. "It's me or you, Jack."

They looked at each other. Then Larnin's bony fingers went down and closed on the Colt butt and the long barrel came up, clean and shining in the sun.

The posse came into Monte Vista at high noon. They rode wearily. Stetsons tilted against the glare, wetting grit-caked lips. The tall loose-limbed rider sat straight, scanning the dusty main street. The silver star winked against his black vest.

They were passing the telegraph office, when a man came running out. He wore a deputy's star. He waved a slip of yellow paper.

"You Rob Tucker? Sheriff down Alamosa way?"

The tall man nodded.

"Still riding the tail of that Reo fella?"

Tucker's eyes narrowed. "You got news?"

The man held out the yellow slip. "They sent that on for you. Said you'd pass this way, maybe want our help."

Tucker snoothed the paper on his thigh. Riders nudged close. "I'll be damned," Tucker said.

The deputy laughed. "That's what I says to my wife, 'That Reo's did it again.' Looks as if your hunting party's over, Sheriff. Seems like that Reckonridge boy is going to live, after all. Come to, early this morning, and said he wouldn't press any charges. Admitted he was starting to draw when Reo fired. Ain't much use arresting Reo when the victim hisself says it was self-defense." The grin widened. "Honest boy, that Reckonridge. Sounds like a nice kid."

"Yeah," Tucker said. "Nice kid."

The riders were silent, then something like a sigh of relief went among them. They hitched ponies and ambled off to the cool shade of the nearest saloon. Tucker dismounted and lit a cigarette. For a long moment, he stared at the match flame. He flung the match to the dust. "The luck of some sidewinders!"

The deputy nodded. "You had a long ride. You're wore thin."

"Can you figure it?" Tucker shook his head. "Here's this Reo, suspicioned of murder in four counties and just when we think he's pinned down, ready to bring to trial, out he slides by the skin of his teeth."

The deputy frowned. Then a thought made him smile. "Say, I got some stuff up to the office. Curl the hair on your chest."

Tucker stared at the dead match. "The luck," he said.

''The luck always rides with him.'' Then he shrugged and grinned back. ''Like you say. It was a long ride.''

They went off along the dry, hot boardwalk. The sheriff's office was at the east end of the main drag. Their backs were turned to the distant San Juan range. They didn't notice the shadows against the sun, the black, picket-winged birds that hovered for a long time above a mountain ledge and then circled down with a slow final grace.

*Best known for his darkly powerful novels about gangster-
ism in America during the twenties, thirties, and forties
(Little Caesar, High Sierra, The Asphalt Jungle), W. R.
Burnett was also an accomplished writer of historical Westerns; such books as* Stretch Dawson *and* Adobe Walls *are
ample proof of his prowess with the Western form. "Nobody's All Bad," one of his few shorts about the Old West, is
a first-rate tale of Billy the Kid and the famous Lincoln
County War.*

Nobody's All Bad

W. R. Burnett

I*m convinced there's a heap of nonsense wrote about this*
here so-called Golden West. I ain't what you'd call a reading man, but since I been old and infirm, as you might say, I
been kind of doing some perusing, and I don't find no truth
in books nohow. Leastways in books I know something
about.

Take these here Western novels now. Hogwash! Plain,
unadulterated hogwash. There's always a vilyun black as
ink, and a hero white as snow, and a sweet little schoolmarm
or sech a matter in the offing, as you might say, and that
there's a Western novel. Even a Mexican'd laugh himself
sick. I'm telling you, life in this here Golden West didn't go
by no formulas. It was a lot better and a lot worse than most
people knows about.

Take that Lincoln County War where Billy the Kid done
his high, wide, and handsome riding. Let one of these here

writing fellers take it up and what do you reckon he'd make of it? A massacre or a holy war, yes, sir, and Billy the Kid'd be a poor misunderstood angel or a demon with a forked tail, spitting fire. 'Tain't in the cards that-a-way, gents. 'Tain't all one way or another; it's mixed. Howsomever, that ain't what I starts out to say. I starts out to tell you about Billy the Kid.

Well, personally, I could never see nothing to get excited about in this here Billy the Kid. Good enough boy, as they grew 'em out here in them days, and as fine a shot as ever used a six-shooter. Kind of a bashful-acting boy, somehow, though he was always a-laughing and a-kicking up his heels, as you might say. Nerve? Yes, sir; that boy had nerve and lots of it. But still there was a God's plenty of men with nerve in these parts, gents. It wasn't no outstanding virtue like sobriety would have been; far from it. But what I'm getting at is this, even if I am shying away from it like a yearling: the truth ain't never been told about young William Bonney, which was The Kid's rightful name, nor never will be.

The Mexicans around these parts are locoed over Billy, El Cheevito, they calls him, and they talks nonsense and rubbish till it gives an old-timer the bellyache. Good enough boy; but no demon and no angel, that's my contention. Maybe there was a hundred boys in this here Southwest as nervy and as plucky as The Kid, but they wasn't put in The Kid's circumstances, as you might say, and so you never hear tell of them.

There's a heap of chance in this world. Things goes by chance a whole lot, I'm telling you, and I've seen plenty. How about that time down to old Alex McSween's adobe in Lincoln when the Murphy boys burnt the McSween boys out and peppered 'em with lead when they come through the door? Yes, sir. Old McSween steps out and, bang! down he goes first pop with his Bible in his hand, so I've heard tell; though a Bible was a queer instrument to be a-carrying in the Lincoln County War.

Out steps a couple of more boys and down they go, full of shot. Yes, sir. Then out steps The Kid and his chances was the slimmest of the lot, as there wasn't a feller in the Murphy faction that wouldn't've give his trigger finger to let some daylight into Billy. What happens? Nothing. Positively nothing. They bans away at The Kid and nary a bullet does he get in his young hide. Nary a bullet from guns fired at ten yards. Now, that's chance, gents. You can't make me believe nothing different nohow.

Other day I was a-talking things over with an old messmate of mine and somehow we got to jawing about Billy the Kid and the Lincoln County War. "There's a special Providence looking after critters like The Kid," says this here old longhorn.

"Hell," I says, "your mind must be a-failing."

"Nothing like it," says my old matey, "I'm telling you I know what I'm a-saying."

Then he relates to me how down Tombstone way old Wyatt Earp, and, gents, there never was a nervier and straighter-shooting feller, walks right up to a passel of Curly Bill's rustlers and bangs away at 'em, and them with rifles at fifteen yards a-peppering at him in broad daylight, and never a crease nor a scratch does he get.

"Howsomever," I says, "that's just luck, like filling an inside straight."

"No, sir," says this stubborn old hombre, "some men has got something on their side excepting luck."

And you couldn't make him believe different effen you argued till doomsday.

No, sir. Books ain't telling the truth, and no wonder when an old hombre like my matey begins talking about a special Providence for bad men. An old hombre that's been every place, from Dodge City, when she was a ripsnorting town, to San Francisco; down the Pecos and 'cross the Rio, lived in Tombstone when she was roaring and in Lincoln when they shot a man a day.

I'll tell you a little story being's you got time to listen, and maybe it'll kind of open your eyes about the Golden West, you being strangers, and maybe it'll amuse you some likewise. Effen not, don't stand on ceremony, as Sheriff Brady used to say, but bust right out with yawns. When a man gets old he gets garrulous with the past and no mistake nohow.

Well, when I was a sight younger than I am at this sitting, with black hair and not this dead white stuff, I was working for a man named Riddle over Lincoln way. Riddle was tangled up with the Murphy faction 'count he was in business with Murphy some; but he wasn't no man for wars and did a lot of lamenting about sech goings-on; a peaceable-like man. But in them days effen you lived in Lincoln County you was in the war whether you liked it or not, as you might say. Neutrality was looked on by both parties as a sight suspicious.

Howsomever, Riddle never actually got in any of the ructions till one day he was over in Lincoln and bumped plumb into The Kid, who was coming out of a bar as old man Riddle went in.

"Asking your pardon," says old man Riddle, who didn't know Billy the Kid from Lucifer.

The Kid laughed and batted him one with the flat of his hand.

"That'll learn you to go around asking pardons, you old snake," says The Kid. Then he turns his back and goes on calm as you please.

That was Billy the Kid, turning his back on a man he'd just whacked across the face, which wasn't healthy in them days nohow. Old Riddle, peaceable-like, as I say, just stood there and looked at this blustering kid, who wasn't no more than nineteen nor twenty, maybe less. And the longer he looked the madder he got, so he ups with his rifle and is all for shooting The Kid when a feller of the name of Willis struck the gun from his hands and planted a knife in him.

"Shooting The Kid in the back, was you!" says this here Willis party.

But old man Riddle don't say nothing. He just climbs up on his horse and rides for home, holding his side. Nervy old crow, he was. When he pulls in I was standing over by the corral, whittling or something, and he says: "War is declared for good and all, boys, and we'll fight till there ain't a McSween varmint left in the county nohow."

* * *

Then he kind of gets a funny look on his face and falls off his pony. That knife went deeper than he calculated and 'fore nightfall he was a dead cattleman.

Well, we buries him over back of the ranch house. There wasn't no cemetery in Lincoln in them days; they usually just buried 'em where they lay effen it was feasible. And we puts up a board, saying: "Elias Riddle. Killed in the Lincoln County War."

Well, we was some inflamed, being as how Riddle was a good man to his hands, and when his brother come in from Santa Fe to take the ranch over we was raring to go, which didn't anger the brother none, as he was a fire-eating kind of feller, noways like the old man. Them that didn't have rifles was supplied by old man Riddle's brother, and he 'lows as how they can start shooting any time.

Lem Cowan was my matey then and a mighty square feller he was, though apt to get full of nose paint and shoot things up some. He used to be friendly with this here Billy the Kid and rustled cattle with him a whole lot in Old Mexico, but since the killing of old man Riddle he was dead set against him and went around saying he'd pay off that slinking varmint as soon as he got square with Willis, the feller that got old man Riddle.

Well, Lem Cowan sure enough made good on the Willis end of the deal. He shot him so full of holes out on the Riddle range one day that he wouldn't hold water nor liquor neither no more than a sieve. But Lem got sort of overconfident and boastful, as you might say, and one day he ran square into The Kid on the streets of Lincoln and 'fore you could chalk your cue he was shot by The Kid, who shot first and talked afterwards. The Kid could pull a six-gun and shoot accurate 'fore you could get your hand towards your gun. He was sure hell for quickness.

Well, some Murphy boys took Lem into the Murphy store and propped him up on the counter to die, but he didn't die none, which fooled everybody, including himself, and when he got a little better they moved him out to the ranch and put him in the bunkhouse.

That bullet had sure raised the devil in Lem. He couldn't sleep nor eat for thinking about that Billy the Kid person, and him and the new Riddle boss used to spend hours in the bunkhouse a-taking turns cussing The Kid and 'lowing what they'd do to him. Well, the rest of the hands was a little lukewarm about the matter by now, and wise they was, though I'm including myself in that category. What was the sense in a bunch of cowhands getting themselves shot up over a fight that didn't pay no dividends to them neither way?

Course they got pretty riled up at first over the killing of the old man, but time sort of dulls things, and as they begin to forget about the old man tumbling from his saddle and all, they begin to think more about their own hides and less about shooting things up. As I say, I was lukewarm. I was saving my money, figuring I'd go a-prospecting over Little Mesa way, and I was aiming to keep from getting planted effen I could help it. But this here devil of a Cowan, flat on his back in the bunkhouse, called us forty kinds of cowards and he had such a lashing tongue and such a way with him that it wasn't long till we begin to get all het up again, being young fellers and warm-blooded and not particularly relishing being called cowards nohow. But we was playing in luck 'cause things kind of got settled up without us horning in.

One evening up rides a Mexican of the name of Romero, or some sech name, all shot up and bleeding, and he says that Billy the Kid has been run out of town, that McSween is dead, that the troops, nigger troops at that, is a-camping at the edge of town, and that the Lincoln County War is practically over. We take the Mexican back to the bunkhouse to palaver with Lem and get himself tied up and respectable, and we lights out for town.

Sure enough what the Mex says is right. The Murphy boys have done burned old man McSween's house down and killed him, which is a pity, as he was a decent, God-fearing man, effen he was a lawyer, and two or three of the McSween boys is stretched out in the street, dead as might be, and these here Murphy boys is drunk as loons and sashaying and capering about among the dead like a passel of Apaches. Well, we stayed to watch the excitement, being's we had been pretty quiet of late and longing to work off our energy some place, and then we rides home, singing.

Might be a week later, gents, and we're still a sight joyful over the end of the Lincoln County War, and riding in from town full of nose paint and contentment. It was a mighty fine night with a full moon and a nice breeze, and we was just kind of idling along, when up the trail comes some feller, hell bent for election, rides past us like a cyclone, and yells: "Ketch me, you sons-of-guns. I'm Billy the Kid, and I'm looking for excitement!" Well, he got it. We all blazed away at once with six-shooters and rifles and down went his horse, but up he got and 'fore we knowed what the play was he'd winged two of our horses, including mine, and had vanished, clean vanished, gents, like as if he'd flew away.

I was so cussing mad I extricates myself from my horse, which is kicking up a big fuss and getting ready to die, and starts after The Kid. I hear him thrashing his way down a hillside where he'd vanished, and I bangs away at the noise, then goes after him.

Well, the boys shout for me to come back and raise almighty hell yelling and whooping in that quiet night, but I'm that mad and locoed 'cause I lost my pony I don't know a thing excepting to get the brazen varmint that done the shooting. I'm getting farther and farther away from the boys all the time, and pretty soon I can't hear them noways, and all I can hear is a feller running like holy hell and a-thrashing through the brush. I don't know how long I kept hotfoot after that Billy person, but by the time the east began to get light I'd lost him. I was still on the Riddle range but way over to the eastward, and I had heard some talk lately about some Mescaleros that had got disgruntled-like and left their reservation, but that was way off to the south, so I just rolled up in my coat to sleep some 'fore I made tracks for the ranch.

* * *

It might have been two hours later or sech a matter when I wakes up with a start, hears some yelling and carrying on, and sees a man hotfooting it down a little ridge not a quarter of a mile off. It's this here Billy the Kid. I can recognize him easy, and he's in a almighty big hurry about something, and I see what it is when a couple of Injuns stick their nobs up over the edge of the ridge. Yes, sir. Here I was right in the middle of that passel of locoed Mescaleros which had skipped their reservation.

I was cold and chilled, and I wasn't looking for any such ructions this early in the morning. But I seen I was in for it, so I looks to my rifle and yells to The Kid. He sees me and kind of stops and considers for a spell. He ain't in such a good fix nohow. Injuns on one side of him and one of old man Riddle's men on t'other, but blood is thicker than water, and Injuns is Injuns, so he joins up with me, ducking and running.

The Injuns is holding a powwow up at the edge of the ridge, and they don't interrupt themselves none excepting to take a pot shot at The Kid or me once in a while just to keep us interested. But Injuns can't shoot nohow and that far away it's plumb ridiculous. Up comes this Billy the Kid, his face red from running, grinning from ear to ear and showing his big teeth.

"How many Injuns is they?" I says.

"Seven or eight," says Billy. "Was that a good pony of yourn?"

"It surely was," I says, "and I don't thank you none for your gunplay."

"I was loaded up with jig-juice," says Billy, "and my blood was up; I'm plumb sorry."

Well, we crawled up into the hills just across from the Injuns and got our backs up against a rock wall and a big boulder in front of us. The Injuns was still powwowing over on the ridge and popping at us every now and then just to relieve their feeling, I reckon, 'cause they wasn't doing nothing but wasting powder.

"Looky here, pardner," says The Kid, "you're a Riddle man, ain't you?"

"I am," I says, "and I been chasing you all over hell and gone."

"Well," says The Kid, grinning, "here I be."

He was a danged ingratiating feller and I kind of took a shine to him.

"Looky here," he says, "let me take that rifle and dust some of them Injuns."

"Nope," I says, "use your six-gun."

"Can't," he says, "the range ain't right and I dropped my rifle some place or another."

"Pretty careless, ain't you?" I said.

"Right smart," he said and picked up my rifle and was sighting it when I took it away from him.

"Use your own gun," I says. But, gents, effen he didn't talk me out of that gun I'm a shoemaker, and good thing he did, too, 'cause while we was arguing a couple of young bucks started veering off to the right, figuring to flank us, I reckon. Effen he didn't get 'em both with two quick shots!

Yes, sir, mighty good shooting it was and him a-grinning and a-smiling all over his face with his big hat pushed back.

"Good gun," he says, handing it back to me.

Them Injuns 'peared to lose heart, as you might say, after that snap shooting and snuck over, not taking no chances, and picked up their comrades and disappeared over the hill.

"Injuns ain't worth shucks nohow," said Billy.

We sat there behind that boulder till round noontime, kind of expecting them Injuns to come back or do something and not wanting to walk into no ambuscade, but they never showed up.

"Well," says Billy, "I'm getting powerful hungry and a little water wouldn't hurt none."

So we footed it down across the valley and made Seven Mile Spring toward evening. We just walked along side by side and not saying a word, mind you, but me thinking plenty how I ought to take this desperate character, as they say, and turn him over to the proper authorities. But I don't know. I kind of took a shine to The Kid and, besides that, being's I'm a truthful man and ain't got no reputation to keep up now that I'm about ready for eternity, this Billy person wasn't the kind that you march off to jail nohow and a gun in his face didn't mean much to that hombre; and effen you understand me, I kind of lost my ill feeling toward this Billy person since him and me fought off them Injuns together, yes, sir.

Well, after we'd soaked ourselves with water down at the water hole, Billy says: "I'm on my way, mister; so long."

"So long," I says.

And there he goes, turning his back on me and walking off as unconcerned as you please just as effen him and me was the best friends in the world and I hadn't been chasing him all over hell and back the night before. At the top of the ridge he looks back and sort of nods, and that's the last I ever see of that so-called bad hombre, Billy the Kid.

Well, gents, that's the last of Billy the Kid in person in this here chronicle, but it ain't the last of him in another form, as you might say. It was two hours later and dark; I was hoofing it for the ranch when I hears a sight of horsemen coming across the vega and me not knowing whether it be Injuns, McSween remnants nor what, till Tom Kane opens his big mouth and yawns, then I yells to 'em.

"By God," says Riddle, "we thought you was done for sure enough; been a-hunting you since sunup."

"I had a brush with some hostiles," I says, "and it delayed me a whole lot."

So Tom Kane took me up behind and we made tracks for the ranch, talking and jesting about them Mescaleros and sech, till one of the hands says: "Did you ketch up with that varmint Billy the Kid?"

This here hand was just joking, you see. Well, I didn't know what to say, but being, generally speaking, a truthful man, I says: "Yep, me and The Kid stood off a bunch of Mescaleros meaning no good, killing two."

"What!" screams Riddle. "Where is this Billy person?"

"Done gone on," I says.

"Gone on!" yells Tom Kane. "Effen that don't beat all

with your matey Lem Cowan still laid up with The Kid's bullet.''

"Well," I says, "I 'lows as how since we fought off them Injuns they ain't no sense nor profit in us being nasty with each other."

"You draws your pay tonight," says Riddle.

Well, I wasn't none too popular around that ranch, gents, as I reckon you can figure out for yourselves. Riddle pays me off and tells me to cut myself out a pony besides 'cause he owes me a bonus, and Tom Kane brings me my saddle that he brung in offen my dead pony.

In the morning I'm out saddling my pony when I see Lem Cowan coming out of the ranch house where he's been sleeping lately 'count it's quiet, and he's pale and staggery, but he's got a six-gun in his hand and he says: "I'll learn you to go consorting with that killing varmint, you Judas!" And he bangs away at me, but being weak and shaky-like, he misses me by a mile and then the boss comes up and takes the gun away from him and carries him in the house, 'cause he don't weigh no more than a hundred pounds. But he kicks and squeals mighty lifelike.

I gets on my pony right spry 'cause I know that gunplay is contagious, like measles, and I don't want no well men taking shots at me, 'cause some of them Riddle boys can shoot.

"Good-bye," I says, waving my arms, and off I go galloping, hell bent for election.

Well, that's about all of my story, gents, excepting that Lem Cowan and me turns out to be pardners after all and goes a-prospecting together over Little Mesa way and finds the Old Red Cougar Mine, where we made our pile. Yes, sir. And Billy the Kid got himself shot up a whole lot over Sumner way by Pat Garrett, sheriff in them days, who used to be his bosom friend, and nobody was a-looking for him to be the feller to get The Kid nohow.

Well, as I was saying, there's been a heap of rubbish wrote about this so-called Golden West. There's no truth in books, gents, and little knowledge in the heads of them that writes 'em. Wasn't a matter of vilyuns and heroes and herowines in these parts. No, sir. It was all jumbled up so bad it would take God almighty himself to cut out his own cattle and leave the rest to the devil. Do you see how I'm aiming?

A prolific writer of pulp Western stories in the forties and fifties, H. A. De Rosso was a master at portraying the seamier side of Western life without ever mitigating, or apologizing for, its harshness. The motives of his heroes are usually mixed, and their victories, if indeed they do triumph (a good many do not even survive), are almost always bittersweet. These unusual qualities are clearly in evidence in the best of his fiction—the novels .44, *The Man from Texas*, and *End of the Gun*, and the powerful story which follows.

Back Track

H. A. De Rosso

At *high noon they rode out of the timber. There below* them, at the edge of the small plain, lay the village, its tan *jacals* seeming unreal and toylike at this distance.

"San Miguel," Llano Lane said. "Nine years, Dave, isn't it?"

Recollection brought no nostalgia to Dave Merritt, not yet. "About that," he said.

"That was after the S.P. job, wasn't it?" Llano Lane said. "We were here a month. It was a nice place to lay low in."

"Let's hope it still is," Merritt said.

Lane threw Merritt a look. "The only time a deputy comes to San Miguel is to collect the taxes. What you so jumpy about?"

Don't you know, Merritt thought, especially after Spencerville? The coming of the end. Don't you feel it, too?

Aloud he said nothing.

Lane shifted his weight in the saddle. A hand rose and rubbed his craggy nose. "I wonder if they still remember us."

"No one ever forgets Llano Lane," Merritt said. A little bitterness crept into his voice but it was not intended for the man but for the situation. He felt Lane's sharp look again.

"Forget Spencerville," Lane said. "There's just the two of us now but we make a good team. We'll have our days again."

Maybe we will, Llano, Merritt thought, but you want to know something? I really don't much care. I feel too tired and old to care.

Aloud he said, "Whatever you say, Llano."

The horses moved on. The clopping of their hoofs hung an instant in the air and then was gone like forgotten memories . . .

They rode into San Miguel from the north. Several mongrels came yapping to greet them and Lane's sorrel shied once and kicked out and sent a dog tumbling and squealing. After that the dogs kept their distance.

From open doorways and glassless windows, dark, impassive eyes watched the two tall riders. A hush seemed to gather, so that the clopping of the horses' hoofs on the hard-packed earth of the street rang clarion clear.

Too many dark trails, Merritt thought while the skin twitched and crawled on his shoulders. The ghosts of too many dead men. The coming of the end. Don't you feel anything at all, Llano?

In front of the cantina of Elfego Vara they reined in. Llano Lane stepped down and brushed at the dust on his arms and thighs. The eyes still watched with that secret stolidity.

Elfego Vara dozed behind his plank bar. The years had not been too good nor too unkind to him. A little more fat around the middle and a smattering of gray in the coal black hair and a slight sallowness in the complexion.

Spur tinkle woke him. He blinked his eyes rapidly to clear

them of the mists of sleep and then watched the two tall men with a puzzled look of semirecollection.

"Tequila, Elfego," Lane said. His voice seemed to boom in the hushed dimness of the cantina.

A wrinkle formed between Elfego's eyes as he poured the drinks. He glanced from one to the other of the tall men, a glimmer of recognition deep in his eyes but never quite coming through.

Lane grinned. His teeth looked very white, framed by the black beard. "Nine years ago, Elfego," he said. "We spent many pesos here in your cantina. Look behind the beard. Don't you remember Llano Lane?"

"Llano Lane," Elfego breathed, eyes widening. There was both fear and awe in his voice.

Merritt threw down the tequila, and while it burned his throat and stomach he looked about, searching the dimness for what might be there but wasn't, this time. Deep in his mind something stirred which he could not define. A fragment of forgotten memory that left him vaguely uneasy.

"We wish a place to stay," Lane was saying. "A good *jacal* for me and my compadre. You remember the señor Merritt, do you not?"

"And the others?" Elfego Vara asked.

A flash of Spencerville passed before Merritt's eyes.

"There are no more," Lane said. "One *jacal* is all we need."

Yes, Elfego, just one *jacal*, Merritt thought. Dandy Jim Hayes and Johnny Forrest and Flint Quarternight and Ben Lord and Sundance, they don't need *jacals* or anything anymore.

"More tequila, Elfego," Lane said.

This one did not burn quite as much. Merritt searched the dimness of the far corners, the dimness that seemed to have diminished, and now his spirits lifted and he did not care so much anymore.

"What are you waiting for?" Lane said.

"Señor Llano. Pardon. I grieve to ask. But I have five little mouths to feed. The money. I grieve."

Lane laughed, quietly but with a ring to it like the ring of blue steel. "Did I leave you unpaid nine years ago? Have I any debts from that time? Is not the word of Llano Lane good with Elfego Vara? Go and find us the *jacal*. We are tired and wish to sleep. *Andale pronto.*"

Yes, Elfego, *andale*, Merritt thought, and forget about money. I have a gold eagle. Llano has even less. Forget about money. If we'd had better luck in Spencerville— *Andale*, Elfego.

"Of a certainty, Señor Llano," Elfego Vara said. "The *jacal*. *Pronto*. You wait here."

His sandals whispered like lost secrets as he padded across the earth floor to the door. His body blocked the light an instant. Then the sun was bright and clean where it touched the threshold . . .

Llano Lane stretched and sighed. "Man, but it's good to have a roof over your head," he said. "No more sleeping out, in the brush, in the timber. No more of that for a while."

Dave Merritt stood at one of the glassless windows of the *jacal*, looking out. Somewhere inside him something ancient was whispering, but all he caught was the hiss of sound. He could not make out a single word.

"What's come over you today, Dave?" Lane asked. Gray eyes weighed and pondered. "Relax. We're safe here."

Merritt said nothing.

"No one comes here," Lane went on. "No one bothers these people. Leave them alone and they'll leave you alone. We had it good that other time, didn't we?"

"We had money that other time," Merritt said.

Lane was silent a moment, struggling with his thoughts. When he spoke it was very softly. "These *pelados* know better than to cross Llano Lane. They might not hear much of the outside world but they've heard of me."

"We had money that other time," Merritt said again, "and we were worth less. Money gives some cowards courage."

Lane gave that laugh with the ring of steel. "Why are you

so worried? I'm the valuable one of the pair. What did that poster we saw yesterday say? Five thousand for me but only one thousand for you. The price has gone up since Spencerville." He laughed again.

Spencerville, Merritt thought. It doesn't bother you one little bit, does it, Llano? Do you think we can go on forever? The coming of the end, Llano. Don't you ever feel it?

"Sit down, Dave," Lane said. "Relax. Me, I'm going to sleep."

He lay down on the pallet on the floor and closed his eyes, and shortly he was breathing the soft, muted breath of sleep. His hand lay on the handle of his pistol. He never slept any other way . . .

Merritt felt the ancient stirrings in his mind as he walked through the village. Memory upon memory returned as he passed each hut. Eyes watched from everywhere, but he heard not a single greeting, though word of him and Lane must have already circulated through San Miguel. The eyes just watched, passively, patiently, neutrally right now.

He found it at the far end of the village, the house of Agustín Prado. The years had changed it little except for a few more pit marks in the adobe. Goats were still penned behind the hut and the pepper trees still whispered gently in the wind.

He wondered what it was that had led him here. Memories, yes, of a few sweet moments, but they had been only a few of many and had never really meant anything to him. There was something more, an ancient hunger and yearning perhaps? He could not understand a thing like that.

The woman was bending over the hearth. Creak of leather and spur jingle told her he had entered, and she straightened with a small gasp and came around ponderously. It was not until he looked in her eyes and studied the shape of her mouth that Merritt recognized her.

"Margarita," he said.

The years and child-bearing had made her breasts massive and widened her hips and added flesh all over her. They had also put a sullen resignation to the burden of life in her face.

She eyed him without speaking, frowning the while, and he knew that she had not yet seen beneath the brown beard.

"I'm Merritt," he said.

Her face brightened. "Ah, yes, the señor Merritt." Then sullenness blanketed it again. She went on eyeing him.

Merritt looked about. Gloom hung like thin smoke in the room, and in the dimness, standing together, he could make out the varying sizes of four children. They watched him with a somber, open curiosity, watched him and the pistol in the holster at his side.

"Agustín?" Merritt asked. "Your father?"

"Dead."

Something skipped in him. Was it a heartbeat? A foreboding?

"And Ana Lucía?" he asked.

"Dead."

This time he knew definitely there had been a pause in his heartbeat, and he could not understand because it had never been like that, for him.

"I'm very sorry," he said, and glanced again at the children, drawn there by something beyond his ken.

"Sorry," said Margarita, and her tone rose, and now the cross that she convinced herself she bore made her voice tremble. "After nine years you return and say you're sorry."

He was frankly puzzled. "I do not understand. Your father, your sister—" He did not know how to finish.

"Yes, my sister. She is dead these many years but she left something for you. Something for you to remember her by."

"I really do not understand, Margarita."

"Anita," she said, and the tallest of the children stepped forward to stand beside her. "Look at her, Merritt. Look at her eyes. They are blue, Merritt, the only blue eyes in San Miguel . . ."

That night he slept very little. It seemed that every time he dozed he found himself in the hut with Margarita and the children, especially the blue-eyed one who stood there so somberly still, staring up at him while something old and fierce and frightening stirred in him.

"I have a good husband," Margarita was saying, a whine in her voice, "but we have three of our own to feed. Still she is my sister's flesh and blood. We clothe her and feed her but it is so hard. And now we have another on the way."

His throat was dry and pained him when he spoke. "Ana Lucía—How did she die?"

"A plague. Anita was not yet one year old. My father died that way, too."

He stared at the child who stared back at him. In the gloom he could not make out the look in her eyes. Something strange and new yet hauntingly familiar stirred in him and for an instant a feeling akin to panic chattered in him.

"It has been so hard," Margarita was saying. "But my Pedro is a good man. We will take her in, he said. She will be as one of our own. But it has been so hard, so little money, so little—It has been very hard."

He took his eyes from the child's face and glanced at her dress. It hung loosely over her body, and it was ragged and torn in two places and it was none too clean.

"I thought since she is yours," Margarita was saying. "Anything will help. Even a little. After all, she is yours. Look at her eyes. As blue as your own. A little would help."

The cold breath of an ancient wind brushed by him. Was there really so little time left?

"Deny her," Margarita was saying, and her tone said that the cross she bore weighed heavily now. "Deny her, then. We will manage. Somehow, no matter how little, how poor, we will manage."

He did not know what prompted him to do it. His hand reached out, awkwardly, intending to touch the child only lightly on the head. She shrank, eyes widening, and then quick as a cat she ducked under his arm and was past him with a swift pattering of bare feet and gone out the door and he was standing there, turned half around, hand still outstretched, watching the door that showed him only sunlight and emptiness . . .

* * *

"I've been thinking," Llano Lane said. He sat at the table in the *jacal,* drawing phantom patterns on the tabletop with a finger. "I can see all the mistakes I made in Spencerville. The next time there won't be any mistakes."

Merritt felt his fists clench, and he opened them, hoping that Lane had not noticed.

"I guess I got a little cocky," Lane said. "I had a bunch of good boys and everything I tried came off real slick. A train in Kansas, another in Oklahoma. Everything I tried worked without a hitch. I thought because I had some good boys all I had to do was ride into Spencerville and then ride right on out."

Merritt stood at the window, watching the leaves of a cottonwood fluttering in the breeze. There was something akin in his own heart, a flutter that seemed to urge, Hurry, hurry. Hurry for what? he asked himself and found no answer.

"I thought I would do something that had never been done before," Lane was saying. "Knock off two banks at the same time. We were seven good men and I figured it could be done. But I was wrong. I made mistakes but I see them now. Next time there won't be any mistakes."

A sense of futility swept over Merritt, leaving him weak and shaken. His eyes lowered, to the dust of the street, but he was looking beyond that and seeing only the endless blackness of the abyss.

"We rode in in one bunch," Lane said. "That was the first mistake. We were recognized. They blocked the streets and we had to shoot our way out. Next time it won't be like that." Gray eyes picked up Merritt's back and examined it. "Are you listening, Dave?"

"Where will you get five more men?" Merritt asked. "You'll never get another five as good as them."

"I know," Lane said, "and I won't even look. Next time there will be only two. Just you and me, Dave . . ."

Down in the thickets along the creek she sat on a fallen tree in sullen brooding. A worn path led him there. She was so lost in her child's world of grief and resentment that she did not hear him. Only at the last moment did she glance up at him towering over her. He saw her thin body gather, ready to flee, and his heart ached in fear of this and he stopped abruptly. That seemed to reassure her but she stayed all gathered and tensed, watching him with a dark suspicion.

"I won't hurt you," he said. "I'd never hurt you. You know that, don't you?"

She watched him with wide eyes. There was a measure of fear in them but there was more, much more. They reminded him of an old woman's eyes which had seen all there was to see, all that was dark and evil. There was no innocence here.

"Don't be afraid of me," he said. "I won't do anything to you."

The eyes took on a glitter like secret laughter. At him? They were an old woman's eyes, all wise. Did she know him for what he was?

"I want to talk to you," he said. "I'm your—father."

He thought he heard laughter, mocking, scurrilous laughter. But her face remained grave. Her lips had not moved. The laughter had been borne on the winds of time, the winds of memories and shame and reproach.

"Margarita told me you were bad," he said. "She told me she had to punish you because you stole a piece of silver. Don't you know it's wrong to steal?"

He stopped because in the long, haunting corridors of time mocking laughter was shrieking. He became aware that the palms of his hands were wet and that his face was warm. Was it because the old woman's eyes watched him so allknowingly?

"Anita," he said, sweating now while he listened to that laughter shrilling in scornful glee, "it isn't right to take something that belongs to another. Don't you understand that? You wouldn't want any one to take something that belongs to you, would you?"

He stopped. What could she have for any one to take from her? A ragged dress that had probably been given her grudgingly. Certainly nothing else.

"You should mind Margarita," he said. "She is good to

you. She has others but she takes care of you, too, and you should mind her and be grateful for that. Do you understand, Anita?''

The eyes watched him, not frightened anymore, but cunning and still suspicious.

"Anita," he said again, "will you try and remember what I've told you? Won't you tell me that you'll mind me?''

The old, wise eyes glittered, full of wariness. The mouth remained grave and still. He stood and watched while back in the paths of time reproach and remorse gathered, and when he thought the cruel laughter was about to begin again he turned and walked away . . .

"It'll be just the two of us," Llano Lane said. "In Spencerville.''

"Spencerville?" Merritt swung around, mind suddenly full and aching from that other time. "Are you crazy, Llano?''

Lane laughed that laugh with the ring of steel. "Why not?" Excitement laid a sheen over his eyes. "No one will expect us to try it there again, not after what happened. That's the last place in the world they'd expect us to try.''

Something dismally chill crawled across Merritt's shoulders, but still he started to sweat.

"Just the two of us," Lane said musingly, eyes far away toying with something that still was not clear to him. "And we'll hit both banks, at the same time. You just watch, Dave. It'll work this time.''

"We'll never make it," Merritt said. "How can we? We failed when we were seven. How are we going to do it with only two?''

"We'll fool them," Lane said. "We'll disguise ourselves. That's the only thing I have to figure out. What the disguises are going to be. But I'll get it. Nothing ever stumped Llano Lane for long.''

Merritt turned back to the window and watched a barefoot boy leading three goats through the village. He kept seeing those eyes, old woman's eyes.

Lane was silent a while, gray glance studying Merritt's back. After a pause, Lane said, "What's on your mind, Dave?"

Merritt stared into the distance and the past. That frantic urgency breathed on him again. Hurry, hurry, it pleaded. Hurry how? he asked and heard no answer.

Lane kept watching him. "Something's eating you," Lane said. "If I didn't know you better I'd say you were scared, but you never were scared of anything."

"It's nothing, Llano," Merritt said. "I'm all right . . ."

This was her world, a child's world of fancies and dreams and exquisite joys, down here among the thickets that shielded her from watching eyes and set this world apart from that other world that held so little. She knelt on the ground and built little mounds of sand with her hands. This must have afforded her pleasure, for she was making small, crooning sounds and Merritt stopped a while and listened. It was the first time he had heard her voice.

When he started ahead his spurs tinkled, and this warned the child and she leaped to her feet and whirled, all in one flash of movement. She stood there poised on the balls of her feet, ready to flee, so Merritt halted.

"It's only me," he said. "Don't run away."

The child watched him, eyes wide and wary.

"I brought you something," he said, extending it toward her. "See? It's a doll, a rag doll. I bought it from another little girl."

She hadn't wanted to sell. She had cried and raised a fuss, but when he offered her father the gold piece it was done.

The child's eyes fixed on the doll and stayed there, mesmerized. But she did not move.

"Here," he said, taking a step ahead. "It's yours. I'm giving it to you, Anita. Here. Take it."

The two small hands that she reached up trembled. Her face said that she did not believe this to be true, that she expected him to snatch the doll away at the last moment. But she reached her hands up anyway.

"Take it," Merritt said.

She grabbed the doll and pulled it from his grasp swiftly as though afraid that he would not let go. She clutched it to her breast and looked up at him with shining eyes, not old woman's eyes but the shining, guileless eyes of a child. Her mouth twitched in a brief, wan smile. Then her face was grave again.

"Anita," he said. "I'm not like other men. I'm not free to go where I please. I'm no longer free to do as I wish."

The urgency in him cried, Hurry, and for an instant he could have wept. The time was so short. He knew it was short. He could feel it in the chill crawling of the skin of his shoulders.

If only Llano would forget Spencerville. That was too risky. Maybe some other place. Some other place, and the money he got there he would use to put her in a good home where she would have good clothes and good food.

I wish I did not have to steal and possibly kill for you, Anita, but there is nothing else for me. If they take me alive I'll hang. I'm sure of that. There's nothing else I can do.

He dropped to one knee in front of her. "Anita," he said and then stopped, for he could not expect her to understand. She stood there, hugging the doll, watching him gravely, and sudden impulse made him stretch out his hand to touch her. She winced as his hand moved and then stood her ground bravely, but he could see the shadow of fear deep in her eyes. Reluctantly, sorrowfully, he withdrew his hand without having touched her.

He rose to his feet. "Be a good girl, Anita," he said woodenly. "Mind Margarita. Be good."

He turned and started back to the village. The winds from out of time were very cold and melancholy now . . .

Llano Lane sat at the table in the *jacal*, cleaning his pistol. He ran the rod through the barrel, and the cloth came out clean. Holding the pistol up to the light, he squinted into the barrel. Then he chuckled.

"I've got it, Dave," he said. "It just came to me. You remember that small Amish settlement north of here? Jericho, I think it's called. There's our answer, Dave."

Merritt said nothing. He stood in the doorway, looking out. He felt as cold and detached as the flesh of a dead man but he was sweating.

"We'll trim our beards the way they trim theirs. We'll steal a couple of outfits from them and ride into Spencerville like that, a couple of Amish preachers." Lane chuckled again. "Who'll ever think it's us? I told you I'd find a way."

Lane started on the cylinder, running the rod through the chambers. "No one will give us a second thought," he said. "The Amish don't carry guns. They don't go around robbing banks." He chuckled. "Man, is Spencerville going to be in for a surprise."

Merritt turned from the door. A sudden spasm set him to trembling but it was quickly gone. Then all he felt were the cold winds of time and doom.

Anita, Merritt thought, if I was sure Spencerville would work, if I was sure—But we can't go on forever and I want to make sure. For you.

Lane held the cylinder up against the light and peered into the chambers. "Well, what do you think of it, Dave?" he asked. "You haven't said."

The time for talking was done, Merritt thought. Words meant nothing any more. There remained only brutality and death.

"I'm sorry, Llano," Merritt said as he drew his pistol and fired . . .

The wind sweeping across the land was cold against his shoulders, and he hunched them to shield the child who was now sleeping in his arms. With sleep the little body had finally relaxed and now nestled against him with a softness and warmth that caused him to marvel. This new wonder almost made him forget Llano Lane, slung across the saddle of his sorrel there behind.

The lights of Fort Benson, where he had a sister who would take Anita, glistened like jewels in the night. He rode into town the back way and made direct for the sheriff's office. A lamp glowed inside, and Merritt reined in his black and dismounted very carefully so as not to awaken the sleeping child.

The sheriff was dozing but Merritt's steps woke him, and he came to, eyes batting in startlement as they took in the tall man with the sleeping child in his arms. Merritt's pistol rapped hollowly as he tossed it on the desk in front of the sheriff.

"I'm Dave Merritt," he said. "Llano Lane is outside, dead. I killed him. I've come to give myself up and collect the reward . . ."

The "mighty big bandit" of the title is Cole Younger, sidekick to Jesse and Frank James—and the events narrated here are those which follow the James gang's famous raid on the bank of Northfield, Minnesota. The result is a particularly fine and exciting story from the pen of one of the best of the contemporary Western writers, Henry Wilson Allen, better known under his pseudonyms of Clay Fisher and Will Henry. Among Allen's many achievements in the field are four Western Writers of America Spur Awards, including two for Best Historical Novel: From Where the Sun Now Stands (1960) and Gates of the Mountains (1963).

A Mighty Big Bandit

Clay Fisher

*I*t was a real nice day. Early fall, woodsmoke hazing the air, nippy in the shade, dozing-warm in the sun, quiet as cotton both in and outside town. For me, I wasn't fighting it. A man doesn't get many vacations in my line and I was making the most of this one. It was up in Minnesota, a fairly decent piece from the Chicago office, my idea being to get as far away from my work as possible for a Pinkerton. Trouble was, some friends of mine from Missouri had the same idea—with trimmings. They not only wanted to get as far from their work as possible, but as fast. When that rattle and slap of gunfire broke loose in town, it brought me bolt upright in the old fishing skiff that was drifting me down the little Cannon River, just outside Northfield.

I stand something like six four with my boots off, which they were right then. Stretching, I could see over the road bridge, down toward the square. There was a shoot-out going at the First National Bank, and it looked to me as if the local folks had ambushed themselves a couple of tinhorn bank robbers. I have been more wrong, but precious seldom.

Bank robbers, yes. Tinhorns, not quite.

I thought I recognized the last man out of the bank, even from the distance. Big fellow, rough-cut, burly, yet graceful and quick as a buck deer. Time he and his pals had cleared the doors and were mounted up, two, three of them had been knocked clear out of their saddles and the remaining six of them, the big man riding last, were hitting it on the flat gallop for the Cannon Bridge.

It occurred to me, along about that time, that this was the same bridge I was drifting toward. Now, I had no sure way of knowing who they were, even though the burly one looked familiar. But I did know one thing; since I was in the same business—on the other side—they might know me. It took me rather strongly that it would be a profitable idea if I rowed like crazy and skinned in under that bridge until they had pounded across it. Pinkerton or not, I was on vacation. What's more, my gun was in the spare room out at the farmhouse where I was staying, and furthermore, my mother had raised a cautious son. Not bright maybe, but outstandingly careful. I went under that bridge like a water skater looking back over his shoulder at a walleye pike.

I will say that I have done very few smarter things in my time.

The five lead bandits hauled up at the bridge not ten counts after I disappeared under it. They sat there reining and holding down their lathered horses, waiting for the big man to come up. He didn't keep them long, and I had, sure as sin sells high, recognized him right. It wasn't anybody but Thomas Coleman Younger, and what he had to say to the little squint-eyed fellow leading the bunch would have frozen the ambition even of Horatio Alger. Cole had a voice like a he-bear with a bad cold, anyway. I will tell you that it surely came through to me clear and meaningful that fall day in Northfield, Minnesota.

"Dingus," he said, "no posse in sight yet, what's your hurry? Now, you want we should split up, or stick together?"

Names are certainly interesting. It all depends where you hear them. In some places, like the boys' privy back of the old schoolhouse, a dingus was one thing. Here, in Northfield, right atop a shoot-out bank robbery, it was another. Like, say, a pet nickname for Jesse Woodson James.

Yes sir, that was it. The James gang. And the better part of seven, eight hundred miles from Missouri. I will tell you, mister, I was sweating like a 2:01 trotter in the third heat.

"Split up," whined Jesse, in that reedy, wild voice of his, which all us Pinkertons had heard described a hundred times. "We'll meet, like planned, back at the slough. Six o'clock, sunset. Come on, let's ride!"

They put the spurs in deep, going over that board-floor bridge to beat Pickett's last charge. When the dust died back, they were gone, and I crawled out from under the bridge shaking fit to shed my teeth.

Well, sure enough, six professional friends from the Show Me state, and any one of them would have struck me dead quicker than a cottonmouth water moccasin. I had to get into town pretty fast, then. Positive identification of its members within five or ten minutes of the robbery could put the James-Younger gang out of business before nightfall. I knew only Cole personally, but the others were familiar to me from wanted flyers. Far as I knew, I would be the only man in Minnesota who could say for certain who had busted the Northfield Bank. Vacation or not, I had to put what I knew on the wire, or start looking for other work. Being a detective for twenty years sort of warps a man's morals. He gets to thinking he's got to do right.

The telegraph office was next to the bank. A pretty good crowd was already jamming up in front of it by the time I puffed in from the river. I used a few elbows and squeezed in the door, which, being held shut from the inside by two shotgun guards, wasn't easy. The guards were surprised enough that they let me get up to the telegrapher, who jumped up and had at me as if I'd insulted his wife's cooking.

"Hold on there, buster!" he yelled. "Just who the hell you think you are?"

"Special Investigator, Pinkerton, Chicago Office," said I. "Got something important I'd like to put on that wire of yours."

"Not a chance, mister," he growled. "We're holding the key open. Just had a bank robbery here. Gang's headed south."

I gave him a bone-dry look.

"So I noticed," I said.

That sharpened him up. "You notice anything else, mister?" he asks, mighty suspicious. The two shotgun guards moved in on me, right then, too. So I gave them all an innocent nod and straight, sober look.

"Seems I did, now you mention it," I answered.

"Yeah? Like what maybe?"

"Like who robbed your bank maybe."

"All right, Mr. Smart-alec Special Investigator: like who maybe robbed our bank?"

"Oh, like Jim, Bob, and Cole Younger maybe. And Frank and Jesse James. Maybe."

He walled his eyes and got a little desperate, at that.

"Mister," he said, "if you're trying to be funny—"

I gave him a bobtailed nod.

"You put it on that wire," I told him, "and see how funny it sounds."

Having said which, I excused myself and started for the door. There I had to hold up and add a PS.

"And when you've put it there," I said, "sign it 'Yancey Nye.' "

That put up all of their eyebrows, and gave me the chance to shoot them a proper sneer of superiority. But you can't trust those Scandanavian hayseeds.

"Well, by damn!" said the telegrapher. "*The* 'Yankee Nye'?"

"Naw," I soured up quick, "you're thinking of Yankee *Bligh*. He's another fellow. Works down to Kentucky and that way. Always playing up to the boss and getting his name in the papers. I said 'Nye,' N-Y-E, Yancey Nye, you got it?''

"Sure," he said. "Hell, we thought you was somebody."

Well, that's the way it goes. I huffed on out of there and up to the livery barn, where I had my rented rig. It was not over fifteen minutes after I'd climbed out from under the Cannon River Bridge that I was ambling that old buggy horse back out to the Nils Swenlund farm, where I was boarding. Past getting a little nap before the evening fishing, I hadn't a plan in the world. There wasn't any Pinkerton accounts in the bank losses, and I was still on vacation. That's what I thought. But I hadn't consulted with my six outlaw friends from Missouri. Nor with one little seven-year-old Swede farm girl from Minnesota; a little girl who had more pure nerve than any outlaw or gunman I ever went up against in my whole life.

Jenni Swenlund was her name, cute as a blond mouse with her taffy braids and peasant jumper. Half an hour later I was standing with her in the barn lot saying good-bye to Nils and Mrs. Swenlund, who were setting out to be with a neighbor woman whose time it was that day. The good folks were some worried about me and the kid getting on by ourselves, so I was easing them off about it.

"Now, you all run on," I smiled. "Take all the time you need with that new baby over yonder. Me and Jenni will make out just dandy. Likely, she can show me where that big lunker is hiding out down by the bridge."

Mrs. Swenlund was still fretted, but gave in some.

"Well, if you're sure now, Mr. Nye."

"Sure, I'm sure," I waved. "Now you all get a move on. That baby'll be old enough to vote before you get started."

That got a smile out of her, and away they went, them waving back and the little girl throwing them kisses and good-byes until they were lost down the county road. With that, she turned to me, all business.

"Come on, Mr. Nye," she tells me. "Thank goodness

they're gone. Now maybe we can get some work done around here.''

"Work?" I dug in my heels. "Now, whoa up, there, princess. I didn't contract to farm this forty."

"All right, you want me to show you where that old lunker is down by the bridge, or don't you?" she demanded.

"Why, sure," I stalled, "but—"

"No buts, Mr. Nye. You just come along and help me hay the mules and get in the afternoon eggs—or else."

I threw her a quick grin and a surrender wave. "Yes, ma'am!" I said. "Show me the way. I'd rather pitch hay to mules than kiss a pretty schoolteacher."

Well, we got into the barn and went to work, me haying the mules, Jenni shagging the old hens around and looking for floor eggs. Hearing an extra loud squawk from one of the barred rocks, I looked around and saw Jenni trying to get it down off a high roost.

"What's the matter, Jenni?" I grinned. "That old biddy giving you more argument than you come prepared to handle?"

She stopped reaching and fetched me a disgusted look.

"Not if I get my hands on her, she isn't!" she told me. "She's broody and doesn't belong in here." She made another dive for the bird, which flopped off the roost and out the nearby front window of the barn. Jenni made a last grab for her as she sailed out the opening. Then she stopped short, threw a scared glance out the window, and ducked back down below its frame. "Mr. Nye," she says, low-voiced, but calm as custard, "come here and look out yonder."

Well, I started over to her grinning half-foolish and wondering what little-girl something had gotten her all stirred up about that old chicken.

"What'd she do?" I said, coming up to the window. "Lay an egg on the jump?"

I hadn't any more than gotten this empty-headed remark past my grown-up's grin, than I took my own glance out the window. I pulled back from it as though somebody had jabbed me in the eye with a hayfork. I grabbed Jenni and clamped a hand across her mouth and plastered her and my-self back against the barn wall. Then I whipped a second look out the corner of that window just to make sure I'd seen what I'd seen.

I had.

It was Cole and Bob Younger and the sixth man of the gang, the only one I didn't know, riding their sweated horses up the Swenlund lane, slow and watchful yet desper-ate and strung-up as wounded game. I could see they must have seen the Swenlunds take off, and figured the place was deserted. Since they were watching the house mostly and not the barn, I was sure they hadn't seen Jenni and me. But there was doubt enough to wring me wet before they pulled their horses to a halt in the barn lot, midway of us and the house.

Bob was real bad hit. Cole and the other man were siding him, holding him on his horse. Cole, that great bear of a man with his gray eyes, curly brown hair, pleasant look, and friendly way, was showing blood in half a dozen places, but still sitting straight and bossing the retreat. The other fellow, swarthy as a foreigner, with a heavy black beard and fore-head no higher than a razorback hog's, didn't look to be hit anyplace. Cole was first to speak, his voice, even though he was hurt so serious, gentle and soft as ever.

"All right, boys, looks like them folks did come from this here farm. We'd best look around to make sure, though, that there ain't nobody else to home."

"Well, let's not be all day over it," snarled the unwounded man. "We got to meet Frank and Jesse and your brother Jim come sundown. You heard Jess."

Cole clutched Bob closer.

"Pitts," he said, "Frank and Jesse will wait. That's why I sent Jim with them; to see that they did."

Charlie Pitts! I ought to have recognized him. I'd seen that mean-animal face on a dozen wanted flyers. I was slipping. But Pitts wasn't. Again, he snarled at Cole.

"Your brother Jim! Bushway! He ain't going to hold Jess and Frank up none. He's bad hurt as Bob, here. Maybe worse." He paused, then added with a sneer. "By the way, how come you Youngers took most of the lead back yonder?''

Cole withered him with a hard stare, and a soft reply.

"Could be, Pitts," he said, "that we waited for it a mite longer than you other boys."

Pitts scowled back stupidly. He was a human brute, not up to the outlaw class of the Jameses and the Youngers.

"Go on," ordered Cole. "Check the house. Find what you can of bandages and medicine for Bob. I'll hold here with him and the horses till you get back. Hop it."

Pitts slid off his mount and went cat-footing it up to the house. Jenni pushed my hand away from her face, giving me a big-eyed look that made me cold inside.

"What's the matter, Mr. Nye," she whispered. "Are they real bad men."

"They're not men, honey," I murmured. "They're animals, hunted animals. You understand?"

"Yes, but they're hurt, Mr. Nye. They need help." She shook her head. "Can't you see they're wounded, Mr. Nye?"

"Sure enough, honey," I said, desperate to get it through to her what danger we were in, "that's right. They're wounded, and a wounded animal will kill you. Now, don't you argue with your Uncle Yancey, Jenni. You just show me where that hayloft ladder is. I don't see it, and we're going to need it, powerful bad."

"But, why—" she began, femalewise.

I grabbed her hard and talked the same way.

"Now, you look out that window again and you tell me what that man looks like that's coming from the house. You're only a little girl but I want you to look at that man real good. Careful now; don't let them see you."

She nodded and peeked out. I could see Pitts coming toward Cole and the horses, and I could see Jenni watching him. He was walking with his bent-kneed crouch and his silent snarl. He came up to his horse and pulled his Winchester from its scabbard, putting his revolver back in his belt.

"All right," said Cole, "now the barn. And hurry it; Bob's bleeding terrible."

Pitts growled like a feeding dog, wheeled, and came toward the barn doors, not ten feet from where we crouched at the window. Here came a killer. Even a child knew it.

"Come on, Mr. Nye," whispered Jenni. "The loft ladder is yonder back of the feed room."

We scrambled up that ladder and lay down in the deep hay on the loft floor just in time. There was a two-inch crack in the loft floorboards, through which we could watch below, and my eyes were as big as Jenni Swenlund's as we both did so.

"Don't even breathe loud," I told her. She bobbed her braids and gave me a pale, small grin and a pat on the hand. I never knew a kid like that, before or since. She had more sense and spirit than any grown-up I ever worked with.

Down in the barn, now, it had got so quiet you could hear the manure flies buzzing around the mules. Of a sudden there was a crash of splintering wood and the doors, hasp and all, flew apart. Charlie Pitts, who had kicked them in, came stalking forward levering the Winchester. He looked behind the feed room and into the mule stalls, turned to the door and called to Cole.

"All clear, bring him in; nobody here, neither."

Cole came in carrying his young brother, Bob, in his arms like a child. Behind him, the trained Missouri thoroughbreds walked in quick and close as hunting hounds.

"Shut the doors," said Cole, "and give me them things you got from the house." He put Bob down in the clean straw of the stall beyond the mules—the one square under where Jenni Swenlund and I lay in the loft. "Easy, now," he said to Bob, "we're going to get you cleaned up, now. Lie quiet, boy, it may hurt some."

Bob, barely conscious, groaned his reply, and Cole went to work on him. Pitts, having seen to the horses, came and stood over them, breathing hard and nervous. Up above, Jenni and I lay flat as two mice with the cat walking past. The stillness got so deep there was no chance even to whisper anymore, and I had to pray the little girl would know to go on keeping stone-still. That she finally couldn't, was no fault of hers. A short straw got under her nose, and it was either move a hand to brush it away, or give a loud sneeze. She made the right choice but in shifting her arm to use the hand, her elbow brushed a little streamer of hay dust down through the crack in the floor. I grabbed her and rolled sideways, just as Charlie Pitts flashed his .44 Colt and drove three shots through the boards where we had been.

I looked at Jenni. She was all right, but had both hands over her mouth to hold in her fright. This was all to the good; now she *knew* that death was standing down there below. I gave her a squeeze, a nod, a pat, and the best grin I could manage under the circumstances. She returned the nod, her eyes bigger than a brace of china-blue milk saucers.

"All right!" snarled Pitts, "whoever's up there, come on down. And come mighty careful."

I didn't know what to do but put finger to lips, warning Jenni to make no answer.

"You coming down," asked Pitts, "or am I coming up?"

For me to reply, and to start down that ladder, would draw me certain death. Somehow, Jenni sensed that. Before I could clap a hand over her mouth, she called down.

"Just a minute, mister, I'm coming—"

I had to let her go, then, but I did it knowing that Cole Younger would never let harm come to a little child. But Cole was still bent over Bob. The minute Jenni appeared at the head of the ladder, Pitts, the crazy man, fired blind, just at the movement of her bright little dress. By grace of God it was a clean miss, and the next instant Cole had leaped across Bob and hit Pitts so hard it drove him clean across the stall and over a tool bin, flatsprawled.

"You feebleminded idjut," he roared, "it's only a little bitty girl!"

Pitts got up, wiping the blood from his mouth.

"She ain't too little to talk," he snapped.

As he said it, he raised up his revolver to fire again. Cole near broke his arm taking the gun away from him.

"You'd shoot a *kid?*" he said incredulously.

Pitts bared his teeth.

"I'd shoot my own kid, were it come down to him or me. We ain't leaving no witnesses behind, Younger. You know Jess's orders on that."

Cole turned him loose, called up to Jenni real soft.

"Come on down, honey. Be tolerable cautious, now. Them ladder rungs look looser'n a old horse's teeth."

Jenni smiled sort of pale-like, and started backing down. Pitts moved in, took hold the ladder, gave it a vicious shake.

"Get a move on, you little brat!" he rasped.

Jenni gave a low cry, lost hold of the ladder, fell clear to its foot. Cole jumped Pitts like a mad grizzly. He very nearly mauled and beat him to death before he was stopped from it by Jenni asking him to please not hit the man anymore, as he likely hadn't meant to hurt her!

Cole dropped Pitts and crouched over her. He dug out his bandanna, awkward and fumbling.

"Here, honey," he said, "leave me wipe away them great big tears."

Noticing an old piece of shaving mirror nailed to the stall partition, he reached it down and held it up for Jenni to see her face.

"Lookit, there, at what them streaks of saltwater are a'doing to your dimples!" he grinned.

She grinned back, but Cole lost his smile the next minute. He was seeing something else in that mirror, and it was me peering over the edge of the loft above. I could see his face, too, the way the angle of the glass was, and our eyes met for one dead-still second. Then, Cole just shook his head and muttered soft as ever.

"My, my, the things a person does see when he ain't got his pistol cocked."

Pitts, limping over just then, scowled black and ugly.

"What'd you say?" he demanded.

"Nothing," answered Cole, "to you."

Pitts glared.

"Well, then, I'm a'saying something to you. Same as I said before. We ain't leaving this kid here."

Cole got up from Jenni's side, his gunhand shifting.

"You're dead right we ain't, Pitts. Not bad hurt the way she is. I'm staying with her."

Pitts shook his shaggy head, small eyes glittering.

"All right, you're welcome to stay, Younger. Stay and get strung up by your lonesome. Me, I'm making it on to Frank and Jess while there's yet time. Stand aside."

Now it was Cole's head that shook slowly.

"Not without Bob, you ain't going no place. He's fixed good enough to ride, now, and you're taking him along."

Here, Bob raised up in protest, but Cole put him down.

"Hesh up, Bob. You're going. I'll meet you all at the slough come sundown, like planned. The little girl's my affair, though. You ain't putting your neck in no rope for me, nor her."

Bob knew the lateness of the hour, both his and the gang's.

"All right, Cole," he said. "We'll wait for you."

"Yeah," sneered Pitts, "at least five minutes."

Cole put hand to gun butt, gray eyes nailing Pitts.

"Get Bob on that horse and get him out of here," he said.

Pitts, too, knew the time of day by now. He only nodded and helped Bob up on his mount. Bob swayed, then steadied. He said, "I'm all right, Cole," to his brother, and Cole said, "Move out, Bob, and God bless you." The two outlaws walked their horses to the lane, then put them on the lope and were gone down the county road in seconds. Cole, turning away from the barn doors, looked up and said quietly,

"All right, Mister Pinkerton man, come on down and come friendly—"

When I had got down, he looked at the empty place where my pistol ought to be.

"Why, Yance," he said, "I'm surprised at you. You don't hardly look decent without your working tools on."

I winced and grinned. "I'm supposed to be on vacation."

"Oh. Well, now, I'm a heap relieved, Yance. I thought maybe you had retired."

"Looks like I ought," I answered, pretty dismal. "You mind if I have a look at the little girl, Cole?" He nodded it was all right, but I held up a minute. "One thing," I said. "You recognized me in that mirror just now. How come you didn't let on to Pitts?" He shrugged, embarrassed.

"Aw, now, Yance, you know we was in the same Missouri outfit. I cain't turn on a fellow Confed'rate soldier."

"Cole," I said, "you're in the wrong business for a man with normal sentiments like that."

"Now, shecks, you know what I mean, Yance. Cold-blood murder like that damn Pitts was a'talking for that pore little thing yonder. Why, that's downright sinful!"

"It sure is," I agreed. "Let's look to her before you bust out bawling. She's passed out cold."

"Sure, Yance, sure." He went with me, and we both got down beside Jenni Swenlund. I gritted my teeth when I saw the leg. Cole looked at me, frightened.

"It's broke compound," I said. "That means when the bone shoves out through the skin like this. Give me your bandanna."

He border-shifted his Colt to his left hand, dug out the bandanna, passed it to me.

"You going to put a twist on her, Yance?"

"Got to. She'll bleed out, if we don't. First we got to get that bone back in if we can. Lay hold her ankle. She may twitch pretty sharp."

As Cole put his big hands on the little leg, Jenni opened her eyes and looked up at him.

"He won't really hurt me, will he, mister?" she asked.

Cole glared at me. I thought he'd drill me then and there.

"She heard you!" he accused. Then he patted her braids careful as though they were glass. "Now, now, honey, he was only funning," he said. "Why, if he was really to hurt you, Uncle Cole would blow his head off." He glanced up at me, nodding softly. "Go ahead, Yance. And, remember; 'Uncle Cole' ain't funning!"

It was maybe an hour later. We had her on the bed in her folks' room up to the house. She was unconscious again and looking pale as a ghost. Cole was patting and stroking her hair, scared half-sick. He still had his cocked Colt in his off-hand, keeping it on me while he fretted over Jenni. I knew I had him where the hair was short, no matter.

"Well, Cole," I challenged, "what you going to do?"

He just groaned with his helplessness.

"Yance," he confessed, "I purely don't know."

"Well, you better do something, and pretty quick."

"You mean about her, don't you, Yance?"

"And *you,* Cole," I answered. "Can I see you outside?"

Cole Younger was not a brainy man, but a gentle-humored big bear, simple in both mind and imagination. Decisions were beyond him, but he understood warnings. He got up.

"Rest easy, now, honey," he told Jenni. "I got to be gone a bit, but I ain't leaving you. Don't have no fears."

Outside the door, I looked at him hard as bedrock.

"You notice that fresh bandage?" I said. "It's all blood again. Soaked knee to ankle in thirty minutes. She don't have a doctor, Cole, she's going to die."

He was in a place where his own life was on the line, too, yet he didn't take two breaths with his answer.

"Yance," he said, "happen I let you ride inter Millersburg and fetch back a doctor, will you guarantee you won't tell I'm out here?"

I had to tell him, no, and he agreed.

"I reckon not," he said sadly. "It wouldn't be no different nor lying, and I never knowed you to lie in your life."

"It's not your life we're talking about, Cole," I reminded him. "You better think of something fast."

He cringed as if I'd hit him with a whip. Turning, he went back in the room, staring around it in desperation. I watched him and, of a sudden, saw his face light up when he spied an open wardrobe full of Mrs. Swenlund's things.

"Yance," he said, whirling on me, "you ever get married up? I disremember."

"Nope," I said warily, wondering what was in his slow mind. "Why you ask?"

He beamed happy as though he had proper sense.

"Well, then, your wife won't mind seeing you in the company of a strange woman, will she?" He jabbed the Colt

toward the wardrobe closet. "Start handing me out them fe-
male unmentionables!"

I looked at him, then at the farmwife's clothes.

"My God," I said, "you really mean a *strange* woman,
don't you?"

"Heavens to mercy, no!" he vowed, widening his catfish
grin. "We'll make a mighty handsome couple, you'll see."
He flicked his glance to the bed and saw that little Jenni had
come awake. Swinging his herd bull's bulk between me and
the girl, he growled with deadly coyness, "*Won't we*,
Yancey dear?"

Since he had shoved the Colt three inches deep in my
belly with the question, all I could do was grunt and give in.
"Whatever you say, *dear*," I agreed, and started handing
him the unmentionables.

Now it was the main stem, Millersburg, Minnesota; a
typical dirt-street hick town. Up the center of the road,
creaking in from the farm country, came the narrow, high-
side corn wagon, canvas cover laced over its bed. I was
driving. On the seat with me was Cole Younger, dressed in
Mrs. Nils Swenlund's Sunday best. The outfit was complete
with starched petticoats, overshawl, flowered print dress,
poke sunbonnet. Yet despite the heat of the day, Cole had a
buggy blanket over his knees and was snuggled up to me
like young love with the lights turned off. Also snuggled up
to me, under the blanket, was the snout of his Navy Colt.
The two old mules plodded steadily. Ahead, the shingle we
were looking for loomed up: I. V. BERQUIST, M.D. Cole gave
me a delicate nudge with the Colt.

"Turn in," he cooed.

"Yes, ma'am," I said, and *gee*-ed the mules down the
right-hand alley, to the doctor's rear yard. There was a back
door to the office, and Cole slid down off the seat and
knocked on the panels. Dr. Berquist opened the door a moment later and Cole put the long Colt barrel under his nose
and asked,

"Can you sew up a thirty-six-caliber hole through a
man's head, Doc?"

That thick, hairy arm coming out of that print dress was more than Dr. Berquist had been ready to write a prescription for. "Why, no!" he gasped. "Of course not!"

Cole tapped him on the shoulder with the Colt barrel.

"Then don't make a sound," he said, "and you won't have to try." He shoved him back into his office, following him in. In a moment he was back. "All clear, Yance; bring the little tyke in," he told me. I lifted Jenni out of the straw-filled wagon bed and carried her in. Inside, the doctor ordered me to put her on the table. I did and Cole and me bent over, with him, watching like hawks to see what news showed in his face. Right away we could tell it was bad. But still he didn't say anything.

Cole shot a nervous look at the clock on the wall. It was five P.M. He put his huge hand on the doctor's arm.

"We're short on time, Doc. How long will it take?"

Berquist shook his hand off, scowling.

"It can't be hurried. Not with a fracture like this."

Cole brought the Colt above the tabletop.

"How long, Doc?" he repeated softly.

Berquist stared at him defiantly.

"A half hour at least. Perhaps longer."

"Damn!" said Cole, still soft. "That's dismal!" Yet he never hesitated. Going to the front door he turned the "Doctor-Is-Out" sign to the street, pulled down the shade, came back to the table, looked again at the clock on the wall, said quiet as spider silk, "Go ahead, Doc; and don't make no mistakes."

When Berquist finally put down his instruments and tied off the last bandage, it was five minutes till six P.M. Cole, long out of his woman's clothes, grabbed him and spun him around rough and hard. "She all right?" he growled.

"For now, yes," answered the doctor.

"What you mean, for *now*?"

"Precisely what I said. She will be all right if kept perfectly quiet. If she is moved suddenly, or handled in any way roughly—"

Cole shoved him aside.

"That's enough, Doc. Nobody's going to be rough with

her. Thanks for your help. You'll get your reward in hea-
ven, unless you want it sooner. One peep out of you that
we've been here and—''

Berquist interrupted him, showing no fear at all.

''I doubt you need worry about me following you, Mr.
Younger,'' he said. ''Descriptions are out on all of you, and
others will recognize you as easily as I. Further, every law
officer and local posse in southern Minnesota is already in
the field looking for you and the others. You will never get
out of this state alive.''

Cole scowled, tapped him with the Colt again.

''Just remember that if I don't, Doc, neither does the little
girl. You savvy them sentiments?''

This Berquist had a heavy skull, like all those
Scowegians. He wasn't going to buckle one inch to Cole,
and I moved in quick.

''He means it, Doctor,'' I told him. ''Don't give any
alarm before we're well away. These Missourians are kill-
ers.'' I gave Cole a special look. ''*All* of them,'' I added.

Cole admitted the compliment courteously.

''Regretful, sir,'' he said to the doctor, ''but true.'' Then,
to me, ''Move, Yance. No more palaver.''

I picked up Jenni Swenlund and went out the back door.
Cole followed. He never looked back at Dr. I. V. Berquist.
Outside, Jenni safely stowed in the bed under the tarp, him
and me back up on the seat, he poked me with the Colt.

''Mind what I told the Doc, Yance. Remember, I'll be
back here under the tarp with the little tyke.'' Saying which,
he slid off the seat and beneath the canvas cover behind me.
All I could see of him was the Colt's nose. ''All right,'' he
concluded, ''let's go. You drive one mile south on the
Madelia Road. Turn left at the Hanska Slough signpost.
You got that straight?''

I took a look back at the doctor's office. I thought I saw
the rear shade stir a bit. Taking the hairiest chance of my
life, I repeated his directions in a too-loud voice.

''*Yes, sir! One mile south on the Madelia Road. Turn left
at Hanska Slough sign!*''

He very nearly put that Colt through my kidneys.

"Keep your big mouth shut, Yance," he rumbled, "and dig!"

"What's the great rush, Cole?" I said, mad at being poked so hard and knowing, anyway, he wouldn't dast shoot me just now. "Jesse said six o'clock. That still gives you five minutes."

"Which is four more than *you* got, Yance," he promised, "happen you don't light out, right quick."

I nodded meek enough, and whipped up the team.

So it was we set out from Madelia, my only hope the slim one that Dr. Berquist had heard those loud-repeated Hanska Slough directions and would figure out what they meant. It wasn't much of a hand to back against the likes of Cole Younger. Not to mention the James boys. I've bluffed bigger pots with a busted flush going into four aces. But my real bet was still on Cole, and on what he would do about that little girl under the wagon-tarp with him, when the chips were down. One thing sure. I was going to find out.

The country was desolate, heavily wooded. The slough was brackish, lonesome-looking. Through the ground brush I could see the crude wickiup the outlaws had made. I got only the one glimpse of it. I made out two wounded, much-bandaged men lying inside. Crouched over the fire outside was Charlie Pitts. In the brief look, I saw no sign of the others. If Frank and Jesse were there, they were out in the brush somewhere. As soon as Pitts heard the crunch of our wagon wheels on the slough road, he jumped for his rifle and dove out of sight.

At that time we were maybe a scant furlong from the camp. Coming to the wickiup moments later, we had to pass under a big, low-limbed hardwood. I never thought to look up. The next thing I knew, that crazy Pitts had jumped down off the overhang and hit me with his boots between the shoulder blades, sprawling me clean off the seat and onto the ground. He lit the seat and braced himself to finish me off with his rifle. He didn't get a fine sight drawn. From under the wagon tarp behind him, up reared Cole and laid his pistol barrel across the back of Pitts's hat. Pitts, he just caved in and slid off the seat. Cole slid onto the driver's box, picked up his rifle, stepped to the ground, covering both of us.

"All right, Yance," he said, "get up real careful. Pitts— throw a rope on him."

As the latter growled and went about tying my hands, Cole noticed the two men in the wickiup to be his brothers Jim and Bob, and that there was but three horses on the picket.

"Three horses!" he barked at Pitts. "Where's Frank and Jesse?"

"They've cut out on their own," mumbled the hangdog Pitts. "Said to tell you they wasn't needing no more wounded Youngers to hold them back."

Cole nodded, as though to expect no more from his famous friends. "How come you didn't turn tail with them?" he asked.

"Fat chance! They was gone when I got here. Left the message with your brother. Real question is, what're *we* gonna do?"

"Light out after them, I reckon. Saving for one thing; I got the little girl in the wagon yonder."

"You ain't!" Pitts was absolutely bashed in by it. I took a hunch it was time for me to horn in, but Pitts recovered and reached for his belt gun before I could make up my opening speech. "Well," he said, "we're getting out of here right now, and the kid ain't going with us. I'll see to that, and if you try to stop me I'll cut you in two."

He had the drop on Cole. Moreover, Cole was trapped another way. His own life was at stake and he knew Charlie Pitts was right. To fool around a minute longer with motherhenning Jenni Swenlund was to put them all, including his two wounded brothers, Bob and Jim, in the shadow of the noose. He watched Pitts head for the back of the wagon, that same dumb, desperate look on his face I had seen in the Swenlund bedroom. And in the same way as then, he got a happy light in his eyes at the last second. .

"Hold it, Charlie!" he yelled. "We *got* to take her with us. She's our hostess!"

Pitts whirled around. "Our what?" he said, surprised, and giving me my chance to buy into the game.

"Your hostage," I translated for him. "You know, that's somebody you hold a gun on, so's the other side don't dast shoot. You remember, like in the war."

"Yeah, Charlie," Cole pushed it, "sort of like a pass through the enemy lines. Get the idea?"

Pitts grinned. "Sure," he said, "you bet I do." He shifted his Colt to cover Cole again. "And I'll be the one using that pass. Fetch her out'n the wagon."

With no choice, Cole did it. Meanwhile, I got the three horses off the picket, also given the same option. Pitts turned the third horse loose, hitting him viciously across the haunch with the revolver barrel. He galloped off into the timber. Pitts now mounted one of the remaining two.

"All right!" he snapped. "Tie the kid on this other horse, hard and fast."

"You wouldn't do that!" gasped Cole. "Not even you, Pitts!"

"Put her on that horse," said Pitts, "or I'll blow her brains all over your vest."

Cole and I looked at each other and knew we had to do it. We laced her on real careful, the splinted little leg sticking out straight. She was brave as ever, and smiled and told us not to be afraid, that Pitts wouldn't hurt her. Cole couldn't take that. He moved in close to Pitts's stirrup, starting to plead with him. Pitts lashed out with his spurred boot, catching Cole, full-face, and ripping him like a saber blade. But the act took his gun off me, and I went up onto the wagon seat and jumped from it, at him. He got the Colt on me in midair. The big .44 bullet took me across the meat of my shooting arm, turned me half around, slammed me into his horse's ribs and down onto the ground. He never looked down at me but only yelled, *"Hee-yahh!"* at his horse, and took off leading poor little Jenni's mount behind him on the flat gallop.

They didn't get five jumps on the way to the woods.

Out of that heavy cover came a blasting of posse gunfire that drove Pitts out of his saddle and cut his horse down like it was both done with a mowing scythe. Cole, quick as a cat, ran out and grabbed Jenni off her loose horse and got her back to the wagon and wickiup, the posse not daring to fire, of course. But while he was doing it, I thought I saw a chance, and reached for Pitts's rifle lying on the ground. Out of the brush beside me came a spurred boot I recognized, kicking the gun away. The boot was followed by what was still in it, and its mate; Pitts was again on his feet, only lightly wounded, and having got back to the wagon while the posse was watching Cole and Jenni.

Now there was double hell to pay.

With Jenni put in the wickiup and me ordered in there to look to her, Cole and Pitts overturned the Swenlund wagon and, with the wounded Bob and Jim Younger crawling out to fort up back of it with them, put up a hard return fire, pinning the posse down just about as tight as the posse had them pinned down. Pretty quick a white handkerchief waved from a shotgun barrel across the way. Cole rasped, *"Slack off!"* to his comrades, and a silence thicker than swamp fog settled in.

"Mr. Nye," called a voice, "are you and Jenni Swenlund all right? This is Sheriff Glispin of Madelia."

"We're all right, Sheriff," I answered. "How many men you got?"

"Fifteen. Plus Dr. Berquist from Millersburg. Who are the men with you, other than Younger?"

"His two brothers, Bob and Jim, and Charlie Pitts."

"Will they surrender?"

I looked out at Cole, under the wagon. He shook his head.

"They say not," I replied.

"Well, will they permit you to bring out the Swenlund girl under a flag of truce?"

Again Cole shook his head, again I answered in negative.

"Do they mean to use the little girl as a hostage, then?"

"Yes, Sheriff, that's it, I'm afraid."

There was a long, ominous pause then before Glispin spoke again. And when he did, the pause only got more ominous.

"All right, Mr. Nye," he said. "Do your best."

* * *

The last daylight was going. No sound came from the silent woods. Behind the overturned wagon, Bob and Jim Younger lay with their terrible wounds, but with rifles waiting for the posse to move. Out beyond the wagon a stride, Charlie Pitts lay up back of the dead horse. In the entrance of the wickiup, where he could watch everything, crouched Cole Younger. Darkness would be down in minutes. With it, they had a hairline chance to slip away. But Charlie Pitts, crazed and brutal as ever, could not wait. Leaving his dead horse, he got behind the wickiup without Cole seeing him. Next moment he had broken through its thin backwall of brush and had his Winchester aimed between Cole's shoulder blades.

"You move," he said to the big Missourian, "I'll drill your backbone. You!" he snapped at me, "get that kid up and bring her over to me." I did it, as I had to. Pitts got a brawny arm around her little waist, lifted her off the ground, back to him, as a shield. Backing out of the wickiup, he stepped clear of it and the wagon. "Sheriff!" he yelled across at the posse, "I'm coming through. Get me a good horse ready. One funny move and the kid dies. You got ten seconds."

As he held up, waiting for Glispin's reply, Cole looked at me, nodded quickly, drew, and handed me his revolver.

"All right, Yance," he said. "I'll take his attention; you try to come at him from behind. Good luck, old soldier."

"Cole," I answered, dead straight, "the same to you."

We went out, then, me through the back wall, him by the front opening. Pitts was through waiting for the sheriff. He threw down his rifle, pulled his belt gun, put it to Jenni's head.

"All right, Sheriff!" he shouted, "I warned you!"

His yell was still echoing when Cole moved in on his left flank, stabbing just one word at him.

"Pitts!"

Charlie whirled to face him. Cole began walking slow toward him. Pitts fired into his big body, one, two, three shots, all plain hits. Cole kept coming. Pitts broke. He dropped Jenni and began to run blind. He picked the wrong way to go—straight into me. I came up from behind my bush and put five of the six slugs in Cole's gun into his belly. The jolt took him like sledge blows, driving him by steps clean back to the wagon, where he finally fell. It wasn't a shoot-out, it was an execution. When it was over, I walked up to where Cole was hunched down on the ground, cradling little Jenni in his arms. I stood there looking down at them.

After a minute, Cole glanced up and smiled tired-like. His own wounds, later found to be eleven bullets lodged in that bear's body of his, finally had him anchored. He could not get up, and had to hand Jenni up to me. I took her from him and said quietly, "So long, Cole."

He made a funny awkward little wave in reply. When he did, Jenni smiled and called back to him.

"Good-bye, 'Uncle Cole.' "

He winced like he'd been knifed. Then looked guiltily to right and left, as though to make certain nobody had heard the kid, or was listening to him, or watching. Then he blew her a kiss with his huge paw and muttered roughly.

"Good-bye, little honey, good-bye."

He pulled out his old calico bandanna, the one he'd used to wipe the tears off Jenni's face in the Swenlund barn, and took a swipe at his powder-grimed eyes. He didn't even seem to realize he did it, but sat there staring off after us as we went toward the posse's line, as though he was seeing into another world, and a better one. Maybe he was, I never found out. When Jenni and me passed through the posse line, the firing began again, and I didn't wait to see the end of it.

Later, of course, my line of work being what it was, I did hear about it. It wasn't a good thing, any way you want to look at it, but I wonder just how bad it was, too.

Under Minnesota law of the day there couldn't be any death penalty. After weeks of suffering from their wounds, Jim, Bob, and Cole were given life sentences in the state penitentiary at Stillwater. History will say they were out-laws, thieves, and murderers. Well, maybe they were. It wasn't my job to say. But I know one little farm girl up near

Millersburg who will give you a mighty big argument about one of those three condemned bandits. But, then, why not? He was a mighty big bandit. Thomas Coleman Younger. In my book, as in that little farm girl's, they don't come any bigger.

In addition to such famous novels as Andersonville *and* Spirit Lake, *Pulitzer Prize-winning author MacKinlay Kantor wrote many short stories about the Civil War and the Old West during his long and distinguished career. Some of the best of these can be found in such collections as* Silent Grow the Guns, Frontier, The Gun-Toter, *and* Warwhoop. *"The Last Bullet," a short-short about an outlaw named Jameson and his horse, Poco, is one of Kantor's least known but most surprising and effective tales.*

The Last Bullet

MacKinlay Kantor

Jameson *thought he saw something stirring on the burnt* sullenness of the desert's face. He thought he saw a quiver among the furious slopes of brown and red.

He opened his dry, cracked mouth; his mouth had been open for a long time, but he opened it wider. He tried to say, weakly, "Posse."

It wasn't a posse. Jameson never thought he'd see the day when he'd be glad to have a posse come smoking up to him; but he reckoned that if a man lived long enough, he saw different days from those he had expected to see.

No quiver in the blue, no twisting and dividing in the brown . . . Jameson turned his head and felt the vast, round, hot flame of sky searing his eyeballs. He managed to lift his hand, and in the scant shade granted by the swollen fingers, he tried to find some buzzards. He couldn't find any buzzards. Nothing lived on this dry pan of desertion—nothing lived here but Jameson and Poco.

The man twisted the upper part of his body, and sighed. Poco's head lay against the burning shale a few feet away; when Jameson stirred, the little horse moved his neck with the agony of a movement five hundred times repeated.

"How you doing?" Jameson wanted to ask his horse.

Poco wasn't doing so well, now. He had done well, for the five years Jameson had ridden him. He had taken Jameson hustling out of towns, slapping along narrow mountain roads when the bullets squealed around him. And there was that night in Dundee when the wise little horse waited silently beside a dark doorway, aloof from the stampede of pursuing hoofs, and carried Jameson away with two bullets in his arm.

Jameson said: "Reckon you'd like a drink. So would I."

He had stolen Poco from the Maxwell ranch, clear over south of the Estella Plata Range, when Poco was only a colt; and he left him with a Mexican at a mountain shack for months after that. Jameson had raised Poco on a bottle, so to speak—taught him to blow his nose and keep his clothes buttoned. He was the only kid Jameson had ever had.

Now the heat-warped fingers of the man's hand stole down to find his revolver butt, as they had stolen a dozen times before. He thought, *"Nothing for fifty miles. I ought to have known better than try to ride across. But we made it, other times. No water . . ."*

His hand trembled as he exposed the cylinder and saw the solitary undented cartridge cap that reposed on the hot surface of powder-grimed steel. One chamber was vacant; Jameson never kept a shell under his hammer. There were five shiny little wafers looking at him; four of them were marred by hammer strokes.

The blue sky came down and struck him across the face. It was a red sky—now it was yellow—now white. "Old sky," he wanted to say, "do you see any posses? I sure would like to see one."

Poco's ears fluttered, and he tried to whinny. Still there was moisture in his muzzle, and one bubble formed there,

and then it went away. It was mighty strange that there could
be any moisture in either of them, after the hot day and the
cold night, and the day before that.

Jameson said, "One of us went wrong. That was a bad
slide. I reckon you might have seen that crack in the rocks,
but I ain't blaming you. You've seen plenty I've never
seen."

His mind went away from him for a while, and came
speeding back amid the hearty hoofs of phantom horses.
There were men in this fantasy; enemies who came to gather
him in, and all the time they laughed at him.

The mystic enemies said, *"Why did you do it, Jimmy
Jameson? You ain't never killed anyone. Time was when
you were mighty charitable with what you took off the road.
You're a bad man, but a lot of people like you. . . ."*

They said in this parched dream that formed within his
mind, *"It wouldn't have been hanging. We're the law. We
know. We've burned powder and shoved lead at each other,
but you ain't really got a bad name. Maybe you'd have spent
a couple years behind bars, but that's all. You shouldn't
have tried the Llano Diablo. No water in the Llano Diablo.
Nobody goes there. . . ."*

He thought that the posse circled him, and then dismounted to pat Poco's red-hot flank and to moisten Jameson's own lips with cool, wet salve from a canteen. *"You're
an awful idiot,"* said the posse. *"Here you are; your horse
has got a broken back, and it looks as if both of your legs is
busted, too. Can't either of you move. Can't even crawl.
Not even coyotes go out on the Llano Diablo. . . ."*

Now he awoke from his dream, and he had the gun in his
hand. Twice he put the muzzle against his own temple, and
twice he fought successfully to keep his finger from tight-
ening. His horse watched him with glazing eyes; again it
tried to lift its head.

"No," Jameson thought, *"I can't! It's hell for me, but I
reckon it's double hell for you."*

Once more the desert became a pasture, and in it he saw a
corral—a lush green place where Poco trotted toward him
stiff-legged, knobby-kneed, his eyes young and coltish.

"Sugar?" said Jameson aloud, now to his darling. "You don't get none. I ain't going to ruin your teeth. I got a piece of apple here. . . ." and his hands played with the thick, wiry mane. "Reckon someday you'll be a mighty fine horse."

The sky changed from white back into yellow and orange. The shadow of the steep stone ridge grew longer; it went past the two suffering shapes—the swollen mass of living horseflesh—the dry-skinned man who lay beside it.

"Not another night," said Jameson. "I can't stand it. Pity there ain't two shells."

Again the muzzle found his temple, but the horse still looked at him.

Jameson breathed softly. "Okay," he croaked. He remembered something about the Bible and a merciful man being merciful to his beast, but Jameson would never call Poco a beast.

He inched forward, suffering horrors until he felt the barrel sinking against Poco's ear cavity, soft and warm and silky despite all endurances.

"Be seeing you," he said, and pulled the trigger. The gun jumped loose from his hand, after it was over. . . .

He did not know how many dreams possessed him, but not many; the night came closer every second. And then his ears picked out a faint scrambling, a sound of sliding gravel. Hoof rims scraped the burnished gray rocks.

They rode up; they were angels in leather and flannel; they wore guns. They would carry Jimmy Jameson behind the bars. But still they were angels.

The sheriff was on his knees beside him.

"Can't understand it," Jameson whispered. "So late. Nobody comes . . . Llano Diablo."

The sheriff looked at the dead horse. He shook his head, even while his hands moved to his water bottle.

"One shell," Jameson said. "It was him or me. Poco needed a break."

The brown, lined face of the sheriff bent closer, and there were other faces behind. Water touched Jameson's lips.

"I guess you got a break yourself, this time," the sheriff

said. "We hadn't come across your trail, and we agreed to ride back to Dundee. We were just turning our horses, behind that hill, when we heard you shoot."

There were other kinds of lawbreakers in the Old West, of course, than hard-bitten bank robbers, rustlers, and gun-slingers. It takes an encounter with one of those hard-bitten bandits to prove this fact to young Corey Waters, and to teach him that there can be a fine line between the law-abiding citizen and the outlaw. Bill Pronzini is the author of close to 30 novels and more than 250 short stories, many of which deal with frontier themes. Among his Western novels are The Gallows Land, Duel at Gold Buttes, *and the forthcoming* Starvation Camp.

The Posse from Paytonville

Bill Pronzini

*W*e'd been riding for most three hours, northwest from Paytonville toward the Owl Creek Mountains.

There were seven of us in the posse. Jim Chalton—acting sheriff with old Tom Rebor gone to Casper—rode lead. And there was Jake Lyman, who owned the Paytonville General Store where I worked as a stockboy; Dan and Ike Nealy, the town blacksmiths; Cal Tyrell, a hand for the Cable Bar spread down to Riverton; and Jud Kinnett, who was a teller in the Wyoming Territorial Bank, where Mr. Howard Page had been president.

I'm Corey Waters, and I was the one had found Mr. Page that morning. I'd been just opening up the rear entrance to the general store, the way I do at seven every morning, when I heard two, three gunshots come from the bank down the way. I started to run along the back alley, and just as I did that the back door of the bank flew open and this man come out with a pistol in his hand. He was half-turned toward the far end, but he saw me coming along the alley and took a quick shot at me. The bullet chewed up sod off on my left, and I ducked down in the shadows of the nearest building.

I didn't get a look at his face, because it had happened so fast, but I did see he was tall and wore a black hat and black denims and a fancy buckskin jacket.

I was afraid he would come after me, but he just ran off down the alley and turned the corner toward Shelton Street. After a minute or two, I went to the bank, and inside I found Mr. Page lying there on the floor of his private office, with blood all over him and two bullets in his chest. He was still alive, and when I knelt down beside him he told me the name of the man who'd done it to him.

It was Lafe Adamson, who was wanted in Wyoming and Montana and Colorado for bank robbery and murder. Mr. Page had recognized him from a poster he'd seen once in Laramie. But he'd made the mistake of trying for the gun he kept in a drawer of his desk, and Adamson had shot him twice and then run out without getting a cent of the bank's money from the safe.

Mr. Page died right after he told me that.

Well, I ran to Mrs. Piper's boardinghouse, where Jim Chalton lived, and got him out of bed and told him what had happened. He was plenty sick and upset, the same as I was, because Mr. Page had been just about the best-liked citizen in Paytonville. He was a fair man, and a generous one, and you could get a loan from him without collateral and a lot of fuss. He trusted folks around Paytonville, and they never made him regret his faith in them.

Only now he was dead, and you could see the hate that was festering inside Jim Chalton and some of the other townspeople when they found out. I could feel it myself, even though I'd only known Mr. Page for a short time. My ma and me had moved to Paytonville, where we had kin, just six months before; we'd come down from Billings just after Pa died, two weeks after my eighteenth birthday.

Jim Chalton rounded up as many men as he could find on short notice—the six of us and himself—and we set out maybe an hour after I'd found Mr. Page. We couldn't be sure which way Lafe Adamson had headed once he'd left town, but Chalton found a plain circular on him from the Pinkerton Agency. It said he'd used the Owl Creek Mountains a time or two to hole up in, so it was good logic he'd try for there again. They were maybe a five-hour ride from Paytonville.

There was only one road leading to the section of the Owl Creeks where Adamson was known to hide out; we set out along there. We had no way of telling if we were right or not in our figuring, but we had to take the chance that we were. There was no time to check any of the other roads around Paytonville, what with Adamson having that hour's start on us.

We kept riding, and the sun grew paler and paler, and now here we were, with the Owl Creeks rising straight ahead of us on the hazy blue horizon. We hadn't seen any sign of Lafe Adamson at all so far.

At the top of a rise, we halted to rest our horses, looking down at the peaceful scene spread out below—a little valley with an ice-blue lake in its center. My horse, and the others, could smell the mountain-fresh water down there; they raised their heads and began to nicker softly.

Jim Chalton leaned forward with his hands resting on the pommel of his saddle. He was lean and spare, with long curling hair and a bushy mustache and a narrow mouth that never smiled much. I didn't much take to him—he was kind of bullying sometimes, and acted as if he were the sheriff instead of Tom Rebor—but you had to admit that he knew how to lead men. He had been in command the whole time back in Paytonville, and on the road, too.

He said, "Reckon we'll let the horses drink when we get down to the lake. We been pushin' 'em pretty hard."

But before we could set out again, a sharp echoing sound drifted up from the valley. Chalton and the rest of us

stiffened, listening. The noise came again, and it was the report of a pistol, all right; you couldn't mistake that sound.

A third shot rang out, and then a fourth and a fifth. I
peered down into the valley. It seemed to me the gunfire was
coming from a stand of cottonwoods near a stream to the
right of the lake, southwest. But I couldn't see anything of
who was doing the shooting.

Chalton spurred his horse, motioning to the rest of us, and
we followed him down the sloping trail into the valley. I
heard two more shots as we rode, then nothing at all except
for the wind and the pounding of hooves.

When we reached the lake, Chalton cut to the right along
the grassy bank and into the cottonwoods. I saw his hand fly
up as we came into the little glade near the lake's edge. I
hauled back on my gelding's reins, bringing him up. And
then I could see the figure of a man lying sprawled face
down on the grass. He had a Colt Army revolver in one
hand, but he wasn't moving.

Chalton swung out of his saddle, with his own pistol in
his hand, and ran to the man's side. He knelt there and
turned him over. The fellow's jacket was open in front, and
there was blood high on the left side of his bare chest where
he'd taken a bullet.

The rest of us dismounted and made a ring around Chalton. "This is him, Lafe Adamson," Chalton said. "He's
wearing the clothes Corey here described."

And he was: he had on the black denims and the fancy
buckskin jacket I'd seen in the alley behind the bank. The
black hat was lying off on one side.

Jake Lyman moved up next to me. Short and squat, he
had a bright red face that everybody said came from too
much whiskey drinking at the Brass Rail saloon. But he had
always treated me pretty well. "That right, Corey?" he
said. "This the man you saw come running out of the
bank?"

"Well, I never saw his face," I said. "But I couldn't mistake that buckskin jacket and that hat. They're the same."

"That's good enough for me," Ike Nealy said. "The bastard dead, Jim?"

Chalton leaned his head close to Adamson's chest. Then he raised up again and looked at the rest of us. "Still alive," he said. "The wound don't figure to be too bad."

I looked around the glade. Adamson's horse, a big bay, was nibbling grass at the far end. "No sign of anybody else," I said. "Who do you think shot him up like that, Mr. Chalton?"

"Reckon it don't matter none," he answered. "Whoever done it is likely a mile gone from here by now."

"Shouldn't we try to find out?" I asked. "Shouldn't we look around for him?"

"Time enough for that later, boy."

"Later?" I said. I didn't like what I saw in his eyes.

"After the hanging," he said.

My throat was dry of a sudden, and there was a cold feeling in the pit of my stomach. I looked at the faces of the others; they were all grim and without expression. Then I looked down at Adamson lying there on the grass with his eyes shut and the blood staining his buckskin jacket.

"You're not going to . . ." I couldn't say it.

"That's just what we're going to do, boy," Chalton said. "We're going to have justice done right here and now. Save the county expense of a trial and a public hanging."

"But he's wounded," I said. "He's unconscious."

"So what, boy?"

"You can't hang a wounded man!"

"No? What would you have us do with him, then?"

"Tie him on his horse and take him back to Paytonville," I said. "The law will punish him . . ."

"Suppose it don't?" Chalton said. "Suppose he gets himself some smart lawyer, and they hoodwink a judge and jury? What then, boy?"

"That won't happen," I told him. "This is 1896, Mr. Chalton. Times have changed. There's no need for the lynch law anymore."

"What about that fella in Cheyenne last spring?" Chalton asked me. "Killed two men in a Wells Fargo holdup, and some fancy-pants lawyer got him off free and clear."

I opened my mouth to say something, but Jake Lyman put

a hand on my shoulder. "Corey, I don't like the idea of a lynching any more'n you do. But, damn it, Jim's right. This man is a killer, a menace to decent folk in these parts. He killed Howard Page this morning, one of the finest men in the whole state of Wyoming and a close friend to all of us. He don't deserve no better than a rope here and now."

"Damned right," Dan Nealy said. "I can't see no wrong in hanging a man done what Adamson done."

"That goes for me, too," Cal Tyrell said, and Jud Kinnett and Ike Nealy nodded their agreement.

I was shaking, and there was sweat streaming down into my eyes now, even in the coolness of the glade. I bit my lower lip, looking at all of them in turn. They were different somehow, or maybe it was me who was different; I felt as if I didn't know any of them, as if they were all strangers.

A lynch mob.

Pa had been a lawyer up in Billings, and I remembered him telling me once about a lynching he'd seen in Spanish Fork, Utah, back in the early 1870s. He'd described the faces of the men to me as they'd looked just before the hanging and during it, and the faces of these six men were just that way. It was as if they'd all been filled up with the need for revenge, and that they couldn't be rid of it until they'd committed the same kind of crime as the man they were hanging.

I didn't know what to do. I hadn't been scared riding with the posse on the trail of Lafe Adamson, but I was scared now. I didn't want to be a part of this—I didn't want it to happen at all—but I knew that it was going to happen and that there wasn't anything I could do to stop it.

Jim Chalton said to me, "Fetch my saddle rope, Corey."

I shook my head. "No," I said.

"Fetch it, boy."

"No!"

"You going to disobey me?"

"I don't want any part of this!"

"Leave him be, Jim," Lyman said. "He's just a boy. He don't understand."

"Then it's time he did."

"Just leave him be. I'll get the rope. The sooner we're done with this, the better."

"I reckon you're right, at that," Chalton said. He looked at me, and then he put his hand in the middle of my chest and shoved. I staggered backward, went down on the seat of my pants. Chalton came up and stood over me spread-legged, with his hands on his hips.

"Go hide your face, boy," Chalton said. "Go somewhere and hide your face."

I got to my feet and backed away from him toward the lake. He stood there like that for a time; then he turned and went back to where the others were.

Cal Tyrell and Ike Nealy brought the bay from the other side of the clearing and put Adamson in the saddle. They didn't bother to tie his hands. They led the bay under one of the cottonwoods, then stood one on either side holding Adamson so he wouldn't fall off.

I watched Jake Lyman bring Chalton his saddle rope, and I watched Chalton fashion a hangman's noose. He kept moistening his lips while he was doing it; his eyes were bright. There was no sound at all in that glade, except for quiet breathing and the sigh of the wind.

I couldn't take any more of it, then. I turned away and ran into the cottonwoods and box elders that grew along the mouth of the stream, where it emptied into the lake. The undergrowth was heavier there, and the trees grew closer together, and after a minute or two I couldn't see the glade at all. But I kept running along next to the stream, feeling sick and confused. I just wanted to get away for a little while, even though I knew I would have to go back to get my horse—go back and see Lafe Adamson hanging from that cottonwood, because I knew they wouldn't cut him down.

What stopped me running was sight of the big black horse nuzzling grass where the trees thinned out next to the stream. It was saddled, and there was the stock of a rifle showing in the scabbard. I'd never seen it before.

I started forward again after a couple of seconds, touching the unfamiliar butt of the old Colt Peacemaker Jake Lyman had given me in Paytonville before we'd ridden out. The thought was in my head that maybe the black belonged to the man who had shot Lafe Adamson, that maybe he was still around somewhere. I peered into the surrounding growth, but I couldn't see anything—not until I had almost reached the horse.

Then I saw the dead man.

He was lying on his stomach with both his hands dug into the soft grass, as if he'd been trying to drag himself toward the black. I swallowed hard, looking off to the side. The path he'd made through the short grass from the woods was just visible, further along than where I'd come.

I knelt down and put my hand under his chest. He was dead, all right. He'd taken one bullet in the belly, another through his left side. He was tall and craggy, wearing a gray sackcloth shirt and corduroy trousers and fancy black boots; there was no pistol in the holster at his belt.

Something bulged in the dead man's shirt pocket. I reached down and wedged out two things with my thumb and forefinger. One was a solid-gold, hunting-style pocket watch; the other was a thin leather wallet. I opened the wallet, and inside there was a card identifying the owner as a Mr. Andrew Grantham. It said he was a Pinkerton detective with the Denver office.

Well, now I understood. He must have been tracking Lafe Adamson for some time, and had chanced upon him here at the lake. The two of them had fought it out, with each taking a bullet. Grantham had crawled through the woods when he'd heard us coming, not knowing who we were, and tried to reach his horse. But he'd died before he could.

But then I noticed that the back lid of the pocket watch had come open in my hand. I could see a cameo photograph of a man and a woman and a boy about my own age on the inside of the lid, and that there was an inscription on the dust cover. I held it up close to my eyes.

The inscription read, *"Mother and Father and Their Loving Son, David."*

The man in the photograph was Andrew Grantham; but he wasn't the man who lay dead in front of me. He was the wounded man in the glade—the man Jim Chalton and the others were hanging as Lafe Adamson!

Shock took hold of me and I jumped to my feet. I had to stop them; I had to! I ran back through the woods as fast as I could run, stumbling through the thick undergrowth. And as I ran I knew what had happened at the lake before we'd gotten there. It wasn't hard to figure out.

Adamson had somehow gotten the drop on Grantham when the two of them came upon one another. The outlaw had known I'd seen him escaping from the bank that morning and could identify the clothes he was wearing, but that maybe I hadn't got a good enough look at him to identify his face. So he'd thought if the posse that came after him was to find the body of a man wearing his clothes, we'd figure that was Adamson and call off the hunt. He'd probably planned to take Grantham's body up onto the road somewhere, so we'd be sure to find it. It didn't matter that we'd learn the truth later on, because by that time he expected to be holed up safe in the Owl Creeks.

So he'd forced Grantham to switch clothes with him. Only before he could kill the Pinkerton man, Grantham had got hold of a gun and they'd shot it out. Adamson, knowing it was the posse coming, had crawled away and died there by the stream. Leaving Grantham alone in the glade, unconscious.

It seemed like forever before I came bursting out of the trees and into the clearing again. They were putting the hangman's noose around Andrew Grantham's neck, pulling it tight; Jim Chalton was standing by the bay's left flank, his hand upraised for the slap that would send the horse bolting out from under the Pinkerton man.

"Stop!" I yelled, running toward them, waving my arms over my head. "That's the wrong man! You're hanging the wrong man!"

They all turned to look at me as I came running up. Chalton said, "What in hell? How can this be the wrong man?"

I thrust my right hand out, feeling a funny mixture of relief and anger inside me, and slapped the gold pocket watch and the leather wallet into Chalton's palm.

"Look at these!" I shouted at him. "This man is Andrew Grantham, he's a Pinkerton detective. The real Lafe Adamson is lying dead in the woods back there, near the stream."

Chalton's face clouded with uncertainty. "It . . . it ain't possible that he—"

"Look at the photograph in the watch."

He looked at it, and the others looked at it. They looked at the wallet identification. They looked at the man slumped over the neck of the bay, with the noose looped around his neck, and then they looked at the watch again. They looked at one another, and they looked at me.

Jake Lyman's red face had gone white. "You're right, Corey. My God, you're right! We . . . we almost hanged a lawman."

Chalton took a hesitant step toward me and put out his hand to touch my shoulder. He didn't seem so big now, so cocksure of himself; he didn't seem like much of a man at all. "Corey, boy, I . . ."

I backed away, staring at him, at the others. And then I turned and ran to my gelding and swung up into the saddle.

I rode long and hard, and it was late afternoon when I finally reached the little cottage I shared with Ma on the outskirts of Paytonville. Right away I packed all my belongings and took them out and strapped them onto the gelding's flanks. Ma wanted to know where I was going, but I couldn't tell her. I didn't know myself. I said I had to get out on my own—I was 'most nineteen now—and that I hoped she understood; she said she did, and she didn't argue. She could see my mind was made up.

Then I rode out of town southeast, and I didn't look back. I figured I could get a job in Laramie or Cheyenne, and when I did I could send for Ma to come live with me there.

I knew one thing sure.

I could never be coming back to Paytonville.

Stealing a horse was considered a hanging offense in the Old West; but every man is entitled to one mistake, and there were worse things a man could be than a horse thief. . . . Arthur Moore has published many Western stories and novels, among the latter such strong titles as The Burning Sky, The Kid from Ricon, *and* Trackdown.

Horse Thief

Arthur Moore

*T*he air was very still. As his roan horse picked its rambling way down the rocky hillside, Logan could see beneath him the low ranges of barren and twisted hills that swept down to the desert floor. The sun's slanting rays bathed the tortured crevasses in a golden light; the shale gleamed like molten metal. Clumps of shaggy mesquite and sage blended into velvet with the distance, and on the horizon the faint smudges of mountains faded into rose gray. Above, the smoky trails of high clouds were slowly turning pink.

Logan glanced at the red sun and picked the silver turnip-watch from his vest pocket, clicked the lid open and studied the black numerals briefly. He closed the lid with a snap and slipped the watch back into its pocket. It would be dark in an hour.

He straightened in the saddle, feeling the unaccustomed stiffness of his right leg. It was healed now, but the bullet had gone in just below the knee. The doctor had said it would always be stiff.

The hill leveled out slightly and he reined in. The sharp

sounds of the horse hooves on granite ceased and the still-ness settled down.

He sat, motionless, staring at the desert. Beyond that waste of parched sand and dry arroyos was Dos Rios, two or three adobe hovels and perhaps a dozen board shacks with chickens stirring up the dust in the wide trail that ran through the village.

Tomorrow or the next day he would meet Buckeye and Shorty there. He sighed and reached for his makings. Buck-eye and Shorty were eager to get back into action after the long lay-off. As their leader, he had written them from Lawsburg directing them to meet him in that lonely spot.

They were grimy, alert as panthers, quick to anger, wild and uncaring. Logan rolled the brown cigarette deftly, put it to his lips and snapped a sulphur match with his thumbnail.

He turned in the saddle, easing his stiff leg, and looked back over the way he had come. He'd deliberately picked Dos Rios as their meeting place. This side of the desert was home range to him. This was where he had grown up. It held certain memories of which his two partners were unaware. He had wanted to see it once more. He frowned at his leg. From Dos Rios they would ride south to the border. He might not ride this way again.

Pushing back the brown Stetson, he leaned on an elbow. His long face had lost its deep tan during his stay in the house at Lawsbury where his leg had been operated on. His narrow eyes were dark and perceptive amid the hundreds of tiny wrinkles. His black hair was long and he wore his mus-tache drooping to the corners of his hard mouth beneath a straight nose. A not unhandsome face but for the mouth.

He'd had no fear that anyone would recognize him. He'd left this territory long ago, when he was seventeen, two years after his mother had died. With her passing his father had become a bitter, harsh man. Logan wondered what he might have done if he had met his father on the street in Lawsburg.

He looked at the cigarette and brushed ashes from his thigh. The town was a good fifty miles behind him. The hill where he sat was the southern edge of the huge Beecher

Ranch, the last cattle range until one crossed those distant hills beyond the desert.

He smiled sardonically into the hazy distance and dropped the cigarette. Pushing with his knee, he turned the horse's head toward the bottom of the hill. All this was behind him now.

A clump of cottonwoods stood forlorn in the ravine far below, their dusty green leaves brilliant in the dying sun. Automatically his eyes darted here and there in search of a spot where he could lay up for the night. There should be water in one of these canyons. The spur jingled as he moved his stiff leg awkwardly, touching the animal's flank.

The horse shied at the unexpected thrust, then stumbled on a shelving bank of crumbling shale. Logan ducked low, pulling up the roan's head. A growl came from his throat and he slipped his foot from the stirrup as the animal plunged and went down heavily. He rolled free in the dust and got to his feet with a limping twist. The horse was on its side, kicking and rearing in pain, its leg broken in a crevice of the rock.

Logan cursed savagely. He ran to the horse's head. The frightened roan whinnied and struggled, blood pumping from the fracture. A single glance told him that nothing could be done. He drew his walnut-handled Colt regretfully. The single shot rang out in the stillness like a cannon's roar.

The boy came from a draw only a hundred yards away. Logan stood looking at him in surprise, his hand slapping at the dust on his Levi's. Then he waved his arm and called out. The boy sat tensely on a big bay gelding, looking him over, obviously quite as surprised as Logan at finding another rider in this wasteland.

The boy nudged the bay at last and came forward slowly, the long shadows moving with him like rippling fingers on the rocky hillside.

He was perhaps sixteen, tanned and bright-eyed. His revolver rested lightly on the saddle horn.

Logan ignored the gun.

"Howdy," he said cordially. He indicated the fallen roan horse with a shrug. "Reckon I'm afoot."

The boy nodded warily, taking in the long tail on the horse. "You from Lawsburg?"

"Bought this here cayuse there," admitted Logan. "I'm drifting south. Just passin' through." He put his hands on his hips and gazed down ruefully at the horse. "Don't that knock the thread off the bobbin?" He grinned at the boy, who slowly put the gun away.

"I'm Logan," said the older man. He squinted at the setting sun. "Time to make camp anyway." He set to work to pull the saddle off the dead horse.

The bay was skittish at the smell of blood. Its rider had to calm him, backing away from the scene.

He wore a faded blue shirt under a heavy mackinaw. His cheap Stetson was torn at the brim, and long, unkempt reddish hair was pushed back over his ears. His face was tanned and lined with dust. He had a short nose which made his upper lip look longer, and a square, determined jaw.

He kept his eyes on Logan, taking in the solid bulk of the man's shoulders, the slim hips and the well-worn holster. He urged the bay closer and peered at the brand mark on the roan horse, nodding faintly as if satisfied with the other's explanation.

Logan worked swiftly, aware of the scrutiny, pretending not to notice the boy's vigilance. He turned and dropped his saddle.

"Step down and share the feed-bag," he invited. "Got plenty grub. Mighty glad to have company."

The boy looked back briefly and swung down from the saddle, his every action tense and hesitant.

"Name's Johnny," he said. He didn't offer to shake hands. He looped the reins of the bay horse over a mesquite branch.

"Glad to know you, Johnny." Logan glanced about and pointed to an outcropping of granite. "Yonder's a likely spot," he said. "We can make us a little Injun fire and be right cozy."

He slung the saddle over his shoulder, picked up the blanket roll and strode limping to the outcropping. The boy stared at the red arc of the sun on the distant horizon and followed slowly, his hand pressing the gun at his side.

Logan put down the load and nodded to the youngster, "Spread your soogins in there, Johnny. I'll get us some java goin'." He stumped busily, gathering dry sticks.

Johnny looked after him for a moment, brushed his sleeve across his eyes wearily and went back for the bay.

The older man bustled with the blackened coffeepot. He sliced strips of bacon and fried them over the tiny fire. In the distance a coyote cried hollowly at the round, pale moon.

Logan divied the food solemnly and stood up to eat out of the skillet. The night was settling down, clear and silvery. The desert was a misty blur and soon the coyote was joined by another.

"Never started out to be a drifter," said Logan. He squatted down by the low fire. "Things figger that way, I guess. I'm headin' south along the border. Got a friend down there. Reckon I'll take a job till winter."

"Me, I ain't got no folks," Johnny said. He picked at the food. "Driftin's good enough. Reckon I'll ride chuck line till I find a roost."

"Shouldn't do bad," the other agreed. "Plenty ranches south. Good rains last year." He put the skillet on a rock and rolled a cigarette. "You could likely find one where I'm headin'. I'd admire to pay you for a lift far's Dos Rios, anyway. That bay of yours could handle two easy."

"Reckon he could," said the boy nervously. He glanced at the horse, hobbled in a shallow draw below the outcropping.

"We got us a deal then," said Logan and smiled. He added another twig to the fire, noting Johnny's instant watchfulness, and peered up into the dark sky, wary of smoke.

From long experience Logan had hidden the cookfire in a pocket of the rocks. The glow would not be visible more than a hundred yards in a single direction. The restless lad was running from something, he decided. He had noted the brand on the bay as soon as the boy had ridden up. The Beecher Ranch didn't sell horses to drifters.

"A man don't like to lose his cayuse," Logan said conversationally. He stared down the hill toward the shadowy mass of the cottonwoods, apparently unaware of Johnny's quick glance. "Sure would dig him a hole if I had a shovel. Them buzzards gonna be pickin' at him come dawn."

Johnny glanced at the sky as though seeing the sinister birds circling in the sun.

"We oughta get us a early start," he said. He grinned shortly. "That there desert goin' to be hotter'n a bobcat."

"Reckon." Logan smoothed his mustache with two fingers. "Could be I shouldn't ask, but ain't you just a mite jumpy, kid?"

Johnny stiffened. His hand swept back toward his gun, but Logan outdrew him easily. Casually he flicked open the loading gate of the Colt, drew back the hammer and spun the cylinder.

"Well now," he said, "don't that beat the ticks off a yearlin'? I forgot to reload this here pistol."

He ejected the empty shell he had used on the roan horse. Picking another from his belt, he calmly slid it into the cylinder, carefully turned the cylinder so the firing pin rested on an empty chamber and reholstered the gun.

"Don't seem like a young feller ought to be so jumpy," he said slowly. He looked directly at the boy. "I ain't the law, Johnny. You got somethin' on your mind?"

Johnny frowned and bit his lip.

"You kill a man?"

The boy shook his head. His square jaw was set but he looked tired.

"Could be the bay, then." Johnny's eyes told him he was right. Logan cocked his head on one side. "Must be a good reason—"

"Sure was," Johnny said bitterly. The words came out with a rush. He seemed to be glad to get them off his mind. "I was ridin' for old man Beecher." He jerked his head. "That there's his range, biggest spread hereabouts. Anyways, I was joshin' with some of the boys yestiddy when old Beecher come along. He thought I was makin' fun of him. And I never even seed him comin'—"

"I've heard of him," said Logan softly. "Tough old bastard."

"He don't give nobody a chance to explain," growled the boy. "You do it Beecher's way or you ain't workin' for him. Anyways, he had me run off the ranch. I didn't have no cayuse and he didn't even give me my back pay."

"Just like that, huh?"

"Just like he was a king or somethin'. Owed me a month's wages."

Logan sighed. 'That's why you took that there bay horse?"

"He owed me," said Johnny wearily. "I figger we're even. Reckon I shoulda gone to the sheriff." He pushed back his torn hat. "If he'd believed me, that is."

Not with Beecher shovin' him," said Logan acidly. "Think I'd figger the same way." He got to his feet stiffly. "You're right, Johnny; we'll be gettin' an early start."

He glanced at the desert and limped around the rocks to the top of the little hill, staring at the shadowy backtrail. Nothing moved there. He reached for the makings and paused. A match could be seen for miles in this air.

Beecher would press the sheriff, he thought, and a posse would be trailing the boy. Maybe even now they were back there somewhere in the darkness, waiting for the first light. What was Beecher's would remain Beecher's. When they caught Johnny it would be all over. Horse thieves got a quick rope. Johnny was only a kid, and he had gotten even the only way he could. But Beecher would say he was a horse thief. Beecher would win again.

Logan looked back toward the little camp. The boy had got a bad break. There was nothing wrong about him. He could spot a wrong-un a mile off. Johnny didn't have the earmarks. He smiled to himself then. It was funny he should be interested in what happened to the kid.

Buckeye or Shorty would have shot the boy off the horse when he first appeared out of the draw. If they'd needed the bay, they would have taken it. Maybe he was interested because the boy reminded him of something.

He fingered the black mustache absently, putting his

weight on his good leg. Johnny had been dealt the same bob-tailed flush he himself had held a long time ago, and on this same range. That was the way it was when a cowboy started running. The first time it might be justified.

After that it became easier and easier to slide downhill, especially when the law seemed to be on the other side. But one day he'd stop running, suddenly. A bullet or a rope. Then they'd throw him in a dry stream bed and cave in the banks on him. Logan turned about and clumped awkwardly down the hill to the camp.

Johnny had put out the fire and was rolled up in the soogins. Logan picked up his own blanket roll. "Anybody see you take that bay horse, Johnny?"

"Don't figger so," said the boy. "Saw a feller in the distance, though. He couldn't have knowed it was me."

Logan grunted and shucked his gun belt. He placed his hat within reach and sat with his back to the rocks.

"Get yourself some sleep," he said softly. "I'll watch awhile." He drew out the bag of Bull Durham and rolled a cigarette.

He had smoked two cigarettes before the boy began to breathe deeply and regularly. Then he opened his warbag, scrounged up an old blank envelope, and tore it carefully into a neat square. He found a stub of pencil and with the light from a match, meticulously wrote out a bill of sale for the dead roan horse, dating it two weeks past.

With the stealth of an Indian, he placed the bill of sale in Johnny's hatband, then he sat back and rolled another cigarette.

The moon was low on the horizon when he finally stirred. Johnny slept peacefully. Logan rolled his blankets, put on his hat and belt and stole from the camp. He took Johnny's saddle and left his own, an even swap. He carried these around the hill and came back for the bay horse, slipping the hobbles and leading the animal to the saddle.

He was far out on the desert when the first pale streaks of light appeared in the east. He reined in and looked back grimly. The posse would find Johnny now. The buzzards would see to that. But when they found him, they'd also find a strange dead horse which the boy had a bill of sale for. No matter how old man Beecher raved, the sheriff and the posse wouldn't go against that evidence. Johnny would be off the hook. Logan had a feeling the lesson would be enough for the boy.

He sighed and glanced at the cold dawn, pulling out the turnip-watch. It was an old watch, the silver was tarnished and scratched, but as the first sparkling rays of the morning sun reached him, he could make out the inscription in flowing letters that half circled the inside of the case. "To our son, Logan Beecher."

"My Brother Down There" is the tense, savage tale of a manhunt in the wilds of Colorado, in which both the hunters and the hunted are dominated by the primitive elements in man's personality. It won first prize in an annual contest conducted by Ellery Queen's Mystery Magazine *in 1953, was later anthologized in Martha Foley's Best American Short Stories of the Year, and was eventually filmed as* Running Target. *It may well be the finest of all of Steve Frazee's high-quality stories and novels, and that makes it something very special, indeed.*

My Brother Down There

Steve Frazee

Now *there were three left. Here was the fourth, doubled* up on his side at the edge of the meadow grass where the wind had scattered pine needles. His face was pinched and gray. Big black wood ants were backing away from the blood settling into the warm soil.

Jaynes turned the dead man over with his foot. "Which one is this?"

Holesworth, deputy warden of the state penitentiary, gave Jaynes an odd look.

"Joseph Otto Weyerhauser," he said. "Lifer for murder."

Deputy Sheriff Bill Melvin was standing apart from the rest of the posse. He had been too deep in the timber to take part in the shooting. He watched the little green state patrol plane circling overhead. It was a windless day. The voice of the mountains spoke of peace and summer.

Joseph Otto Weyerhauser. Spoken that way, the words gave dignity to the fugitive who lay now on the earth in the pale green uniform that had been stolen from the wash lines of a little filling station a hundred miles away.

Sid Jaynes was a beefy man with dark eyes that glittered. Jaynes had not known who the convict was and he had not cared. The green pants and shirt, when Weyerhauser tried to run across the head of the little meadow, had been enough for him.

"He played it like a fool," Jaynes said. "He could have stayed in the timber."

"You made $12.50 with each one of those shots, Jaynes." The deputy warden's voice ran slowly and deliberately.

"Let the state keep their twenty-five bucks," Jaynes said. "I didn't come along for that." His rifle was a beautiful instrument with a telescopic sight. The dead man lay beside a sawed-off shotgun and a .38 pistol taken from a guard he had slugged with a bar of soap in a sock. "Why didn't he stay in the timber, the damn fool?"

"They're all city boys," Warden Holesworth said. "He was heading for the highway."

It put you on the wrong side of your job to make a comparison between the dead man's short-range weapons and the rifles of the posse, Deputy Bill Melvin thought. Weyerhauser had been one of four prison escapees. He had taken his big chance with the others, and here the chance had ended.

That was all there was to it; but Melvin wished he did not have to look at Weyerhauser or hear any more from Jaynes, who was always the first man to reach the sheriff's office when the word went out that a manhunt was on. Jaynes, who ran a garage, never came when help was needed to find a lost hunter or a wrecked plane.

Sheriff Rudd spoke. Sheriff Rudd was a veteran of the

open-range days of men and cattle. He stood like a rifle barrel, tall and spare. His face was bony, with a jutting nose.

"There's three more," the sheriff said. "All tougher than Weyerhauser." He squinted at the green plane, now circling lower in the trough of the mountains. "Call that flyer, Melvin. He's buzzing around this basin like a bee in a washtub. Tell him to get up in the air. Tell him about this and have him call the patrol station over the hill and see if anything has popped there."

Deputy Melvin started back to the horse with the radio gear. Jaynes called, "Ask him if he's spotted any of the other three."

Melvin paid no attention.

"One twenty, ground party, Stony Park."

"Ground party, go ahead."

"Get some altitude. You're making Sheriff Rudd nervous."

"What does Rudd think I am? There's a hell of a wind up here. What happened?"

"We got Weyerhauser. Dead. Call Scott and Studebaker on the roadblocks."

"Stand by," the pilot said.

Melvin leaned against the mare. She moved a little, cropping grass, switching her tail at deer flies unconcernedly, while Melvin listened to the plane call across the mountains. Jaynes's sleeping bag was on the crosspieces of the pack saddle, put there to protect the radio from branches.

Jaynes walked over. "Has he spotted—?"

"I didn't ask," said Melvin.

"Why not?"

"He would have said so if he had."

"Well, it won't hurt to ask. Maybe—"

"Go collect your twenty-five bucks, Jaynes."

"What do you mean by that?"

Jaynes did not understand. He never would.

"Ground party, One twenty," the pilot said. "Negative on all roadblocks and patrol cars."

"Thanks, One twenty. Call Studebaker again and have an

ambulance meet us at the big spring, east side of Herald Pass, at one this afternoon.''

"Okay." The plane began to climb. Melvin watched until it gained altitude and shot away across the timbered hump of Herald Pass.

"That's a hell of a note," Jaynes complained. "Guys like me come out here, taking time off from our business just to do what's right, and you don't even ask whether he's spotted the others or not.''

Melvin pulled the canvas cover back over the radio. "Four times twenty-five makes a hundred, Jaynes. What are you going to buy with all that money?''

"I give it to the Red Cross, don't I!''

"You mean that first twenty-five you knocked down—that little forger? I remember him, Jaynes. He came out of a railroad culvert trying to get his hands up, scared to death, and you cut loose.''

Jaynes was puzzled, not angry. He said, "You talk funny for a deputy sheriff, Melvin. You sound like you thought there was something nice about these stinking cons. What are we supposed to do with them?''

Melvin went back to the posse. Deputy Warden Holesworth had searched the dead man. On the ground was a pile. Candy bars, smeary and flattish from being carried in pockets; seven packs of cigarettes.

"One down and three to go," Jaynes said. "Where do we head now, Sheriff?''

Sheriff Rudd looked around the group. Two or three of the men sitting in the grass had already lost stomach. Rudd named them and said, "Take that sorrel that's started to limp and pack Weyerhauser up to the highway.''

"At the big spring on the east side," Melvin said. "There'll be an ambulance there at one o'clock.''

"I've got to get back myself," the deputy warden said. "Tomorrow I'll send a couple of guards out. We can fly in Blayden's hounds from up north—''

"I don't favor hounds," the sheriff said. "Keep your guards, too, Holesworth. The last time you sent guards we had to carry 'em out. You keep 'em sitting in those towers too much.''

"That's what they get paid for, not for being Indian guides and cross-country men. To hell with you." They grinned at each other. Then Holesworth gave Jaynes another speculative glance and helped lift Weyerhauser on to the lame horse.

That left seven in the posse. They divided the cigarettes. Small ants went flying when someone gave the pile of candy bars a kick. One chocolate bar, undisturbed by the boot, was melting into the earth beside the other stain.

Two days later Sheriff Rudd cut the trail of three men whose heelprints showed *P* marks in the center. Rudd swung down and studied the tracks, and then he took the saddle off his gelding.

"What's the stall?" Jaynes asked. "That's the track of our meat, Rudd."

"A day and a half old, at least. Give your horse a rest." The sheriff sat down on a log and began to fill his pipe.

Melvin walked beside the footprints for several steps. He saw the wrapper of a candy bar lying on the ground. Four days on candy and desperation. The poor devils. Poor devils, hell; the candy had been stolen from the filling station where they had slugged a sixty-year-old man, the desperation was their own, and they were asking for the same as Weyerhauser.

Melvin looked up at the gray caps of the mountains. They ran here in a semicircle, with only one trail over them, and that almost unknown. If these tracks with the deep-cut marks in the heels continued up, the fugitives would be forced to the forgotten road that led to Clover Basin. From there the trail went over the spine at 13,000 feet.

It was a terrible climb for men living on candy bars. Melvin went back to the resting posse, saying nothing.

"Clover Basin, maybe?" Sheriff Rudd asked.

Melvin nodded.

"Why haven't the damn search planes seen them?" Jaynes asked.

"There's trees and rocks, and the sound of a plane engine carries a long way ahead." Bud Pryor was a part-time deputy, here now because he had been called to go. He was a barrel-chested man who could stop a barroom fight by cracking heads together, but he didn't care much for riding the mountains. And he didn't care at all for Jaynes.

"Any other stupid questions, sharpshooter?" Bud Pryor asked Jaynes.

The sheriff got up. "Let's go."

They rode into the first of the great fields of golden gaillardia at the lower end of Clover Basin. The buildings of the Uncle Sam Mine hung over the slope at the upper end like gray ghosts. Rudd stopped his horse. The others crowded up behind him.

Motion started at the highest building and sent small points out on the slide-rock trail. "Hey!" Jaynes cried. Both he and Melvin put glasses on the tiny figures scrambling over the flat gray stones. Two men in green uniforms. Two men who ran and fell and crawled upward toward the harsh rise of Clover Mountain.

Jaynes let his binoculars fall on the cord around his neck. He raised his rifle, sighting through the scope. Some sort of dedication lay in his glittering eyes, some drive that made Melvin look away from him and glance at the sheriff.

Rudd, however, without the aid of glasses, was watching the fleeing men on the eternal stones of Clover Mountain.

Jaynes kicked his horse ahead. "Come on!"

"Get off and lead that horse awhile, Jaynes," the sheriff said. "You've knocked the guts out of him already the last few days."

"There they are!" Jaynes gestured with his rifle.

"And there they go." Rudd got down and began to lead his horse.

"Now what the hell!" Jaynes twisted his face. "They're getting away—farther out of range every second!"

"They're a mile airline. It'll take us the best part of two hours to reach the mine," Sheriff Rudd said with weary patience. "And then it will be dark. Go on, Jaynes, if you want to, but leave that horse behind."

"It's mine."

"You'll leave it behind, I said."

Jaynes looked through his scope and cursed.

"Three came in here," Bud Pryor said. "Go on up and kick that third one out, Jaynes. He's there."

"How do you know?" Jaynes's voice was not large.

Pryor's thick lips spread in a grin. He was still sweating from the last steep hill where they had led the horses. "Gets chilly mighty quick in these high places, don't it?"

Rudd started on, leading his horse. It was dusk when they closed in on the bunkhouse of the Uncle Sam Mine, working around from the rocks and coming closer in short rushes to the toe of the dump. Jaynes and Melvin went up the dump together until their heads were nearly level with the rusted rails that still held rotting chocks.

"I'll cover you from here," Jaynes said. "This scope gathers light so a man can't miss."

Melvin raised his head above the dump. An evening wind drove grouse feathers across the yellow waste toward him. He saw a rat scurry along the ledge of a broken window and then sit still, looking out. Inside, two or three others squealed as they raced across the floor.

Melvin scrabbled on up and walked into the bunkhouse. Two rats carrying grouse bones ducked through holes in the floor. One half of the roof was caved in, but the other end, where the stove sat with its pipe reduced to lacy fragility, was still a shelter.

The stove was warm.

Here, for a time, three men had stayed. They were city-bred, and so this man-made shell seemed the natural place to take shelter. No outdoorsman would have sought the rat-fouled place, but the escaped prisoners must have received some small comfort from it.

Instinctively they had huddled inside this pitiful ruin for the security that all pursued mankind must seek. And now, caught by the dusk and the silence, looking through a window at the mighty sweep of the high world, Bill Melvin was stirred by a feeling for the fugitives that sprang from depths far below the surface things called logic and understanding.

"What's in there?" Jaynes called.

Melvin stepped outside. "Nothing."

Jaynes cursed. He climbed to the dump level and stared at the dim slide-rock trail. He fondled his rifle.

Pryor's voice came from the lower buildings, high-pitched and clear, running out to the walls of the great basin and echoing back with ghostly mockery. "Nothing in any of these, Sheriff!"

"Let's get on the trail!" Jaynes yelled.

"Come down here," Sheriff Rudd said, and both their voices ran together on the darkening rocks around them.

Melvin and Jaynes rejoined the others. Melvin was dead-weary now, but Jaynes kept looking at the slide-rock, fretting.

"We can't get horses over that slide-rock at night," Rudd said. "And maybe not in daylight. We'll camp here to-night."

"And all that time they'll be moving," Jaynes objected. "Are you sure you want to catch them, Sheriff?"

"They'll be feeling their way down the worst switch-backs in these hills," Rudd said. "On empty stomachs."

"Like hell!" Jaynes said. "They've been living like kings on grouse."

"One grouse," Melvin said.

"They must be getting fat." Rudd pointed to the floor of the basin. "We'll camp down there and give the horses a chance to graze."

"And make this climb again in the morning," Jaynes said disgustedly.

Dew was gathering on the grass when they picketed the horses. All the chill of the high-country night seemed to have gathered in the enormous black hole. They ate almost the last of their food at a fire built from scrubby trees.

Jaynes cleaned his rifle before he ate. He rubbed the stock and admired the weapon, standing with the firelight glittering in his eyes.

"What will that pretty thing do that a good Krag won't?" Bud Pryor asked.

Jaynes smiled and let the answer gleam in the reflection of the flames.

"Somebody will have to start out tomorrow for grub," the sheriff said. "How about it, Jaynes?"

"I can live on the country," Jaynes said.

"Yeah." The sheriff unrolled his sleeping bag. "One hour each on guard tonight. Not at the fire, either. Stay out by the horses. I'll take it from three till dawn."

Jaynes peered into the darkness. "You think the third one is around in the rocks, huh?"

"I think the horses can get all tangled up. The third man went over the hill a long time ago," Rudd said.

"How do you know that?" Jaynes asked.

"Because I'm betting it was Marty Kaygo. He's the toughest and the smartest. He wouldn't sit in that eagle's nest up there, hoping nobody comes after him."

"Kaygo, huh? What was he in for?" Jaynes stared toward the gloomy crest of the mountain.

"He killed two cops." Rudd took off his boots, pulled his hat down tightly, and got into his sleeping bag. "He killed them with one shot each." The sheriff was asleep a few moments later.

Jaynes set his rifle on his sleeping bag and began to eat. "Who are the other two?"

"Don't you even know their names?" Melvin asked.

"What's the difference if I don't?"

Maybe Jaynes was right. It had to be done, one way or another; names merely made it harder. "Sam Castagna and Ora L. Strothers," Melvin said. "Castagna used to blow up rival gamblers for a syndicate. Strothers specialized in holding up banks."

"Ora L. That's nice and gentle, a con having a name like that," Jaynes said.

"Don't you give him the right to have a name?" Melvin asked. "Don't you give him the right to be a human being?"

Jaynes looked blank at the anger in Melvin's voice.

"What is it with you, anyway? You and Rudd both talk like it was a crime to send those bastards rolling in the grass."

Rolling in the grass. That was exactly what had happened to Weyerhauser when Jaynes's second shot ripped through his belly.

Melvin walked away from the fire suddenly, into the cold dark layers of the night. The possemen were sacking out. Jaynes squatted near the fire alone, eating, a puzzled expression on his face. Bud Pryor, stripped down to long underwear and his boots, came over and stood beside the flames for a few minutes, warming his hands.

Dislike of Jaynes and a sort of wonder mingled on Pryor's fleshy face. He parted his thick lips as if to speak. But then he felt the fire and settled into his sleeping bag, grunting.

The night was large and silent. Up toward the knife edge of Clover Mountain two men had scrambled across the rocks, crawling where slides had filled the trail. Two men running for their lives.

Melvin kept seeing it over and over.

Castagna's sentence had been commuted to life just two days short of the gas chamber. Strothers had never killed a man, but he was cold and ruthless. Marty Kaygo, who must have gone across the hill before the others, was in debt to the law 180 years. This was his third escape from prison.

They were all no good, predators against society. But . . . In the solemn night, with the tremendous peace of the mountains upon him, Bill Melvin stared uneasily at the line which must run from crime to punishment.

Ordinarily, he did not allow himself to be disturbed like this; but Jaynes, scraping the last of his supper from a tin plate, had kicked over the little wall that divided what men must do from what they think.

"I'll take the first watch," Melvin said.

Jaynes came out from the fire. He spoke in a low voice. "It's only nine o'clock. Barker's got a flashlight. We could slip up on the slide-rock trail—there's patches of snow there—and see for sure if they all three crossed."

"Why?"

"If one is still here, he'll try to slip out of the basin tonight. We could lay out in that narrow place and nail him dead to rights."

"I'll take the first watch." Melvin walked deeper into the night, trembling from high-altitude fatigue, mouthing the sickening aftertaste of Jaynes's presence.

"Why not, Melvin?"

"Go to bed!"

Sometimes a healthy man does not sleep well at great altitudes, and so it was with Melvin this night. When Jaynes relieved him, Melvin heard the beefy hunter going down the basin past the horses. He knew that Jaynes would make for a place where he could command the narrow entrance to the basin, and that he would lie there, patiently, his rifle ready.

Melvin wondered if his eyes would glitter in the dark.

Jaynes stayed his watch, and the watch of the man he did not waken for relief.

Dawn slid across the peaks. Light was there when dew and gloom were still heavy in the basin. The sheriff and Pryor cooked the last of the bacon and opened the last two cans of beans.

Jaynes saddled up and led his horse toward the fire before he ate. "What kind of rifle was it this—what was his name, Kaygo?—stole at the filling station?"

"A .30-06," Rudd said. There were pouches under his eyes this morning, and he looked his years. He stared through the smoke at Jaynes. "New one. He took five boxes of shells, too, Jaynes. They're hunting cartridges."

"I've got a few expanding noses myself," Jaynes said. "Let's get started."

Rudd spat to one side. "You're like a hog going to war."

Bud Pryor laughed. The other manhunters stared at Jaynes or at the ground. They seemed ashamed now, Melvin thought, to be a part of this thing. Or a part of Jaynes.

Pryor said explosively, "I'll go in after chow today, Sheriff. Me and Jaynes."

"No!" Jaynes said. "I can live on the country. Me and Melvin can keep going when the rest of you have to run for a restaurant."

Rudd said to Pryor, "You and Barker, then. It's closer

now to Scott than it is to Studebaker, so we'll split up after we cross the hill. Try the radio again, Melvin. Maybe nobody will have to go in.''

"No contact," Melvin said, later. "When we get to the top, we can reach out and make it.''

They took the slide-rock trail from the dump at the side of the bunkhouse. In passing, Melvin noticed that the grouse feathers were almost entirely blown away.

Seventy years before, jack trains had used the trail; but now the years had slid into it. The posse led their horses. Sparks from steel shoes in the stretches where the ledge still showed drill marks; a clattering and a scramble, with the horses rolling their eyes when they had to cross the spills of dry-slippery rocks.

In the snowbanks, the tracks of three men; and one man had gone about a day before the others.

There lay the ridge, half a mile ahead. On the left, where they traveled, the mountain ran down wildly to ledges where no human being would ever set foot.

They lost the little radio mare. She slipped and fell and then she was threshing over and the slide-rock ran with her. She struck a ledge and was gone. The rocks kept spilling down a thousand feet below.

Rudd patted the neck of his frightened gelding. "There went a damn good little mare.''

Jaynes said, "They don't exactly give those radios away, either. My sleeping bag cost sixty-two bucks.''

They came out on the wedge-top and went down three switchbacks to let the horses take a blow out of the wind. A dozen lakes were winking in the sunlight. The mountains on this side ran in a crazy pattern. Every major range in the United States runs north and south, with one exception; but from the pinpoints where a man must stand, the north-south coursing is often lost or does not exist at all.

There was no highway in sight, no smoke, just the vast expanse of timber with the gray-sharp slopes above and the shine of beaver meadows where little streams lay separated from each other by ridges eight thousand feet high.

"A regiment could hide out down there all summer,''

Rudd said. "But these guys will most likely keep running downhill, hoping to hit a highway sooner or later."

Jaynes's rifle was in his hands, as usual when he was on foot. He pointed with it. "I know every inch of that country. I've fished and hunted all through it."

"Don't be a fool," Sheriff Rudd said. "I rode that country before you were born, and I discovered a new place every time I went out. And I could do the same for a hundred years." Rudd shook his head. "Every inch of it . . . !"

Jaynes said, "I can find any tenderfoot that tries to hide out down there." He patted the stock of his rifle.

"Goddamn you, Jaynes! I'm sick of you!" Melvin cried. "Keep your mouth shut!"

Jaynes was surprised. "Now, what did I say? Have you got a biting ulcer or something, Melvin?"

"Let's go on down," Rudd said.

Melvin's stomach held a knot that eased off slowly. For a moment he had seen the land without a man in it, forgetting even himself as he stood there on the mountain. But Jaynes would never let a man forget himself for long.

In the middle of the morning the green plane came over and circled them. The pilot was calling, Melvin knew, but they had no way now to listen or call back. After a while the plane soared away over the green timber and drifted on toward Scott.

They struck the timber. Fallen trees lay across the trail, slowing the horses. There were still three men ahead.

"Planes, radios, horses—what the hell good are they?" Jaynes said irritably. "In the end it comes down to men on foot closing in on each other."

"Like you closed in on the Uncle Sam bunkhouse, huh?" Pryor asked. "Hand to hand, tooth and toenail."

"Strip down to a breechclout, Jaynes," Rudd said. "I'll give you my knife and you can go after Kaygo properly."

Barker said, "Yeah, why don't you do that, Jaynes? You big-mouthed bastard, you."

Barker had little imagination. He was a sullen man who would kill the fugitives as quickly as Jaynes. All that motivated Barker now, Melvin thought, was a desire to transfer the cause of his hunger and weariness to another human being. Jaynes had already been marked by him as a target.

"I don't understand you guys, so help me," Jaynes said.

Melvin felt a flash of pity for him; the man really did not understand. What made Jaynes tick probably was as obscure as the forces that had sent the men he so greatly wanted to kill into a life of crime. Somebody ought to be able to figure it out. . . .

The big buck flashed across the narrow lane in a split second. The smaller one that followed an instant later was going just as fast. Jaynes broke its neck with one shot.

The thought of fresh liver relieved some of Melvin's dislike of Jaynes. "Nice shooting, Jaynes."

"Thanks."

"I'll eat that thing without skinning it," Bud Pryor said. He had his knife out already and was trotting ahead.

Jaynes sat on a log and cleaned his rifle while Pryor and Melvin dressed the buck. Jaynes had merely glanced at it and turned away.

"He's larded up like first-class, grass-fed beef," Pryor said. "Lucky shot, Jaynes."

"I seldom miss a running target." Jaynes spoke absently, looking ahead at the trees.

Pryor sent Melvin a helpless look. "It sure looked lucky to me."

"No luck at all," said Jaynes. "It's simple if you have the eye for it."

Pryor made a motion with his knife as if to cut his own throat. He and Melvin laughed. For a few moments Jaynes was no problem to them.

"Sling it on a horse," Sheriff Rudd said. "We can eat when we get to Struthers's sawmill set."

"Struthers? That's one of the men we want," Jaynes said.

"Different spelling," Rudd said. "Jumbo Struthers has been dead for forty years, and the sawmill hasn't run for fifty-two years."

"We could dig him up," Pryor said, grinning, "so Jaynes could shoot him."

For the first time Jaynes showed anger. "Why do you keep digging at me? What are we out here for, anyway? You act like there was something wrong in what we're doing!"

"We're here to bring back three men, dead *or* alive," Rudd said. "Let's go."

The trail expanded into a logging road, with live trees trying to close it out and dead trees trying to block it. Mosquitoes came singing in from a marsh on the left. Already tormented by the snags on fallen timber, the horses shook their heads as the insects buzzed their ears. Pryor kept swinging his hat at blowflies settling on the carcass of the deer. "The good old summertime," he said. "How'd you get me out here, Sheriff?"

"You were getting fat, so you volunteered."

The small talk irritated Jaynes. "We're not making much time," he said. Later, after a delay to lever aside a tangle of dead jackpines, he went ahead in a stooping posture for several steps. "One of the boys ain't doing so good all at once."

Melvin studied the tracks. One man had started to drag his leg; a second one was helping him. The third track was still older than these two. Farther down the road a punch mark appeared in the soil. One man was using a short pole as a cane.

Jaynes wanted to race away on the trail. "We'll have that one before long!"

"Hold up." The sheriff stopped to fill his pipe. "I'd say the fellow twisted a muscle or sprained his ankle trying to jump that tangle we just cleared out. The other one will leave him, that's sure."

"The old ranger lean-to in Boston Park must be pretty close," Jaynes said. "Half a mile, I'd say."

"About a mile," Rudd said.

Melvin knew about it, the big lean-to sometimes used by fishermen and hunters. Man had made it, and the fact would seem important to the men ahead. Considering the tracks of the injured fugitive, Melvin wondered whether the convict would last to Boston Park.

"If he's bunged up as bad as it looks, he's likely ready to quit," Rudd said.

"He won't give up," Jaynes said. "He'll make a stand."

The sheriff narrowed his eyes at Jaynes. "Why will he, if he's hurt?"

"If he's been left at that lean-to, he's the loneliest man in the world right now," Melvin put in.

"Yeah?" Jaynes kept edging ahead. "I'm not walking up on that hut to find out how lonely he is."

"Nobody is," Rudd said. "When we get close, two men will take the horses. The rest of us will cut off into the timber and come in from all sides of the lean-to. He may not be there at all."

The lean-to was set between two trees on high ground, clear of the swamp that edged the beaver ponds. Generations of outdoorsmen had piled boughs along the sides and on top until the shelter was a rust-brown mass. That it had not been burned by a careless match long ago spoke tersely of the nature of the men who came far into the mountains.

Melvin and Sheriff Rudd came to the edge of the trees a hundred yards apart. They waited for Pryor, on the right. Barker and Jaynes were to ease out of the trees on the left, Barker to cover the back of the shelter, Jaynes to prevent escape farther to the left.

There had been a fire recently among the blackened stones before the lean-to. Fine ashes stirred there, lifting to a little wind that rolled across the beaver ponds and whispered through the tall swamp grass.

Melvin saw Pryor come to the edge of the trees and signal with his hand. Barker slipped to the cover of a windfall behind the shelter. He wagged his rifle.

Inside the lean-to a man cleared his throat.

Melvin sank to one knee behind a log.

The sheriff said, "Come out of there! You're boxed. Walk out with your hands up!"

"I can't walk," a voice replied.

"Come out of there. We'll rip that place apart with bullets if I have to ask again."

The brittle needles scraped against each other. A chunky

man whose face was black with beard came on hands and knees from the hut. He was wearing a soiled, torn green uniform, too small for him. One pants leg was gone below the knee.

"Toss your pistol away," Rudd ordered.

"No gun." The man clawed against one of the trees. He pulled himself erect. "No gun, you stinking, dirty—" He started to fall and made a quick grab at the crosspiece of the shelter.

A rifle blasted from the edge of the timber beyond Barker. The man at the lean-to fell. He was dead, Melvin was sure. "Watch him! Watch him!" Jaynes called. "It's just his arm!"

Melvin and the sheriff walked in then. The man had been shot through the left hand, a thick hand, by a soft-nosed hunting bullet. The palm was torn away and the fingers were spread like the spokes of a shattered wheel. The man rolled on his side and put his broken hand under his arm.

"My leg is cracked before." He cursed. "Now look at it!" The leg was really broken now; it had twisted under when the man fell. Melvin searched him and found two packs of cigarettes.

Barker came around the hut. Jaynes arrived on the run. "I could just see his arm when he grabbed for his gun!"

"He grabbed, all right," Sheriff Rudd said. "To keep from falling on a busted leg."

"Oh!" Jaynes stared down. "It looked to me like—"

"Shut up." Rudd yelled at the timber where the two men were holding the horses. "Bring 'em on!" There was a first-aid kit on Melvin's horse.

"Which one is this?" Jaynes asked.

"Sam Castagna." Suspected of seven murders, convicted of one, sentence commuted to life. "Where's Strothers, Sam?"

"Run out on me." With his face against the brown needles Castagna tried to spit explosively. It merely dribbled from his mouth and hung in his black beard. He cursed in Italian, glaring up at Jaynes.

Barker said, "No gun anywhere around the hut. They had

two sawed-offs and two .38 pistols, besides the rifle Kaygo swiped at the filling station.''

The horses came in at the trot. Pryor circled the swamp and plodded through the grass. He looked at the wounded man. ''Castagna, huh? Nice boy who likes to put bombs on car starters. The other two are still going down the trail, Sheriff.''

''Straight to a highway,'' Rudd said. ''Let's patch him up and move on.''

''I'm going to eat here,'' Pryor said, ''if you have to leave me. I'm going to beat the blowflies to some of that deer.'' He began to build a fire.

Melvin and Barker made splints for Castagna's broken leg. They wrapped his hand. He watched them stolidly. When they pulled his leg, he ground his teeth and sweated. Melvin got him a drink of water afterward.

''Thanks,'' Castagna held the cup in a trembling hand, slopping part of the water down his chin and into the thick black hairs at the base of his neck.

''Where's Strothers and Kaygo, Castagna?'' Jaynes asked.

Castagna looked hungrily at the meat Pryor was roasting on a green limb. He lay back on the ground and closed his eyes. There was a depression under his head and it caused his face to tilt straight into the sun. Melvin took off his coat and rolled it under the wounded man's head.

They squatted around the fire, roasting cutlets chopped from the loin with a hand ax, too hungry to bother with a frying pan. Blood from half-raw meat ran down their chins when they chewed.

None of us is far removed from the wolf, Melvin thought; but there is a difference between men like Rudd and Sam Castagna. There has to be. Yet where was the difference between Castagna and Jaynes, who cleaned his rifle before he ate?

Melvin glanced at the gleaming weapon, laid carefully aside on the dry grass. He felt an urge to hurl the rifle far out into the beaver pond.

Sheriff Rudd ground his meat moodily. ''I never used to

stop when I was on the chase. We stop to gorge ourselves while a desperate man keeps going. The difference is he *has* to get away and we don't *have* to catch him.''

"Him? Who do you mean?" Jaynes asked. "Why don't we have to catch him?''

"Oh, hell," Rudd said. "Gimme the salt, Barker.''

"I don't understand what—" Jaynes said.

"Before we leave here, Jaynes, you throw into that pond every damn hunting bullet you got," Rudd said. "I'm going to watch you do it.''

They all looked at Jaynes. He could not grasp the reason for their hostility. "Shells cost money. I'll use that old coffee can over there and bury them under the lean-to. Next fall I'll be through here hunting.''

"Do that, then," Rudd said. "Every damn soft-nose you got." But Rudd seemed to find no satisfaction in the trifling victory.

He knew he was only scratching at the surface, Melvin thought.

The sheriff twisted around toward Castagna. "Some deer meat, Sam?''

"Yeah. Yeah, let me try it." Castagna ate greedily, and then he lost everything before they could get him onto a horse.

The green plane was cruising southwest of them. A few minutes later it came over Boston Park, dipping low. It went southwest again, circling six or seven times.

"Uh-huh," Rudd said.

"He must be over the Shewalter Meadows," Jaynes said. "That's all down-timber between here and there.''

"Not if you know the way from the sawmill set." Rudd swung up. "Catch Castagna there if he starts to fall.''

There were still two sets of mantracks down the logging road. Just before they reached the sawmill site they found a sawed-off shotgun laid across a log, pointing toward one of the sawdust piles near the creek. Under it an arrow mark scratched in the black soil pointed in the same direction.

"Now that's a cute trick," Jaynes said. He sighted through his scope at the sawdust piles, age-brown mounds blending into the wilderness. He was suspicious, but he was confused.

"It reads to me that Strothers wants to quit, and wants to be sure we know it," Rudd said.

"Suppose he's still got the pistol? Suppose it's Kaygo?" Jaynes asked.

"Most likely Kaygo is over there where the plane was circling," Melvin said. Kaygo had left the others at the Uncle Sam Mine. The sheriff, at least, was sure of that, and Melvin had accepted it. Still, he did not like the quiet of the sawdust piles, warm and innocent-looking out there by the creek.

Rudd said. "Come on, Melvin. The rest of you stay here. Take Castagna off the horse and let him lay down awhile."

"I'd better—" Jaynes said.

"Stay right here," the sheriff said.

Rudd and Melvin leaped the creek and tramped upon the spongy surface of the sawdust piles. In a little hollow of the shredded wood they found their man, asleep.

His blond whiskers were short and curly. The sun had burned his face. His green shirt, washed recently in the stream, was spread near him and now it was dry. His heavy prison shoes were set neatly together near his feet.

"Strothers, all right," Rudd said. "Wake up!"

The man was snoring gently. He jerked a little but he did not rouse until Rudd tossed one of the shoes on his stomach. Strothers opened his eyes and yawned.

"What kept you so long?" he asked.

Cold and deadly, the bulletins had read; he had never killed a man, but he had always entered banks prepared to kill. He had studied law, and later, engineering. It was said that he could have been successful in either. Now he sat on a pile of sawdust in the wilderness, ready to go back to the isolation cells.

"Local yokels, eh? I didn't think those lazy bastards of guards would come this far. Got anything to smoke, Constable?"

"Where's Kaygo?" the sheriff asked.

Strothers yawned again. He felt his feet. "Talk about

blisters!'' He began to put on his shoes. ''Why, Marty left us at a rat hole on the side of a cliff day before yesterday.''

''We know that,'' Rudd said.

''That's why I mentioned it.'' Strothers reached toward his shirt.

''Hold it!'' Melvin picked up the shirt. There was no weight in it, nothing under it. He tossed it to Strothers, who rose and began to put it on.

''Where's the other .38?'' Rudd asked mildly.

''The other? So you got Weyerhauser. Can I have a smoke?''

Melvin lit a cigarette and tossed it to Strothers. The sheriff and his deputy glanced quickly at each other.

''I don't know who's got it,'' Strothers said. The horses were coming out of the timber.

He saw Castagna. ''Did you ask Sam?''

The sheriff's eyes were tight. He spoke easily, ''Sam's clean. You look clean. So Kaygo's got it. Why'd you give up, Strothers?''

''Too much of nothing here. No future.'' Strothers grinned, dragging on his cigarette, watching the horses from the corners of his eyes. The surface was smooth, but there was steel savagery underneath. Castagna was a bully who had graduated to bombs on starters and bundles of dynamite against the bedroom walls of gambling kings; Strothers was everything the long F.B.I. reports said.

''You could have given up with Castagna,'' Melvin said.

''That two-bit character! I play it alone.'' Strothers puffed his smoke. ''Do I get some chow?''

''Yeah,'' Rudd said. ''Half-done venison.''

''Raw will be fine, Constable.''

''Walk on over toward the horses,'' Rudd said. ''When I say stop—stop.''

''Sure, Constable. Just don't stall. I want to get home as soon as possible. I'm doing some leather work that can't be neglected.''

Not the usual bravado of a petty criminal—Strothers was too coldly intelligent for that. He was spreading it on lightly for another purpose. He wouldn't have much luck with Rudd, Melvin knew. Let him find it out.

Strothers limped ahead of them. "When my last blister broke, that was when I decided to hell with it."

"Right there, Strothers," Rudd said, when they were twenty feet from the horses. With the exception of Jaynes, the posse was relaxed. The first heat of the chase had been worn from them, and this third easy victory coming toward them was nothing to cause excitement.

Rudd nodded at Melvin, making a circle with his finger in the air. Melvin walked wide around Strothers and freed his lariat from the saddle.

"The great big Strothers, he comes easy," Castagna said sullenly.

Strothers ignored Castagna; his eyes were on the rope in Melvin's hands. Barker and the others looked at Strothers dully, but Jaynes sensed what they did not. He pushed his scope sight down and raised his rifle.

"Never mind!" Rudd said sharply, standing several paces behind Strothers. "Put that rifle down, Jaynes. Drop your pants, Strothers."

Strothers smiled. "Now look, Constable . . ." He was watching the loop in Melvin's hand.

And that was when Rudd stepped in and slammed Strothers to the ground with the butt of his rifle. Melvin drove in quickly then. Strothers was enough for the two of them for awhile, but they got his arms tied behind him at last.

The little automatic, flat, fully loaded, was tied with strips of green cloth from Castagna's pants leg to the inside of Strother's thigh. Castagna cursed bitterly, clinging to the saddle horn with his one good hand.

"Why didn't you search him right at first?" Jaynes demanded angrily.

"It takes more steam out of them to let them go right up to where it looks like it's going to work," the sheriff said. "Build a fire, Pryor. We may as well eat again before we split up."

Strothers chewed his meat with good appetite. He had

struggled like a wolf, but that was done now and his intelligence was at work again. "What tipped it, Constable—the cigarettes?"

"Partly," Rudd said. "You wouldn't have left both packs with Sam unless you figured to be with him soon. That wasn't too much, but I knew you would never go back down the river and let them say Ora L. Strothers was caught asleep and gave up without a fight. You really were asleep, too—on purpose."

"Sure. I got the nerve for things like that. It made it look real." Strothers's good nature was back, but he was not thinking of his words. His mind, Melvin knew, was thinking far ahead now, to another plan, setting himself against walls and locks and ropes and everything that could be used to restrain a man physically, pitting his fine mind against all the instruments of the thing called society.

There was a lostness in him that appalled Melvin. Strothers was a cold wind running from a foggy gorge back in the dawn age of mankind. The wind could never warm or change or remain confined. Compared to Strothers, Sam Castagna was just a lumbering animal that knocked weaker animals out of the way.

"You would have taken Castagna with you, if you could have knocked a couple of us off and got to the horses?" Melvin asked.

"Sure," Strothers said. "We planned it that way."

That was talk to be repeated in the prison yard, to be passed along the corridors of the cell block. Talk to fit the code. But not to feed the vanity of Ora L. Strothers, because it was a lie. Let Castagna, lying feverishly on the ground in Melvin's jacket, believe what Strothers said. Castagna had been left behind to build up the illusion that desperate men would surrender without a fight. That he was injured and had to be left was not primary in Strothers's mind; it was merely helpful coincidence.

"Which one of us was to 've been first?" Melvin asked.

Strothers wiped his lips. "You, I thought. Then I changed my mind." He glanced at Jaynes.

"Yeah," Jaynes said. "I read you like a book. I wish you had tried something, Strothers."

The two men stared at each other. The antagonism that separated them was as wide as the sky.

"I'll bet you're the one shot Sam," Strothers said. "Did you shoot Joe Weyerhauser, too?"

Jaynes did not answer. Watching him, Melvin thought, He lacks the evil power of Strothers's intelligence, and he lacks the strength of natural good. He doesn't know what he is, and he knows it.

Strothers smiled. "I've taken half a million from the banks and never had to shoot a man. You, Snake Eyes, you're just a punk on the other side because you don't have the guts and brains of men like me. How about it?"

Jaynes leaped up. His wasp voice broke when he cursed Strothers. He gripped his rifle and stood with the butt poised to smash into Strothers's face.

"Whoa there, Jaynes!" Sheriff Rudd said, but it was not he who stopped the rifle. With his legs tied and one arm bound behind his back, Strothers looked at Jaynes and smiled, and Jaynes lowered his rifle and walked away. After a few steps he turned toward the creek and went there, pretending to drink.

Barker and Pryor stared at Strothers. "Don't call *me* any of your names," Barker growled.

Strothers looked at him as he might have glanced at a noisy child; and then he forgot them all. His mind was once more chewing facts and plans, even as his strong teeth chewed meat.

If this man had been led by Marty Kaygo, what kind of man was Kaygo? thought Melvin.

Rudd said, "I'll take everybody in but you and Jaynes, Melvin. Do you feel up to staying on the trail?"

There was no place where a plane could set down to pick up Castagna. Two and a half days out, Melvin estimated. Rudd would need five men to keep an eye on Strothers day and night. They were out of food, too.

"All right," Melvin said.

Jaynes had overheard. He came back from the creek. "I'm staying, too."

Strothers smiled.

"I'll send the green plane over Shewalter Meadows three days from now," Rudd said. "With grub. Now, what else will you need?"

"Send me another coat," Melvin said. "Send Jaynes another sleeping bag. We both better have packs, too."

The sheriff nodded. He put Strothers on a horse and tied him there. They lifted Castagna to the saddle again. He was going to suffer plenty before they reached the highway. Castagna looked at Melvin and said thickly, "Thanks for the coat."

Strothers smiled at Melvin from the corner of his eyes. The smile said, Chump!

A hundred yards down the creek a logging road took off to the left, and there went the tracks of Marty Kaygo. Melvin and Jaynes walked into second-growth timber. The sounds of the horses died away. Under his belt Melvin was carrying the pistol he had taken from Strothers.

Jaynes said, "I damn near smashed that Strothers's ugly face for him."

"Uh-huh."

"You can't hit a man tied up like that, not even a pen bird."

"No."

"Of course not," Jaynes said.

The road began to angle to the right, along a ridge.

"This won't take us straight to where the plane spotted Kaygo," Jaynes said. "Let's cut into the timber."

"I'm staying with his tracks. I don't know what that plane was circling over."

The road turned down the ridge again, on the side away from Shewalter Meadows. Kaygo's tracks were still there, but Jaynes was mightily impatient. "I'm going straight over the ridge," he said

"Go ahead."

"Where will I meet you, then?"

"At the Meadows."

"You sure?" Jaynes asked doubtfully.

"This old road runs into one hell of a swamp before long. I'm betting he went to the Meadows, but I'm going to follow his trail all the way."

They separated. Melvin was glad. He wanted to reduce the chase to the patient unwinding of a trail, to an end that was nothing more than law and duty; and he could not think of it that way so long as Jaynes was with him.

Where the swamp began, Kaygo had turned at once up the ridge. There was something in that which spoke of the man's quality, of an ability to sense the lie of a country. Most city men would have blundered deep into the swamp before deciding to turn.

Jaynes was right about down-timber on the ridge, fire-killed trees that had stood for years before rot took their roots and wind sent them crashing. Melvin went slowly. Kaygo had done the same, and before long Melvin noticed that the man had traveled as a woodsman does, stepping over nothing that could be walked around.

Kaygo would never exhaust himself in blind, disorderly flight. What kind of man was he?

Going down the west side of the ridge, Melvin stopped when a grouse exploded from the ground near a rotting spruce log. He drew the pistol and waited until he saw two others near the log, frozen in their protective coloration. He shot one through the head, and five more flew away.

Now an instrument of the law had broken the law for a second time during this chase; but there were, of course, degrees of breakage. A man like Strothers no doubt could make biting comments on the subject.

Melvin pulled the entrails from the bird and went on, following Kaygo's trail. The man had an eye for terrain, all right. He made few mistakes that cost him time and effort, and that was rare in any man crossing unfamiliar, wooded country.

A woodsman at some time in his life? Melvin went back over Kaygo's record. Thirty-five years old. Sixteen of those years spent in reformatories and prisons. An interesting talker. Athletic. Generally armed, considered extremely dangerous. Approach with caution. The record fell into the glib pattern of the words under the faces on the bulletin board in Rudd's office.

Gambles heavily. If forced to work, seeks employment as clerk in clothing store . . . There was nothing Melvin could recall to indicate that Kaygo had ever been five miles from pavement.

The sun was getting low and the timber was already gathering coolness in its depths when Melvin came out on a long slope that ran down to the Meadows, two miles away.

Where the sun still lay on a bare spot near a quartz outcrop Melvin stopped, puzzled by what he saw. The mark of the steel butt-plate of Kaygo's rifle and the imprint of his shoes, one flat, the other showing no heel print, said that Kaygo had squatted near the ant hill; four cigarette butts crushed into the ground said that he had been here for some time.

Coolness had diminished activity of the ants, but they were still seething in and out of their dome of sand and pine needles; and Kaygo had squatted there for perhaps an hour to watch.

It was Melvin's experience that some perverseness in man causes him to step upon ant hills or to kick them in passing. This one was undisturbed. Kaygo had watched and gone away. Melvin had done the same thing many times.

What if I have and what if he did also? he asked himself. Does that change what I have to do? But as he went on, Melvin kept wondering what Kaygo had thought as he squatted beside the ant hill.

Near dusk Melvin lost the trail where the wide arm of a swamp came up from the drainage basin of the Meadows. But Kaygo was headed that way, Melvin was sure. One gentle turn too far to the left, back there on the long slope, would have sent Kaygo into the ragged canyons near the lower end of the Meadows.

He must have spotted the place from the top of Clover Mountain; but seeing from the heights and finding from a route through timberchoked country are two different things.

Kaygo had a fine sense of distance and direction, though. I can grant him that, Melvin thought, without feeling anything else about him to impede my purpose. The purpose—and Melvin wondered why he had to keep restating it—was to bring Marty Kaygo out, dead or alive.

On the edge of Shewalter Meadows, where the grass stood waist-high to a man all over the flooded ground and the beaver runs that led to the ponds out in the middle, Melvin stopped behind a tree and scanned the open space. There was only half-light now, but that was enough.

Beavers were making ripples in the ponds and trout were leaping for their evening feeding. The Meadows lay in a great dog-leg, and the upper part was cut from Melvin's view by spruce trees and high willows. The best windfalls for sleeping cover were up there, and that was where Jaynes would be, undoubtedly.

Let him stay there tonight alone. Sooner or later Melvin would have to rejoin him, and that would be soon enough. Melvin went back into the timber and cooked his grouse. He ate half of it and laid the rest in the palm of a limb, head-high.

The night came in with a gentle rush. He dozed off on top of his sleeping bag, to awaken chilled and trembling some time later. The night was windless, the ground stony. Melvin built up the fire and warmed himself by it before getting into his sleeping bag.

Dead or alive. The thought would not submerge.

One Kaygo was a vagueness written on a record; Melvin had learned of another Kaygo today. They made a combination that would never give up.

If Melvin had been here just to fish and loaf, to walk through the dappled fall of sunshine in the trees, and—yes, to be caught away from himself while watching the endless workings of an ant hill; to see the sun come and go on quietness; to see the elk thrusting their broad muzzles underwater to eat; to view all the things that are simple and understandable . . . then, he knew, he would be living for awhile as man was meant to live.

You are Bill Melvin, a deputy sheriff. He is a man called Kaygo, an escaped murderer.

Dead or alive . . .

He came from dreamless sleep when the log ends of the fire were no longer flaming but drizzling smoke across a bed of coals. He felt the presence near him by the rising of the hackles on his neck, from deep memories forgotten by the human race.

Carefully, not breaking the even tenor of his breathing, he worked one hand up to the pistol on the head shield of the sleeping bag.

The man was squatted by the fire with a rifle across his knees. His hair was curling brown that caught a touch of redness from the glow of embers. The light outlined a sandy beard, held steady on wide cheekbones, and lost itself in the hollows under massive brow arches. The man's trousers were muddy, at least as high as the knees, where the fabric was strained smooth by his position. They might have been any color. But there was no doubt that the shirt was green.

The face by itself was enough.

It was Marty Kaygo.

He was eating what was left of Melvin's grouse.

He turned the carcass in his hands, gnawing, chewing; and all the while his face was set toward the shadows where Melvin lay.

Slowly Melvin worked the pistol along the edge of the ground until, lying on his side, he raised it just a trifle. The front sight was a white bead that lined across the coals to Kaygo's chest. Melvin's thumb pushed the safety down.

Long rifle cartridges, just a spot of lead that could sing over space and kill. Kaygo, the cop-killer. Speak to him, tell him to put up his hands and let his rifle fall. If he swung the rifle to fire, the pistol could sing and kill.

From where came the whisper that fire and food must be shared even with a deadly enemy? From the jungle all around that might pull them both beneath its slime an instant later?

The sabre-tooth and the great reptiles were out there in the night. And men were men together, if only for a moment. The jungle was not gone, merely changed.

Melvin let the pistol rest upon the ground.

Marty Kaygo rose. He was not a tall man. Even in his prison shoes he moved lightly as he stepped to a tree and replaced the carcass of the grouse. He grinned, still looking toward where Melvin lay.

And then he was gone.

Melvin lay a long time before he fell asleep again.

When he rose in the bitter cold of morning, he went at once to the dead fire. There were the tracks. He took the grouse from the limb. One leg was untouched.

Staring out to where the first long-slanting rays of the sun were driving mist from the beaver ponds and wet grass, Melvin held the chilled grouse in his hands.

What's the matter with me?

The truth was, Jaynes was Melvin and Melvin was Jaynes, great developments of the centuries; and Kaygo did not fit where they belonged. But . . .

Melvin shivered.

He went out of the timber into the sunshine, and he sat down to let it warm him while he ate the rest of the grouse. There before him, leading through the gray mud out toward the wickerwork of the beaver dams, were the tracks of Kaygo. He had crossed the boggy ground by night, walking the beaver dams above deep water, returning the same way. It was not an easy feat even in daytime.

I wish I could talk to him, Melvin thought. I wish . . .

The shot was a cracking violation of the wilderness quiet. It came from somewhere around the dog-leg of the Meadows.

Melvin went back to the campsite and got his gear.

Before he turned the dog-leg, he saw Jaynes coming toward him. Jaynes stopped and waited.

"What the hell happened to you, Melvin?" There was blood on Jaynes's shirt.

"I followed his trail, just as I said I would. You shoot a deer?"

"Yeah. That's one thing there's plenty of here. Kaygo's

around. I saw his tracks in the upper part of the Meadows last night. We'll get him. I know every inch—"

"Let's get at the deer."

They roasted meat, and then Jaynes was impatient to be off.

"Just hold your steam," said Melvin. "We've got another two days before the plane drops chow, so we're going to start drying some of this meat."

"There's lots of deer."

"We'll dry some of this. We don't know where that plane will drop our supplies, or what they'll be like when we get to them. And you're not going to shoot a deer every day, Jaynes."

They cut the meat in thin strips and laid it on the gray twigs of a fallen tree until the branches were festooned with dangling brown meat. Camp-robber birds were there at once, floating in, snatching.

"How you going to stop that?" Jaynes asked.

"By staying here. I'm going to do some smoking with a willow fire, too. Take a turn around the Meadows. See what you can find out. You know every inch of the land."

"I'll do that." Jaynes took his rifle and strode away.

He was back at noon. "Where'd you camp, Melvin?"

Melvin told him.

"Well, he was there, this morning. He crossed the swamp and went back the same way. He's in the timber on this side somewhere. He's getting smart now about covering his tracks."

"What's he eating?" Melvin asked cleverly.

"I don't know, and I don't care. He slept one night under a windfall. Where'd he learn that, Melvin?" Jaynes was worried.

"I think it must come to him naturally. He's probably enjoying more freedom right now than he's had in his whole life."

Jaynes grunted. He eyed the tree that was serving as a drying rack. "Hey! Do you suppose we could pull him in with that?" He looked all around at the fringe of trees. "Say we go down into the timber on the other side and then circle back to that little knob over there . . . About three hundred and twenty-five yards.'' Jaynes rubbed the oily sheen of his rifle barrel. ''One shot, Melvin.''

''You think he's hungry enough to try it?''

''He must be.''

''The birds will scatter our meat.''

''Part of a lousy deer, or one jailbird! What's the matter with you, Melvin?''

The venison was not going to cure before the plane came in and Melvin knew it. He had stalled long enough.

They went a half-mile beside the lower Meadows. On the way Jaynes stepped sidewise to jump into an ant hill and twist his feet; and then he went on, stamping ants loose from his shoes. ''He must be hungry enough by now.''

They went back through the timber and crept behind a log on the little hill across the field from their camp. The smoky birds were having a merry time with the meat.

Now Jaynes was patient. His eyes caught every movement across the park, and his position did not seem to strain his muscles. They stayed until the shadows lowered cold upon their backs. It was then that they heard the rifle shot somewhere in the lower Meadows, two miles away.

''He's got his own meat.'' Melvin laughed.

Jaynes rose. ''What's so damn funny about it?''

Melvin had wrapped his undershirt around a venison haunch, but the blowflies had got to it anyway. He brushed the white larva away.

They roasted meat and ate in silence.

Marty Kaygo was still around Shewalter Meadows. They cut his sign the next day, and they found where he had killed the deer. The convict was here, and it seemed that he intended to stay.

Jaynes was infuriated. And he was speechless for awhile when they returned to camp that night and found that Kaygo had stolen Melvin's sleeping bag.

''Who are the tenderfeet around here?'' Melvin laughed again.

''You don't act like you want to catch him! By God, I do, and I'll stay here all summer to do it, if necessary!''

"To catch him?"

"To kill him! I'm going to gut-shoot him for this little trick!"

"You would have, anyway." There was no humor now in Kaygo's stealing the sleeping bag.

The plane came in on the afternoon of the third day. Clouds were scudding across the peaks and the pilot was in a hurry to beat out a local storm. He banked sharply to look down at the two men standing in the open dryness of the upper Meadows.

He went on east, high above the timber. They saw him fighting a tricky wind. On the next bank he kicked out the box. The parachute became a white cone. Lining out with a tailwind boosting him, the pilot sped away toward Scott.

"If he had any brains he'd've stayed to make sure we got it," Jaynes said. "Typical state employee."

A great wind-front flowing in from the mountains struck them with a chill that spoke of the rain soon to follow. Melvin watched the plane bouncing jerkily in downdrafts above the canyons. "The pilot's all right, Jaynes."

"Look at that thing drift!"

They knew for sure after another few moments that the box would not land in the upper Meadows. Melvin said, "Wouldn't it be something if it lit right at Kaygo's feet?"

"Big fine joke, huh?"

They trotted across the creek and down along the edge of the Big Shewalter to keep the chute in sight. They were a long way from it when they saw it splash into the water near the opposite side of the flooded area. An instant later the rain boiled down on them.

"I hope they had sense enough to put the stuff in cans." Jaynes turned up the collar of his jacket.

The ponds were dancing froth now. Through the mist they saw Kaygo run from the timber and wade out after the box.

Jaynes dropped to one knee. He pushed his scope down and began to click the sight adjustment. "Eight hundred yards," he muttered. His rifle bellowed with the thunder on the mountains. "Where'd I hit?"

"I couldn't tell."

The first hard blast of rain was sweeping on. Jaynes fired again, and this time Melvin saw the bullet strike the water to the left of Kaygo, chest-deep now, towing the box to shore with the shroud-lines of the chute.

"About five feet to the left," Melvin said.

Kaygo sprawled into the grass when the next shot came.

"That did it," Melvin said.

"No! He ducked."

Kaygo raised up. Skidding the box over wet grass and mud, he reached timber while Jaynes tried two more shots. Over that distance, through wind and rain, Jaynes had performed well—but Kaygo was still free.

Kaygo's boldness was worth applause, but Melvin felt only a bleak apathy. The end had been delayed, that was all.

"Come on!" Jaynes said.

"Across that open swamp? No, thanks. We'll work through the timber."

"He's got our stuff!"

"He's got a rifle, too."

The box had been fastened with wing-nuts, easy to tap loose. The packs Melvin had asked for were gone, and the jacket, and about three-fourths of the food, Melvin estimated. The sleeping bag had been unrolled. Rain was filtering through the pines on a manila envelope containing a note.

They peered into the gloom of the wet forest. It was no time to press Kaygo hard, and they both knew it.

While Jaynes raged, Melvin read the note.

"Rudd started in at noon today with big posse. He says not to take any chances. He says there were *two* .22 pistols and a hunting knife taken from the filling station."

"That's a big help!" Jaynes cursed the weather, the pilot, and the stupidity of circumstance.

"I told you on Clover Mountain I was sick of you, Jaynes. Now shut up! You're lucky Kaygo didn't slice your sleeping bag to pieces or throw it into the water."

"I'm fed up with you, too, Melvin! You didn't even try to

shoot a while ago. You act like the stinking louse is your brother!''

My brother. The thought plowed through Melvin, leaving a fresh wake. It was not fashionable to speak of men as brothers; you killed your brother, just like anybody else.

They plodded toward camp, carrying the cans of food in their hands. The labels began to soak off. Melvin finished the job on the cans he was holding.

''That's smart,'' Jaynes said. ''Now what's in them?''

''You're right, they're no good to us anymore. A hungry man has to know what he's getting.'' Melvin began to hurl the cans into a beaver pond, until Jaynes pleaded with him.

''Then shut your mouth for awhile!'' Melvin cried.

They went on to camp through a cold rain that soaked into Melvin's soul.

''Soup!'' Jaynes said later, when they sat under a dripping tree before a smoking fire. ''Kaygo's back in the timber having hot coffee and canned chicken.''

Jaynes could not destroy everything, for he had the unrealized power to give laughter. Melvin began to laugh while Jaynes stared at him angrily. Was it the sound of laughter, as well as the smell of fire, that caused the monsters of the long-ago jungle to raise their heads in fear?

''I said I'd get Kaygo if it took all summer. You sit here and laugh some more, Melvin. I'll get him!''

They found the second pack the next morning, empty, hanging on a tree. ''He's cached part of the grub somewhere,'' Jaynes growled. ''He couldn't have put it all in one pack. Smart! He did it in the rain, and now we can't back-track him.''

But they could trail him in the fresh dampness. Kaygo had realized that, too; he had gone far south of the Meadows, and on a rocky ridge they lost his trail. The ridge was a great spur that ran down from Spearhead Mountain, bucking through lesser cross-ridges arrogantly. The lower end of it, Melvin knew, was not eight miles from the highway.

''Maybe he's clearing out,'' Jaynes said. ''He read that note about Rudd. He knows he's going to get it. He's headed for the highway now. Somebody else will get him, after all we've done!''

"Pathetic, ain't it?" Melvin looked at Spearhead Mountain. "Maybe he went that way. He likes mountains.''

"What do you mean?"

"Nothing you'd understand. He's gone toward Spearhead, Jaynes.''

"The highway! I'm going after him, Melvin. If I don't cut his trail by the time I hit Bandbox Creek, I'll come back. Don't sneak off this time and camp by yourself. He could have walked right in on you that night.''

"Yes, he could have killed me, I suppose.''

Jaynes eyes narrowed. "Those tracks beside your fire the next morning—one of yours was on top of one of his, Melvin. He sneaked in while you were asleep, didn't he? And you were ashamed to mention it to me! It's a wonder he didn't take your rifle and sleeping bag right from under you. I'll mention that to Rudd when he gets here.''

"You do that, Jaynes." Harlan Rudd had shared food and fire with outlaws in the old days, and he was not ashamed to talk about it now that he was sheriff. "Get out of my sight, Jaynes, before I forget I'm a brother to you, too!''

"Brother?" Jaynes gave Melvin a baffled look before he started down the ridge.

There was something Kaygo could not have known about this ridge: It appeared to be the natural route to Spearhead, but higher up it was a jumble of tree-covered cliffs.

Melvin stayed on it only until he found where Kaygo had slipped from his careful walking on rocks and left a mark which he had tried to smooth away. Then Melvin left the ridge and took a roundabout, but faster, route toward Spearhead.

He went too rapidly. In midafternoon he saw Kaygo far below him, between two curving buttresses of the mountain. The fugitive was not pushing himself.

While Melvin watched through his glasses, Kaygo removed the stolen pack and lay down in a field of columbines, pillowing his head on the stolen sleeping bag. The wind was cold on Melvin's sweating skin as he hugged his vantage point behind the rocks.

Jaynes might have made a shot from here; he would have tried, although the range was four hundred yards greater than yesterday across the Big Shewalter. Melvin knew his own rifle would do no more than scare Kaygo down the hill.

Like hunting sheep, he thought. You have to wait and try to make them blunder into you.

Kaygo lay there for an hour. He was not asleep. He moved occasionally, but mostly he lay there looking at the sky and clouds.

He was wallowing in freedom; that was it. Damn him! He would not do what fugitives are supposed to do. He insisted on acting like a man enjoying life.

My brother down there, Melvin thought. Yes, and I'll kill him when he comes near enough on the saddle of the mountain.

Kaygo rose at last, but he did not go. He stretched his arms to the sky, as if he would clutch a great section of it. Then he sat down and smoked a cigarette.

The sweat was tight and dry on Melvin. The wind scampered through his clothing. Of course I have to kill him, he told himself. He's found something he loves so much he won't be taken from it any other way.

Kaygo went up at last. Melvin slipped behind the rib of the mountain and climbed steadily. The wind was growing quiet now. There was a sullen heaviness in the air. It would rain again today.

Melvin was far ahead when he took a position among rocks that overlooked the saddle. He could see Kaygo, still in no hurry, coming up the harder way, coming over a red iron dike that had made the notch on Spearhead back when man clutched his club and splashed toward refuge as the clamor broke out in the forest.

It was his job. Society paid him, Melvin reminded himself. Climb faster, Marty Kaygo. You will have your chance to go back where you belong, and when you refuse the job will be done quickly.

The air grew heavily quiet. Melvin blinked when he heard

a tiny snap and saw a blue spark run along his rifle barrel. He rubbed his hand against his woolen shirt. His palm crackled with pinpoint sparks and the fibers of the sleeve tried to follow the hand away. He stroked his hair and heard the little noises and felt the hair rising.

All this was not uncommon on the heights in summer when a storm was making, but Melvin had never experienced it before. It gave him a weird sensation.

Kaygo came into the saddle when the air was fully charged. He jumped when blue light ran along his rifle barrel. He was then two hundred yards away from Melvin. He would have to pass much closer. Kaygo stared in wonder at his rifle, and then at the leaden sky.

He held up his hunting knife. Sparks played upon the point. Kaygo laughed. He raised both knife and rifle and watched the electricity come to them.

A little later he discovered steel was not necessary to draw static from the swollen air. Kaygo's fingers, held aloft, drew sparks. He did a dance upon the rocks, shouting his wonder and pleasure. Strange balls of light ran along the iron dike, and the air was filled with a sterile odor.

This day on Spearhead Mountain, Marty Kaygo roared with joy.

Melvin had never heard laughter run so cleanly. Laughter from the littered caves above the slime; laughter from the tree-perch safe from walking beasts; laughter challenging the brutes . . .

It did not last. The rain came just after the first whistling surge of wind. The bursting air cleared.

Kaygo trotted easily for shelter, his head lowered against the pelt of ice. He came straight toward the rocks where Melvin lay. There was a clatter somewhere behind Melvin, granite slipping on granite, but he had no time to wonder.

"Kaygo!" he yelled. "Drop it!"

The man threw up his head as he ran, and he brought the rifle up, not hesitating.

My brother, Melvin thought. That held him one split second longer, with his finger on the trigger and his sights on Kaygo's chest.

Another rifle roared behind him. Kaygo's legs jerked as he tried to keep running. He went down and his hands reached out for the wet stones. That was all.

Jaynes came limping through the rocks. "I hurt my knee, but I got him, rain and all!"

Melvin could not rise for a moment. He felt frozen to the rock.

At last he came up, slowly.

"You were right," Jaynes said. "He took the hard way. After I left you I got to thinking that was what he would do."

They went across the stones to Kaygo. Jaynes turned him over. "Heart. I said I didn't miss running shots, not very often." That was all the interest he had in Marty Kaygo; and now that vanished, too.

Jaynes slipped the pack from the dead man's back. "Steal our chow, would he! Grab your sleeping bag and let's get out of here. Rudd and the others can take care of the chores now. Four for four, Melvin."

"You're counting Strothers?"

"I wish that big-mouth had tried something."

The rain was the coldest that ever fell on Melvin. He unrolled the sleeping bag and covered Kaygo with it, weighting the sides with stones.

Jaynes started to protest, but near the end he helped. "I guess even Kaygo deserves something. He wasn't a bad-looking character at that, was he?"

All this time Melvin had not looked at Jaynes. Now he picked up Jaynes's rifle. Deliberately, Melvin began to smash it against a rock. He splintered the stock and the forestock. He bent the bolt and he battered the scope until it was a twisted tube hanging by one mount, and he continued to beat the breech against the rock until the front sight ripped his palm and the impacts numbed his wrists.

He dropped the rifle then and stood breathing hard.

Jaynes had cursed loudly at first, but then he had stopped. The hard glitter was gone from his eyes.

Now, in the voice of a man who lives with splinters in his

soul, Jaynes said, ''By God, you're going to buy me a new rifle, Melvin. What's the matter with you, anyway?''

Melvin said nothing. Then together they started down the rain-soaked mountain . . .